Every Why

Shirley Ford

All rights reserved.

Shirley Ford has asserted her right under the
Copyright, Designs and Patents Act 1988,
to be identified as the author of this work.

No part of this publication may be reproduced,
stored in a retrieval system, or transmitted in
any form or by any means, without the prior
permission in writing of the publisher, nor be
otherwise circulated in any form of binding
or cover other than that in which it is
published and without a similar condition
including this condition being imposed
on the subsequent purchaser.

All characters and events are a work of fiction
and any similarities to anyone living or dead
are purely coincidental.

ISBN 9781478152361

Everything that you need or want in your life
will begin to arrive when you're in-Spirit:
The right people will show up,
the financing will materialize,
those around you will be attracted
to your enthusiasm and commitment,
and you'll be a source of inspiration to others.

Quotation from Dr. Wayne W Dyer

Every Why

Chapter 1

March 2008

The woman strained her eyes to check the time on her old Accurist wristwatch, the overhead light in the railway carriage was quite dim. It showed nine o'clock; only another ten minutes until the train reached Strathdown, their final destination. The thought of the unknown filled her with a mix of fear and excitement, but there was no going back, not now. Susan Vizer gripped the letters that lay in her lap and her stomach churned as she gazed unseeingly through the window into the gathering darkness.

'Put them away, it's too late to change your mind.'

With a sigh, Susan turned to her mother, wishing more than anything that she could have come alone. Without answering, she stuffed the letters back in her handbag and turned her gaze once again to the window, from where her reflection, ghostlike, stared back. For the umpteenth time that day, Susan questioned her sanity at what she was about to do.

Both women, at the time were totally unaware of four other women all about to embark on the same adventure, and head to the same destination. All of them inexplicably linked by letters – letters that they felt compelled to respond to. For each one of them, their lives would never be the same again.

Chapter 2

September 2006

Sinking gratefully into the soft cushions of his favourite easy chair, Angus McPhail glanced out of the window at the riot of colour that filled his garden. Rose bushes, fuchsias and sturdy heathers; the scent of which he could still bring to mind, from his walks about the grounds during the summer months. Unfortunately, the ever-encroaching weeds were swallowing the entire garden up.

One of his greatest pleasures was to potter round the gardens, especially in the early mornings, but for the last few months or so it had become increasingly difficult. He was getting old, his mind was still active but his body wasn't so keen.

Twisting awkwardly in the chair, Angus winced as his arthritic joints complained loudly. The house and the estate were far too big for him to run now; he was tired. His attempt at easing the burden several years ago, which involved letting a local couple run one-half of the house as a Bed & Breakfast business was a dismal failure. Neville and Doreen Campbell were enthusiastic amateurs, with no actual experience. Promotion and marketing of their business were non-existent; they expected visitors to find them, even though they were a couple of miles from the main road. Their enthusiasm died along with the lack of money and in the end, they gave up with relief and took early retirement. Now their side of the house stood empty and neglected; yet another reminder of his increasing years. He had no idea what else to do with it. Angus also understood his manager's increasing frustration, but could not raise any enthusiasm for the estate, and his biggest fear was that Hugh Campbell, Neville and Doreen's son would leave now that his parents were no longer around.

Angus's thoughts drifted back to the happy times when he came home after his years at sea and helped his mother run Dunnbray. Was it really twenty years since she passed away? Dunnbray was always a resounding success under her careful hands. Admired by all who knew her, Isobel McPhail was actively involved in the running of the estate right up until her death. Somehow, since she passed away, Angus's enthusiasm and strength to carry on were gradually fading. It was time for the old place to get a new lease of life, before it was too late.

A sharp tap on the door interrupted his thoughts. 'Come in.' He called out, without rising from the comfort of his armchair.

Douglas McKinley, smartly dressed in a dark blue business suit, appeared in the doorway, a thick grey folder in his left hand. Angus indicated for him to take the chair opposite. Over the last eighteen months, Angus had grown to like and respect Douglas.

'Good to see you again my boy, do sit down.' He was very impressed with the amount of information Douglas produced. Angus was very grateful to his solicitors for suggesting him. He had been extremely pleased and thought Douglas worth every penny paid for his services. Pointing to the folder in Douglas's hand he said, 'is your investigation complete? Is everything there?'

'It's all complete Angus, everything you need to put your plan into action.' He smiled and handed the folder over to the old man. He was aware of the importance of that folder to assist in Angus's plan.

After Douglas left, Angus studied the list of names carefully, then lifting the telephone receiver from the small mahogany table beside him, he dialled the all too familiar number. A few minutes later, his call finished, he leaned back in his chair. Finished. There was no going back. He knew a chain of events had begun which would change lives forever. His own life included; as always he thought of his mother and how proud she would have been.

Chapter 3

September 1935

A smile hovered round Archie McPhail's lips as he stood in the doorway watching the remaining mourners disappear down the drive. Thank God, he thought they would never leave; eating his food, drinking his wine, greedy devils. He looked about him. 'It's all mine.' He whispered to himself. 'At last, it's all mine.'

Isobel came and stood alongside him, Andrew, their youngest balanced on her hip. The other two boys were soon at her heels and his familiar feelings of distaste rose as he looked at them all.

'That went well Archie. A great send-off for your father, though I did not expect quite so many people to come back. I am just glad we had enough food.'

Archie did not attempt to hide his feelings. 'They only came out of curiosity, not respect for my father you silly woman. All they wanted was to find out what I was going to do with the place now that I am the Laird.' He patted his large belly before tucking his thumbs into his tartan waistcoat. Laird of Dunnbray, he loved how the title rolled off his tongue. Oh, how he had waited for this moment.

'What *are* your plans now?' asked Isobel, as he closed the door on the wet autumn day.

Archie had been making plans for his inheritance for some time. He took great delight in telling Isobel. 'Week-end shooting parties for all those well-to-do city folk with pots of money and not much sense. Old Hector McTavish does it over near Edinburgh, very successfully too I hear. It can't be that difficult, let them bag a stag or two, keep them well fed, ply them with drink and we can charge a fortune for the pleasure.'

Isobel's heart sank; Archie's plan meant that he would be able to indulge himself in his favourite activity whilst making some money at the same time. He was totally oblivious to all the extra work it would entail, all the cooking, the cleaning, the beds to be changed. Her responsibility of course; she would definitely need help in the house now.

'Would the week-end parties bring in enough money to send the boys away to school?' Isobel asked.

'I'm not wasting good money on their education. I never went to boarding school and I have done all right for myself. They will inherit this place one day when I am gone, that is good enough.'

He glanced at his sons, snivelling brats all three of them - he could not stand kids. Angus was a skinny seven year old, a gust of wind would knock over; chubby Alan, five years old, always whingeing; and Andrew, well, he arrived ten months ago, and not planned by him of course. It was all Isobel's fault and she was welcome to him.

Isobel sighed and left Archie congratulating himself. She knew in her heart that the mourners really did have respect for Allister, more than could be said for Archie. She would miss her kindly father-in-law.

'Come on boys,' she said, heading for the kitchen. 'Let's leave your father to his business.'

Isobel was not stupid; she knew Archie had been more attracted to her father's inn and money than her. The McPhail family had been successful farmers, both with crops and Dunnbray venison and lamb, the meat well known in the area for its quality. Archie unfortunately was not made from the same hardworking stock as his father, who was a well-liked member of the local community. Allister McPhail, thrilled to have a son, envisaged a successful future, but it was not to be. Allister made the money and Archie spent it.

Settling Andrew into his high chair and the boys onto the bench alongside the kitchen table, Isobel gave each of them a plate of leftover cold ham, cheese and chunks of bread, and sinking into the old elm high backed rocking chair by the side of the range, she felt a wave of tiredness sweep over her.

Life was going to become so much worse now that Allister was not around to rein in his son's excesses. Ailsa, Archie's mother had died when he was a young boy and Allister had raised his son to the best of his ability, but he was a difficult child and grew more difficult as he grew to adulthood.

Archie was itching to get his hands on the inheritance. The reading of the will was to be the next day, but he already knew there was not as much as he was hoping He had paced up and down for hours after this news asking Isobel the same questions repeatedly. Where was all the money? Was it hidden somewhere? Did the family solicitors have any idea? They said they did not, but they were lying of course. The questions continually played on his mind and he drove Isobel to distraction with them.

She could not wait for the following morning, when he would finally find out just how much he had inherited, perhaps then he would calm down and get on with the running of Dunnbray.

Allister had only been dead just over a week and already outgoings were being cut to the bare minimum to leave more for Archie's pocket; the first move was to get rid of Dougal McCall the old estate manager, who wasn't needed in Archie's opinion. In fact the real reason was that Archie thought Dougal too friendly towards his wife, harbouring a simmering dislike for the man and took the first opportunity to get rid of him. This was a big mistake in Isobel's opinion.

Isobel gazed into the flickering flames through the range bars, wondering what the future held for her. She was a tall, well-built woman; with striking rather than pretty features, and eyes a piercing blue. She wore her blond streaked brown hair scraped back into a bun, from which curls would escape and frame her face, making her appear at first glance, much younger than she was. Lines were appearing round her mouth, which gave her a serious look, and caused by the continual gritting of her teeth as she silently witnessed Archie's crass and boorish behaviour. She could never understand what persuaded her to marry him in the first place, but it was too late now, she had the children to care for.

The solicitor, Mr Michael Dobson, a dapper little man, anxiously peering over glasses perched on the end of his nose, arrived promptly at eleven thirty. Archie, anxious to hear the news, rushed him into the large sitting room. Isobel, embarrassed for the unseemly haste asked if Mr Dobson would like a sherry, which he gladly accepted. Archie glared at his wife as she poured the drink.

Settling down into one of the armchairs pulled up to the blazing fire, which again, Archie did not think should be wasted on a solicitor, Mr Dobson opened his briefcase and read out the contents of the will. Firstly, the three boys to receive five pounds each. Archie was horrified.

'They can pay for their own upkeep for a while out of that,' he shouted.

Mr Dobson shifted awkwardly in the chair.

'Archie, your father has left that money for the boys; we should put it away for them.' Isobel could not believe how mean her husband could be.

'Yes, we can put it away in my account; now Mr Dobson, what's more important is how much have I been left?'

Mr Dobson picked up his sherry and downed it in one gulp, then told Archie the amount of money he would receive.

Archie collapsed onto the sofa in shock. 'Is that all? I know you said there wasn't as much as I had been expecting, but are you quite sure?'

Isobel did not know what to say and there was an uncomfortable silence for several minutes, then Mr Dobson coughed discreetly and said to Archie. 'I have one more thing to give you,' and handed Archie an envelope, addressed to him in his father's handwriting.

Archie snatched it from Mr Dobson, tore the envelope open and pulled out a single sheet of paper, staring at the hand written contents in disbelief.

'Is this meant to be a joke? Are you making fun of me Mr Dobson? Because if you are then I suggest you leave.' Archie roared, his face contorting with rage. He screwed the piece of paper up and threw it towards the fire. Luckily, he missed and Isobel rescued it and undoing it read the words on the page, silently first and then again aloud.

The secret of Dunnbray is never far away.
Is it under ground? Where the secret can be found?
Find four legs and a tail and the secret will unveil,
Security for Dunnbray always, forever and a day!

Solve this riddle and your money worries will be well and truly over.

'How exciting, a riddle, what do you think it means Archie?'

Turning to Mr Dobson Archie snapped, 'Did you know about this stupid riddle?'

'Yes, your father had to discuss it with someone, but that is all I know, I don't know what exactly is hidden and I don't know where, so please don't ask me any more. I will take my leave of your good selves now, and wish you the best of luck.' His gaze fell on Isobel as he grabbed his briefcase and rushed to the door. He pitied her, and hoped her life would not be too difficult with that unpleasant husband of hers. The less he had to deal with Archie McPhail the better as far as he was concerned.

Isobel showed Mr Dobson out, and then came back into the sitting room to find Archie pacing backwards and forwards once again, muttering to himself. When he saw Isobel, he shouted at her to try and think of all the animals, *four legs and a tail* could describe, that his father might have had as pets. It had to refer to one of the pets; that was Archie's only answer.

'Have his dogs been buried in the grounds, can you remember? When did that last old dog die? What was his name? Was his body buried in the garden somewhere? For goodness sake woman, think.'

'Jasper, that was his name and yes I think he was buried in the grounds. Dougal would have known, probably buried Jasper himself, but you got rid of him didn't you?' Isobel could not resist a small smile, hidden behind her hand of course.

Archie spent several wasted days searching for Dougal's whereabouts, but to no avail, he had travelled south apparently to stay with his family. Then Archie spent more time wandering around the grounds searching for signs of a grave, but again found nothing. Frustration ate away at him as he tried to set up his shooting parties and raise more money. He had lost heart in his plans now that he knew that somewhere, there was money or something of value hidden away. He could not forgive his selfish father for hiding his money. The riddle gnawed away at him for the rest of his life.

Chapter 4

March 2008

To take the lift or stairs, which would be quicker? Susan Vizer decided on the stairs, as the door of her second floor apartment shut noisily and she rushed across the landing. Oops, she had done it again, slamming the door and forgetting about disturbing her neighbours. Only the other day, Mrs Tweedy, the elderly woman who lived opposite, told her that the slamming door woke her up. Oh well, it could not be helped. She was late leaving for work; the third time this week and it was still only Thursday.

Susan ran down the two flights of stairs and crossed the elegant high ceilinged hall with its polished parquet floor to the front door of the apartment block. There was no time to stop and appreciate the beauty of this building today. As she rushed through, she spotted the post on the large hall table, where the postman left the mail for all six residents. Quickly rifling through the pile, she pulled out some junk mail, and a hand written cream embossed envelope addressed to her. She glanced at the envelope curiously, and then shoved it in her handbag with the other post; she would look at it later when she had more time.

Running round the side of the building, shivering in the icy wind blowing across from the Jurassic coast a few miles away, she unlocked the car door and climbed in. Once inside her bright yellow Peugeot 207, she shook out her unruly mass of dark brown curls, rubbed her hands together to warm them and started the engine. Ten minutes later, she was singing along to the radio, oblivious to the other commuters crawling through the morning rush hour traffic. One of her favourites, Elvis Presley was singing 'Good Luck Charm,' she was a great fan of Elvis's music.

Susan's home was a small rented, two bedroom furnished apartment in Poundbury, a couple of miles from Dorchester town centre, where she worked as a property adviser for Harper & Golightly, the prestigious Estate Agents. She loved her apartment and her job, in fact life was good most days; her glass was always half full, the only thorn in her side being her mother. The two of them got on reasonably well considering; in Susan's opinion, her mother relied on her too much, but she was far too kind to ever tell her mother that.

She was still humming as she parked her car and walked the short distance to her work premises, her happy mood dipping slightly as she took her key out and opened up, realising she was going to be on her own and office bound all day. The boss was on holiday and the other member of staff was having some dental treatment so had booked the whole day off. First things first she told herself, as she went into the tiny kitchen at the back, made a mug of coffee, opened a new packet of chocolate biscuits and took two out, knowing that she shouldn't, then sat down at her desk and leafed through the details of the new houses coming onto the market.

It was a busy morning, with people popping in for details of properties, and others with telephone enquiries; and she made several appointments for clients to view houses the following day. She glanced out of the window several times and could see that the weather had warmed up considerably, the sun now shining in a cloudless sky. Unable to resist any longer, and with her stomach growling in hunger, she quickly phoned her mother saying she had an appointment so wouldn't be going for lunch, turned the shop sign to 'closed', pulled on her warm grey woollen coat, and stepped out on to the sunny pavement. Finding a vacant bench in the nearby park, she sat down and opened up the tuna and sweet corn sandwich she had bought from the little shop on the corner.

Her sandwich finished, she closed her eyes against the rays of sun peaking through the branches of the trees, and sat contentedly. A few minutes passed, then suddenly laughter disturbed the peace and opening her eyes she noticed a young couple strolling past, arms entwined around each other, the girl's face upturned and smiling at her partner. They were oblivious of their surroundings, enveloped in their own cocoon of love. A stab of jealousy hit Susan as she watched them; she thought about Steve; they had been like that couple in the early days, where had it gone wrong? Divorced now over five years, there had been one or two men but no serious relationship since.

Shaking her head to remove the depressing thoughts threatening to overwhelm her and remembering the post, she opened her bag up and took out the junk mail along with the intriguing cream envelope. She put the junk mail aside and opened the envelope, finding a single page letter inside. Reading it quickly she wondered what it could mean.

You have been chosen to spend a four week holiday in the highlands of Scotland! she read, but, there was to be *no contact with the outside world*; was it someone's idea of a joke? It could not possibly be genuine could it?

About to throw it in the bin nearby with the other junk mail, she paused, something told her not to. She read it again; why her? Why had she been chosen? Tucking it away in her handbag, she strolled back to the office deciding to show her mother on the way home from work that night.

Chapter 5

A difficult woman to like, everyone said about Phyllis Godwin. Critical to the point of rudeness, she always managed to rub people up the wrong way, even her own easygoing daughter. A member of the Women's Institute for years and a volunteer with Help the Aged, she had many acquaintances but no-one she could call a close friend.

She sat in the kitchen of her two up, two down terrace house in a quiet side street of Dorchester, her lunch half eaten; wrinkling her nose up in distaste, she pushed aside the left over shop bought quiche. Susan had not come for lunch. An appointment, she had said, huh, a likely story. With elbows on the table, she rested her head in her hands for a moment. The pain at the back of her eyes grew worse; she would take some Paracetemol in a minute. Her sleep last night had been fitful; the Iris Gower book she was reading had evoked memories of Bill for some reason.

It would have been their thirty–ninth wedding anniversary this year, if he had not gone and died from a massive heart attack at the age of sixty-two. A widow now for five years, it did not seem that long. She did miss him of course, but not his domineering ways. Life was so much easier now there was more money in her purse. Bill always watched every penny, handing out just enough housekeeping money out of his weekly wages, expecting her to manage and she always had, even though at times it was a struggle. This led her on to thinking about Susan, their only child; she would have loved another one, perhaps a boy, but Bill doted on his daughter and decided that one was enough. Bill's word was final, it always was.

She was so lucky to have a daughter like Susan, who would do anything for her and never complained. Phyllis knew she was often unfair, expecting Susan to take her shopping every Saturday and a ride out to a garden centre on a Sunday, sometimes for lunch to save either of them cooking. Moreover, most days she came to Phyllis's for lunch and even called in on her way home from work. However, it was just so easy to cling on to her daughter; it made the lack of friends seem much less important.

With a big sigh, she roused herself, pushed her feet back into her comfy slippers which had slipped off when she sat at the table, and going to a drawer in the kitchen she opened a small bottle and shook out a couple of headache pills which she took with a drink of water. She donned an apron over her pale blue long sleeved jumper and co-ordinated dark blue pleated skirt; Phyllis always liked clothes to match and took care of her appearance. The paintwork didn't really need a wipe down, but picking up a cloth she thought it would pass the time until Susan called on her way home, and hopefully the headache would clear. Housework, was all she seemed to do these days.

Chapter 6

It was no good, however hard India shoved and pushed, the doors of the full-length wardrobe in her large bedroom refused to shut on the rails of designer suits and dresses, the stacks of shoes and handbags. 'Oh for goodness sake,' she muttered as she kicked the door in frustration; she would have to get rid of some of these clothes, take them to a charity shop, but not today, she could not be bothered.

Wandering into the lounge, she picked up the latest edition of Vogue, taking it with her to the kitchen, idly flicking through the pages, then discarding it the moment she saw a letter addressed to her, propped against a jug of freshly squeezed orange juice on the black granite breakfast bar.

Slitting open the envelope with a long red fingernail, she pulled out a co-ordinated cream embossed letter from a solicitor's office in Glasgow. Reading it, a big grin spread across her face, just as her father made an appearance.

'Look at this Daddy; do you think I should reply?'

Before he even spoke, India knew what her father's reaction would be.

A holiday with a difference' he read aloud. '*All expenses met,* what a load of bloody nonsense. *A life changing experience?* It's another of those Reality TV Shows. Just throw it away.' He strode out onto the balcony of their penthouse apartment.

A few minutes later India joined him, leaning against the ornamental black railings; slipping her hand under his elbow, but saying nothing as they gazed in silence at the boats gliding by on the Thames below. As the only child of Sir Harold Thompson-Smythe, she knew he only wanted the best for her, but it sometimes had its drawbacks. The plusses were enormous of course. The best education, mixing with royalty, boxes at Ascot, worldwide travel, but for all that India was lonely. She voiced that thought aloud.

'Lonely ...' her father looked at her in astonishment. 'How can you be lonely, you have so many friends, why only last week you were invited onto Charlie Fortesque's yacht for ...'

'Yes, a holiday, but that is just it, I don't need yet another holiday. I don't do anything to have a holiday from.' Not wanting to hear about *his* plans for *her* future yet again, she turned and pushed her long blond hair away from her face, kissed his smooth clean-shaven cheek; his recognisable favourite Paco Raban aftershave tickling her nostrils. 'Daddy, let's not discuss this now,' and with a gentle squeeze to his elbow, returned to the kitchen, grinning, knowing she could wrap him around her little finger. He would have forgotten all about the letter by tomorrow and then she would reply.

Chapter 7

Parking her car outside her mother's home, Susan glanced at the neat terraced house, with its gleaming windows, spotless green paintwork and well swept front step that led straight from the pavement into the property. She felt a twinge of pity for old Amy, who lived next door, whose own house front matched her mother's for cleanliness. Amy was forever being reminded by Phyllis how lucky she was to have her as a neighbour.

Susan used her own key to open the door and called, 'Cooee, it's only me Mum.'

'About time too,' was the curt response.

Susan sighed as she looked at the mean spirited woman standing by the dining table, arms crossed. Noticing the ever-increasing deep furrows across her brow, the wrinkles around her eyes, and that down turned mouth, didn't her mother ever smile any more? She was starting to look older than her fifty-nine years.

'Are you ok Mum?'

'I've had a headache all day, can't seem to shake it off.'

'Well I've got something here to cheer you up,' Susan said pulling the letter from her handbag, 'Listen to this,' her face alight with excitement.

'A holiday of a lifetime, four weeks in Scotland', she read, 'What do you think? Intriguing isn't it?'

'Give me that,' said Phyllis as she snatched it from Susan's hand and read the contents. 'I've had one of those as well; you're not going to fall for that are you?'

'Well...'

Phyllis, not waiting for an answer, continued to read aloud. *'A free four week holiday, in a castle, the outcome could be rewarding'* She would never understand her daughter's positive take on everything.

'There is *no such thing as a free lunch,* throw it away. Mine's already in the bin.'

Susan quickly crossed the room and opening her mother's bin, rummaged inside and pulled out the letter, luckily nothing had been dropped on top of it. She smoothed the letter out and yes, it was the same as hers.

'Have you asked Amy if she has had one too?'

'I went straight round, I did not want her replying to something like this, you know how confused she gets, but she had not received one.'

'It is a bit strange don't you think, why we should both get a letter like this? Anyway, what do you think, shall we reply? See what it's all about?'

'I'm putting mine back in the bin and if you've got any sense you will do the same and don't think of accepting the offer and going anywhere without me, how would I manage if you cleared off for four weeks.'

'Why does everything have to be about you, Mum? You are perfectly capable of looking after yourself, if you're going to be like that, I'm off, I'll see you tomorrow.'

The urge to slam the door on the way out was strong, but Susan resisted, it would not achieve anything. Phyllis stood tight-lipped waiting for the door to slam, but it did not. She looked at the other half of discarded quiche wrapped in Clingfilm for Susan to take home and picking it up threw it into the bin. She would give her a call a bit later, maybe, but not until after Coronation Street.

Susan's fingers gripped the steering wheel as she drove home, mind in a whirl, angry at her mother, but intrigued by the letter. Reaching the sanctuary of her small apartment, without meeting any of her neighbours, she sighed with relief as she closed the door on the outside world.

The letter was read and re-read several times before Susan put it away and settled down with a mug of tea and the local paper. Suddenly, the telephone rang, making her jump and almost spill her drink. Knowing whom it would be, her shoulders tensed as she picked up the receiver. There was no hello, no apology for earlier, just 'If you are going to reply to that letter then so am I. I'm not having you go without me.'

There was no explanation for her mother's sudden change of heart, from telling her to throw it away, to this, wanting to come too.

Phyllis, not waiting for Susan to say no, continued in a rush, 'neither of us has had a holiday for years, I have been thinking about it, it might do us both good, what do you say?'

Susan knew better than to argue, what would be the point? 'Alright Mum, if you're sure, I will write for both of us and accept the offer.'

'*Strike while the iron's hot* I say,' and the phone clicked, Phyllis had rung off. Those flipping proverbs, muttered Susan, heartily sick of her mother's sayings.

Putting the paper away, she rummaged in her stuff to be sorted cupboard for the photograph box, pulled it out and after a long search, finally settled on a photo of the two of them on a day trip to Bournemouth the previous summer. It was a sunny day, the sea was a Mediterranean blue and they were both smiling, that made a change, she thought cynically as she popped it into an envelope. Why did they need photos? She switched on her computer and began to type her reply.

Almost a week later, Susan sat at her desk in the empty office, flicking through the property sales for the last couple of months. February and March were always quiet, but spring was just around the corner and sales always picked up then. Ever the optimist, she just knew things would get better.

The mobile ringing and vibrating on the desk interrupted her thoughts, caller ID showed 'Mum.' For goodness sake, what did she want? Phyllis was at Susan's flat doing some much-needed housework. Letting it ring for a few seconds, she flipped the phone open, but before she could say anything, her mother's excited voice shrieked down the line. All Susan could hear were garbled words that she could not make head or tail of.

'Slow down Mum, what are you trying to tell me.'

Phyllis repeated herself, this time slower. 'There's a hand written envelope for you in the post, I bet it's that holiday you wrote about. It has got to be that, you don't get letters from anyone.'

Ignoring the little dig, she replied, 'Don't be silly, it could be anything. I'll be home at lunchtime and have a look, now please get off the phone, I am really busy.'

A few minutes later, her mobile rang again.

'What is it now Mum?'

'It is the holiday, we are going on holiday, there is a letter, and there are two train tickets. I told you that's what it was.' Phyllis could not contain her excitement.

'You shouldn't be opening my post, but is it really about the holiday?' Too intrigued to stay annoyed she said, 'I'll take an early lunch break, be there in fifteen minutes.'

Before Susan had chance to put her key in the lock, Phyllis opened the door, grinning from ear to ear, waving the letter in her face. Susan quickly read the contents.

It was from MacDonald, Scott & MacDonald, who were the same solicitors as before. It thanked her for accepting, and she read on:

First class train tickets to Strathdown leaving in ten days, looking forward to seeing them both. Only ten days! How was she going to get everything organised in such a short time. *A castle; twenty miles from Strathdown;* the address to remain secret, how odd!

'Are we doing the right thing Mum? Are you sure about this?'

'*Nothing ventured, nothing gained,*' was Phyllis's only reply.

Later, after dropping her mother back at her own house, Susan read the letter again. Their train seats had been booked for 20th March. Pacing up and down the lounge, her mind raced; there was her boss to explain to, bills to be settled. Whatever had possessed her to reply? And what did people wear in Scottish Castles? She imagined lots of tartan kilts and thick woolly jumpers.

She rushed into her bedroom and threw open the wardrobe door and gazed at the contents. There were lots of maxi skirts in denim, her favourite, and several baggy long sleeved t-shirts and smock tops. A few pairs of jeans and a couple of coats and some long thick wool cardigans. Any of those would be suitable, she thought, not considering anything elegant for any dinners that might be held.

Never one for dressing fashionably; her ex-husband had done a great job of knocking her self-confidence, always criticising her, so that she now found it easier to merge into the background; absolutely hating drawing attention to herself, not realising that in dressing the way she did, that in itself drew attention to her. Susan was five feet, two inches tall with a slim figure, but no-one would ever know.

Chapter 8

The clock/radio alarm ringing loudly in her ear woke Susan in a fright from a nightmare-filled sleep; she was being chased through dark woods, by a sword-waving highlander in a kilt. He was shouting at her and she was so scared, trying to find somewhere to hide. She lay in bed bathed in sweat as she re-lived the nightmare. Then last night's doubts flooded her mind as she entered the spare bedroom to wake her mother, who had stayed over the night before. She took a shower to try to clear her head. Was she mad? Was bringing her mother the right decision?

The taxi picked them up in plenty of time to catch the train from Dorchester at 07.53. The journey involved three changes of train before they reached their destination later that night.

'My arthritis will play up with all the sitting around. Why do we have to change trains so often? Twelve hours you said the journey takes, that's far too long for anyone, why couldn't they have flown us up?' Susan ignored Phyllis's barrage of questions. The journey would be endless at this rate, why couldn't her mother just shut up for a while. Armed with sandwiches, drinks and magazines they boarded the first train.

With every change of train and platform, Susan's muscles ached more and more as she pulled the suitcases behind her, holdall and handbag slung over her shoulder, whilst making sure her mother kept up. If one more passenger bumped into her with their suitcase or worse still those huge backpacks she would scream. How did they manage to carry those backpacks anyway without falling over backwards? She smiled as her imagination conjured up the sight of a backpacker, lying on his back with legs and arms waving helplessly in the air like an insect.

At last, the final leg of the journey, the Glasgow to Strathdown train. Dropping gratefully into her seat, Susan pushed her hair away from her face, closed her eyes to avoid conversation with her mother and thought about the next four weeks. A relaxing shower and a nice meal would be welcome at the end of the journey, but she still could not shake off the feeling of apprehension growing stronger by the hour. What had she done? What had she got her mother involved in?

'It's too late to change your mind now.'

For God's sake, would her mother never shut up? 'I know it's too late, but I still can't help worrying Mum.'

'You worry too much.'

'Why don't you shut your eyes and have a nap.'

At 19.26, exactly the train pulled into Strathdown station. The sky was darkening and looking around there wasn't much to see. Susan helped her mother down onto the platform, collected the suitcases, and together they walked towards the exit looking anxiously about for any sign of someone waiting to collect them.

A voice with a soft Scottish brogue saying, 'Welcome to Strathdown ladies, your carriage waits,' made them jump and turn round. In the dim light of a street lamp, they saw a tall casually dressed man with dark curly hair reaching to his shoulders, neat beard and moustache, standing by a black people carrier, the side door of which was open. 'Allow me to introduce myself,' he said, 'Hugh Campbell, Estate Manager at your service. You must be Susan and Phyllis; it is so good to meet you. Have you had a good journey? Let me get the cases loaded while you climb in and make yourselves comfortable. It'll take us just over half an hour to get to the Castle; it's too dark to see anything tonight, but I can guarantee you will love the views tomorrow when you look out of the window.'

Phyllis sat back in the seat with her eyes closed; the long journey had worn her out; but Susan leant over the back of the passenger seat and tried to engage Hugh in conversation, asking him for more information. She was dying to know more about their holiday but he was very reticent, obviously did not want to chat and soon she gave up. Tiredness now enveloping her again, she lapsed into silence.

'Here we are ladies,' Hugh suddenly said, making them sit up in their seats and gaze with interest out of the window. In front of them were large wrought iron gates, and a dilapidated board to the one side was just about distinguishable in the gloom. 'Welcome to Dunnbray Castle Hotel,' the almost indecipherable writing said. . Through the gates, a large mansion house was just visible, silhouetted against the skyline. Hugh got out and unlocked the gates, drove through, then jumped out and locked the gates again behind them.

'Why are the gates locked Hugh?' Phyllis asked, sitting up with an anxious look on her face, but Hugh pretending he hadn't heard her continued along the drive pulling up outside the house.

'This isn't a castle; it's just a big house.' Phyllis continued. 'Why did they call it a castle?'

'Shush Mum.'

Susan with her love of historical novels pictured a carriage with four handsome horses pulling up outside and a footman helping a beautifully dressed lady to alight.

Stepping out on to the gravelled drive, their gaze was drawn upwards. The property towered above them, standing three storeys high. Smooth stone pillars either side of the door supported a balcony with ornamental railings. Six curved steps led up to an ornate oak front door. An arched decorative fanlight over the top cast a pool of welcoming light.

'They could do with a darn good polish,' Phyllis said, as she noticed the brass stag's head knocker, letterbox and handle all dulled by neglect. Her eagle eyes missed nothing, even in the semi-darkness.

'Go ahead, the door's open,' Hugh said, 'Edna's getting your meal ready; I will bring the cases in.'

Phyllis pushed the door open, and followed by Susan entered the biggest hall either of them had ever seen, a magnificent room. The warmth from a large fire crackling in the hearth at the far end was a very welcome sight, drawing Phyllis over to stand in front of it, and warm her hands. Large paintings hung on every wall, hunting scenes and landscapes, portraits, probably of ancestors of the castle. One portrait in particular caught Susan's eye, it was of a very striking looking man dressed as a Highlander, gazing out over the landscape with his hand resting on the neck of his horse. Her eyes then took in two enormous brass and glass chandeliers hanging from the corniced ceiling, decorated with sparkling glass beads; wall lights created a dappled pattern on the rug covered stone floor.

Susan's eyes were drawn to the staircase; she crossed the room and unable to resist, stroked one of the stag's heads carved out of oak, which stood proudly on the newel posts. Gazing up at the wide shallow treads, carpeted in a faded tartan design, and the banisters disappearing up into the gloom of a galleried landing stirred her imagination yet again.

'Wow,' she uttered, breaking the silence, 'just look at that, it's like being on the set of one of those historical dramas. We should be in period costumes.'

'It doesn't look very clean from where I'm standing, calls itself a hotel, when it obviously hasn't been occupied for ages.' Phyllis was off again.

'Shut up Mum,' Susan whispered. 'Don't start criticising yet please.'

'Hugh...' Phyllis was just about to point out the state of the place, when she noticed he had unloaded the luggage and was on the point of leaving. Realising he had been spotted, a look of panic crossed his face and he shot out the door raising his hands and shouting to them, 'Edna's in the kitchen, she will explain everything, see you in the morning.' He closed the door quickly behind him. With the sudden realisation of what he was doing, they rushed to the door, pulling it open just in time to see the red taillights disappearing down the drive.

Hugh felt guilty as he drove away leaving them like that. Should he have stayed and explained more? Was it right what Angus was doing? His mobile phone rang interrupting his thoughts; it was Angus asking him if Susan and Phyllis had arrived safely.

Back inside, Phyllis asked, 'Why has he left us?'

'I've no idea; he couldn't get out quick enough could he? Let's go and find this Edna person, whoever she is,' Susan replied, her feeling of apprehension growing by the minute. 'I wonder why she didn't meet us at the door.'

They were just about to enter the kitchen when a short dumpy woman in her fifties, dressed in plaid trousers and black top with severely cut straight grey hair, which she pushed back behind her ears, came towards them, hands outstretched in greeting.

'Come in, come in,' she said as they introduced themselves. 'I am Edna Hill, the housekeeper; you must be famished after your journey.' She smiled, but her blue eyes glinted coldly and Susan shivered involuntarily as they shook hands. 'I've laid on a cold supper for you so that you can relax and help yourselves, but first, would you like to take your cases upstairs to your bedrooms, Susan I have put you in the *Rose* room and Phyllis you have the *Poppy* room, you'll see the names on the doors. I'll put the kettle on ready for a nice cup of tea when you come down.'

'Do it yourself, I see,' said Phyllis.

'Shush Mum, and what a lovely idea having names for the rooms,' continued Susan, struggling up the stairs with their cases. Phyllis followed behind huffing and puffing carrying the holdall. 'Here's your room Mum.' She pushed open the door with her shoulder, put the cases down and looked around. 'This is lovely, I hope mine is as nice as this, look a four poster bed, I've never slept in one of those before have you? There's an ensuite too.'

Phyllis did not answer; she was too busy running her hand along the edge of the dressing table.

'Look at this,' she held out dust covered fingers, 'it must be a very cushy number that woman has here, call herself a housekeeper indeed.'

'Leave it Mum, please, just for tonight, I am tired, don't make a fuss, we can say something in the morning.'

Moving next door to the *Rose* room, they found similar furnishings.

Susan looked around her and smiled. The rooms might look as if they hadn't been used for ages, but they were warm and welcoming and the bedding at least felt clean and fresh as she ran her hand over the sheets.

'Let's have a quick wash and freshen up and then go down, I'm starving,' Phyllis said as she went back to her room.

Susan swilled her face, then looking at herself in the mirror, thought about the reaction she felt on meeting Edna. I do not like that woman, and I don't think she likes us either. Susan reacted very quickly to people she met, instant likes and dislikes; it was an instinctive feeling, one that she had come to trust over the years. A few minutes later, they were back in the kitchen, where they found Edna making a pot of tea.

'That's just what I need, thank you.' Phyllis took a cup from Edna. 'What time is breakfast?'

'Any time you like, just help yourselves. Didn't anyone tell you this is a self-catering holiday? You will find everything you need, but either Hugh or I can pop in tomorrow, and see how you are getting on.' Picking her coat up from the back of one of the Windsor kitchen chairs, she gave them a wave and disappeared. They gazed after her, open-mouthed.

When she finally found her voice Susan said, 'What do you make of that?' She could not believe what had just happened.

'She's just left us here in this great big house all on our own. I suppose we are on our own. Shall we have a look and see? Susan, I don't like this one bit, I'm scared.'

'We'll be alright, Mum, try not to worry, we can't be the only ones here can we?' Susan spoke with a lot more confidence than she felt. 'Let's have that cup of tea and something to eat, then perhaps we can have a quick look round.'

Chapter 9

In his youth, before Archie met and married Isobel, rumours spread that he had caused a local girl to get pregnant. These rumours were never substantiated, but strangely, around the same time, Mary, a farmer's daughter suddenly found work in Aberdeen, a very good job apparently, a ladies maid no less and her father became the proud owner of a flock of sheep and some new farming equipment. Nothing was ever proved, and Isobel and her father were never sure if there was any truth in the rumours and gave Archie the benefit of the doubt.

About fourteen years later, a young girl appeared in the village, her name was Morag; her parents had both died and she was now desperate to find work. Allister heard about her arrival and took pity on the girl offering her a position of housemaid at Dunnbray.

A quiet, hard working girl, Morag eventually married Jack, one of the gardeners and left her employment when she became pregnant. Edna, their one and only child was born, and soon Morag went back to work and many years later when she eventually retired, Edna took her place as housemaid in the big house.

Always aware of her relationship to Angus, Morag never talked about it, she felt it was not her place to do so. The only person she told was Edna, her daughter, when she was old enough, but said that it was to remain their secret; nothing good would come out of telling the McPhail family the truth.

But Edna was a totally different character to her mother, where Morag was kind; Edna had a spiteful edge to her. Morag was helpful, but Edna would do nothing that she considered was not her job. She could be rude and disrespectful. After a time she left Dunnbray and married Joe the local blacksmith, quickly becoming pregnant and producing a son, Jamie, who became the apple of her eye.

When Jamie was five years old, Edna returned to Dunnbray, as housekeeper to Angus, who now needed help. The anger she felt at her mother's and grandmother's treatment was never far from the surface, and she had been determined to get back to Dunnbray one way or another and this opportunity was too good to miss. Angus allowed her to bring Jamie with her during the holidays. She was a strange woman, no one able or even wanting to get close to her. She had confided details about her past to Joe, but he just thought her bitter and out for revenge, and told her to forget the past and look to the future and concentrate on their son, which she did, but not in a good way. She spent hours talking with Jamie, but the conversations always died if anyone approached. She watched everything that went on, and always knew Angus's business.

The bitterness and anger Edna felt ate away at her over the years. She was determined to put Jamie where he rightfully belonged and would stop at nothing to achieve that. The more she plotted his future, the more unbalanced she became. Unfortunately, Jamie was not the brightest of lads and never realised how disturbed his mother really was.

Chapter 10

Removing the lid off the ice bucket, India yelled. 'There is no ice, Consuela, where are you? Get me some ice.'

The evening was unusually warm for March. Opening the sliding glass doors leading to the penthouse patio and carrying her gin and tonic through, she sank into a well-padded garden chair.

Consuela appeared at her side. 'Sorry Miss India, I didn't know you would be back this early, here's your ice.' She placed the ice bucket at India's side. 'Can I get you anything else, something to eat maybe? And here's a letter which came for you earlier.'

'No, for goodness sake just leave me in peace.' Without looking at Consuela she snatched the letter out of the maid's hands, then used the tongs to plop a couple of ice cubes into her drink. Downing it in one gulp, she opened and read the letter, looked at the train ticket enclosed and with her eyes raised to the sky she whispered thank you to an invisible presence. Letting out a shout of joy she rushed into the lounge to find her father.

'Look Daddy, remember that letter I showed you the other day. I'm sorry but I did reply to it and I am to go to Scotland in ten days time, you don't really mind do you?'

'Let me see that. I knew you would go behind my back. I have already told you it's a reality TV show, don't you get involving the family in anything embarrassing; I have my reputation to uphold. I would rather you did not go.'

India adopted the little girl pleading voice, which always worked and said, 'But Daddy, I really want to go, it sounds so exciting and I have been getting so bored just lately, and you wouldn't want me to get a job and work in a shop or anything would you? This might be just what I need, go on Daddy say yes, say I can go, please.'

He knew he could not resist, so replied, 'All right, but the slightest hint that things aren't right, you telephone me, and I'll send the car for you. Do you hear me India?'

'Yes Daddy, thank you Daddy. I love you.' India rushed back to her bedroom, her mind racing with all the things to do before leaving. New outfits to buy, hair coloured and trimmed, pedicure, manicure and a hot stone therapy, a new treatment at her local spa, which she had been meaning to try. And of course a lunch with all her friends to tell them how lucky she was.

Unable to take India to the station himself, Sir Harry arranged for Keith, the chauffeur, to take her to catch the 12.30 from Euston. Dumping her luggage on the pavement Keith drove off, with the excuse that parking outside the station was illegal and he would be moved on by the police, but in reality he couldn't stand his boss's daughter; he was employed to drive Sir Harry around, not that spoilt brat.

India glared after him. He needed to be taught a lesson; she would speak to her father when she got back, he was lucky to have a job, ungrateful man. She picked up her luggage and strode into the station, her air of confidence hiding the nerves that she felt.

The temperature had dropped over the last few days; the cold wind whipped up by the narrow platforms swept India's hair across her face, as she gazed blankly up at an overhead screen, trying to work out which platform she needed. Shivering, she was about to find someone to ask, when a voice beside her said, 'Can I help? Where are you travelling to?' A tall middle-aged man smartly dressed in a dark suit, white shirt and conservative tie stood next to her.

'Preston, Glasgow, then on to Strathdown,' she replied, giving him the once over.

'Platform 5 then, that's my train too. Would you like some help with your luggage?' Without waiting for a reply, he picked up her case and walked with her along the platform. The train was already in, so glancing through the window he quickly found some empty seats and was just about to lift her case in through an open doorway when she said, 'oh no, not there, I have a first class ticket, those seats will be at the front of the train.' She strode off in front of him, climbed aboard and looked at him shocked as he dumped her luggage in the doorway, wasn't he going to put it in the luggage rack for her? What was wrong with men these days?

Douglas McKinley looked at the girl he had recognised on the platform; he should have known better than to offer to help after all the information he had gathered on her.

India watched him from the doorway as he walked back up the platform and boarded the train a few carriages back.

Hmm, smart, well-dressed, educated voice, but only travelling second class, she instantly dismissed him from her mind, stored her case and holdall and found a seat. India was far more used to travelling in taxis, limousines and planes and her heart pounded with the excitement of a long train journey, but she hid it well, nonchalantly taking out her Blackberry and texting her friends as if catching a train was a perfectly natural thing to do.

Several hours later, the train finally pulled in to Strathdown station. Thank God, India thought as she scrunched up her throbbing toes in her stilettos, why had she worn those stupid high heels for the journey. Because you look good, that is why, she told herself as with great deliberation she slipped on the navy jacket, which matched her dress, slung her handbag over her shoulder, took her holdall and large suitcase from the luggage rack, and stepped down onto the platform.

While she waited to be collected, she noticed the man who had carried her bags at Euston; he passed her by with a slight nod of his head, climbed into a waiting taxi and vanished from sight. She idly wondered why he had travelled to this small town and what his business was.

Chapter 11

The endless night was over; the sun's rays could be seen peeping between gaps in the curtains. The bed was comfortable but Susan had tossed and turned all night. She wished she could have got up and made herself a drink, but did not like the idea of creeping around a strange house in the dark, trying to find light switches. She had heard her mother moving about in the night, obviously unable to sleep either. Old properties always seemed to creak and groan as if the weight of the passing years rested on their weary shoulders, but it could be unnerving for someone not familiar with the sounds. With a glance at the travel clock at the side of the bed, she saw it was seven - thirty so decided to get up.

Pulling back the heavy damask curtains, her breath caught in her throat. Hugh had been right about the view. The long gravel drive reached out to gates at the far end of the grounds. Lawns stretching out on either side, interspersed with flowerbeds and trees. On the other side of the boundary wall an avenue of beech trees could be seen disappearing round a bend in the lane, and on either side miles of pine forest, with moorlands beyond and finally mountains on the distant horizon, and was that snow she could see on the top? She screwed up her eyes to focus, but still wasn't sure. She wondered what the mountains were called.

Her eyes dropped to the garden again, and closer inspection showed the grass was in need of cutting, and the flowerbeds were choked with weeds. The garden was in the same uncared for state as the house by the looks of it, and there was a wire fence dividing the garden in two, which seemed an odd thing to do. Someone needs to love this house and garden again was the thought that went through her mind.

She turned from the window and wandered around the room; her feet sank into the thick burgundy carpet, which looked recently laid. She picked up the hairbrush from the Victorian dressing table set, and wondered whose hair it had brushed over the years. Gazed at her slightly distorted face in the antique mirror; moving on to the paintings of hunting scenes hanging on the walls; she was not too keen on stags being chased and killed, but pictures of this style were typical of the era. The room had a warm welcoming feel to it, the radiator was piping hot, but such a shame it was not a bit cleaner. She smiled to herself knowing her mother would be there with dusters and vacuum before the day was out.

She took a quick shower, dragged a hairbrush through her still-damp curls, and dressed in her usual uniform of casual jeans and baggy jumper, then knocking on her mother's door and receiving no reply, she peeped in to find the room was empty; her mother must already be downstairs. She ran down the wide staircase, running her hand gently over the stag's head again at the bottom. Wasn't it all just wonderful? The worries of the night before disappeared in the pleasant light of day as she crossed the hall. The sun, through the windows, creating pools of bright light on the stone floor. Susan entered the kitchen with a happy smile on her face.

Phyllis was sitting at the table, cup of tea in hand, the usual miserable expression on her face and surrounded by all the dirty dishes of the night before.

With a cheery grin Susan said, 'Hi, Mum, did you sleep ok?' Already anticipating what the answer would be.

'No, I did not, once I realised we were the only ones here, and everything creaks and groans, this house is far too big and empty, I don't like it one bit.'

'It's always difficult in a strange place the first night and it is an old place, you have to expect some noises; you'll get used to it and after a few nights, you won't even hear the creaks.' Susan as always tried to jolly her mother along. 'What about the view though, have you had a look, isn't it wonderful? You can see for miles out of the upstairs windows; I cannot wait to explore can you? I am so excited. What have we got for breakfast, have you had a look yet?'

Phyllis did not bother replying, she could not see what all the excitement was about, it was a big old house standing in big grounds, so what.

Knowing she would not get a reply, Susan opened up cupboards, which were full of everything they could possibly need. There was a large selection of cereals, a choice of breads and jars of locally made marmalade and jams. The fridge was well stocked with cheeses, ham, milk, butter and various spreads. 'We are not going to starve that's for sure. Now, I fancy toast and marmalade, does that suit you too?'

'We need to get this lot tidied up first before we create more dirty dishes.' Phyllis pointed to the table.

'It won't take long,' Susan replied piling the stuff into the sink and turning on the hot tap. The hot water was plentiful; she had been pleasantly surprised with how good the shower was, and the radiators were all warm. It felt a cosy house considering its size.

Susan was hoping Hugh would arrive early; there was so much to ask him. 'I'll have to make sure I put his number in here,' she said flipping up the cover on her mobile phone, 'why there's no signal; I noticed a phone in the hall, I'll see if that's working.'

She picked the receiver up, but the line was silent. 'There's no outside line either, we can't call anyone.'

'Don't you remember what the letter said, *no contact with the outside world*, wasn't that the wording?'

'I didn't realise they were that serious, what if there's an emergency? I'll add it to the list to ask Hugh.'

Breakfast over and the kitchen tidied, they decided to explore while they waited for Hugh to arrive. The back door in the kitchen actually led out onto the side of the house, and they agreed to look out there later. A doorway at the side of the kitchen took them into a utility room, complete with storage cupboards, washing machine, tumble dryer and large chest freezer. Lifting the lid of the freezer, they found it well stocked with meats and fish and frozen vegetables.

'There's enough food here to feed an army. I'm surprised there's no dishwasher,' Susan commented, looking around.

'Well, you needn't think I am doing all the washing up either.' Susan just gave her mum a look.

Beyond the utility room was a further room, empty except for a few cupboards and coat hooks around the walls, and another door to the outside, which they thought would probably have been used on wet days, where the men could leave dirty wellies and coats after a day's shooting, or whatever men did years ago. As they turned to go back to the kitchen, they spotted another door tucked away in the corner.

'Where does this lead to then?' Phyllis said opening it up.

'We have a cellar by the looks of it,' replied Susan. 'Shall I go down and take a look?' She fumbled around for a light switch, found it and started down the stone steps; the light didn't stretch very far and as she crept deeper into the dark space, hand on the brick wall to keep her balance and hopefully feel another light switch, her thoughts went into overdrive imagining spiders, mice, or rats even? Not one for swearing usually, she let out a loud 'Bloody hell!'

'Susan, what are you doing down there?'

'It's ok Mum,' she called as her fingers touched another light switch, almost out of her reach on the side wall, she flicked it on and the cellar was suddenly bathed in bright white light, thank God for that. She shouted to Phyllis to come down carefully, because the steps were steep. The lights had revealed rack upon rack of wines and spirits, all covered in a thick layer of dust.

'It doesn't look like anyone has been down here in years, Mum,' she said gazing around in astonishment.

'Do you think we can help ourselves?' Phyllis's enthusiasm perked up a bit as she glanced around hopefully, looking for the sherry; she did enjoy a small glass occasionally.

'The door wasn't locked, so I am sure no-one will mi… what on earth's that?' She jumped as a great clanging sound could be heard from upstairs. Realising it must be the doorbell, Susan raced ahead of her mother up the stairs and opened the door to Hugh. His eyebrows shot up in surprise, she hadn't been particularly smart last night when he had met them at the station, but today she was worse, scruffy jeans, baggy top and her hair, why didn't she do something with it and was that a cobweb he could see?

Susan fidgeted uncomfortably under his critical gaze and pushing hair off her face mumbled something about exploring.

'Is everything ok, are you alright?'

'Sorry, yes thanks, I've just run up from the cellar, there's a good stock of drink down there, will it be alright if we help ourselves to the occasional bottle?'

'Of course, no problem, take what you want. Now, do you need anything else?'

'Hugh, I have no mobile signal, the phone doesn't work, we are self catering according to Edna, it's not very clean and we seem to be the only two people here, it isn't quite what we expected. Do we really have to stay here?'

Hugh reminded her of the letters she had received and that she had agreed to everything, especially *the no contact paragraph*, so what was the problem; of course they weren't going to be the only ones there, it just so happened they were the first to arrive.

'But it didn't mention self catering.' Susan was getting exasperated with Hugh.

'But it did say *a holiday with a difference,* this is what you are getting and you did sign to say you were happy with the arrangements, now either Edna or myself will call everyday so please don't worry and another lady is coming tonight, so you will have some company.'

'How many are expected altogether?'

Hugh told her that there would be five or six in total. The others would be arriving as soon as they could make arrangements. It would have been so much easier if they could all have come together, as some of them now would not be staying the whole four weeks as originally planned. They had families to consider, so it was understandable.

There were more questions from Susan and Phyllis, but Hugh would not be drawn on why they had been invited, who the other women were or why everything was such a big secret and in the end, they gave up. An invitation to join them for coffee was politely declined, Hugh saying he was too busy.

'He doesn't want to talk to us does he?' Phyllis commented after he left. 'He's scared he might let something slip if he stays. Why should he feel like that?' Susan had no answer.

The rest of the day was spent in more exploration of the house. Double doors opening off the hall led into a magnificent dining room with an oak floor, which when given a good polish would look beautiful. In the centre of the room stood a large mahogany table complete with sixteen high backed upholstered chairs. The two carver chairs, one at each end of the table, were so heavy, that Susan could not move them. One enormous mahogany sideboard was full of a complete Georgian dinner service, recognisable by the dark blue and gold decorative band around the white porcelain, and another matching sideboard contained a set of heavy solid silver cutlery. There were drawers packed with neatly folded snowy white linen tablecloths and napkins.

'Just look at all this, wouldn't it be wonderful to dine in here Mum.' Susan ran her hands appreciatively along one of the sideboards, and then discreetly wiped her fingers down her jeans to remove the dust, hoping her mother had not noticed.

Phyllis snorted her disapproval.

Disappointed with her mother's reaction, who was totally incapable of seeing the beauty in anything, Susan continued from room to room. First of all a small, cosy sitting room leading off the dining room, with a three piece suite covered in a chintz fabric, a small fireplace, a china cabinet and two coffee tables, with table lamps. It would be lovely in here with the thick curtains drawn and a fire burning brightly.

'Look at those curtains, some of the rings have come loose and the hems want re-stitching.'

'Something for you to do then Mum, you like sewing.'

'I shall turn into a skivvy in this place if I'm not careful.'

It was Susan's turn to ignore her mother.

On the other side of the hall, to the left of the front door was a much larger sitting room with enough comfy chairs and sofas to seat about twenty people, this room alone was bigger than the whole of Susan's small apartment. Rugs again partly covered the oak floor. This time the walls were hung with paintings of great sailing ships, tossed about on stormy seas. There must have been a connection with the sea at some stage in the house's history. A door in the side wall opened into a small library, which gave off the musty smell of a room unused for some time.

Phyllis ran her hands along the shelves of the bookcases, which covered two complete walls, floor to ceiling. She held out her fingers to show Susan. 'Just loo…'

'Yes, I know they are all filthy, you don't need to keep pointing it out. Perhaps we should look for some dusters and cloths and give the place a clean, it would give us something to do.'

Walking out of yet another door ahead of her mother she entered a narrow passageway, repeating her favourite mantra under her breath, *'Don't let her get to you, don't let her get to you.'* Four weeks was a long time to spend in each other's company; could she cope with it?

To her right the passageway led back into the main hall, but her eyes fell on two more doors nearest to her and she went to open the first one. The handle turned, but nothing happened, she pushed, then pulled but the door wouldn't move, it was locked; that's strange, she thought, trying the second door, which was also locked.

'Why do you think that is?' she said to Phyllis, who by this time was standing behind her.

'No idea, and I have had enough for one day, I am going to give my bedroom a vacuum and dust, I am not sleeping in filth another night.'

Susan sighed as she watched her mother leave, and then re-entered the library. It might smell musty, but there was a lovely peaceful feel about it. A few days with the window open and a good clean would work wonders. She sat in the dark green leather swivel chair behind a huge oak desk, facing the garden, and gazed about her. There was a small fireplace, a matching small dark green leather chesterfield and an occasional table. The polished oak floor, similar to the dining room and sitting rooms, was mostly covered by a large rug. This would make a lovely retreat when she needed to get away from her mother. She felt herself relaxing, her shoulders gradually dropping from their usual position up by her ears whenever she was in her mother's company, and the tension in her neck eased. Yes, she thought, I am not going to let mum spoil this holiday.

She looked out of the window again and seeing the sun shining, decided a walk round the grounds was called for. Walking back through the hall, she threw open the front door and took a deep breath, the fresh Scottish air filling her nostrils. She raked her fingers through her hair and walked towards the circular flowerbed in the middle of the drive, bent down and pulled a few dandelions out. The difference was immediate; all thoughts of a walk disappeared as she pulled a few more weeds out and soon cleared a large area of garden. Daffodils and tulips were struggling to force their way through, their short green shoots just visible. Different varieties of small Hebes emerged and in the centre was a statue of some sort. About to rescue it from its prison of ivy, her work was interrupted, by Phyllis calling out.

'Dinner's ready, you've been out there hours, come on in.'

Not realising how long she had been outside, she quickly washed her hands at the sink, then joined her mother at the kitchen table. Phyllis had rustled up tasty lamb chops with vegetables and gravy and Susan realised she was starving.

'Well done Mum, this is lovely, did you find your way round the kitchen okay, what's it like using an Aga? You've never had one of those before.'

'I've quite enjoyed it actually, that Aga is good; you know Hilda, one of the ladies at the W.I. well, she has one and swears by it, wait 'til I tell her I have cooked on one too, that'll wipe the smug look off her face.'

Did her mother always have to have a dig at others? Susan despaired. Roll on the arrival of more company, perhaps one of them would be more her mother's age and get her to cheer up a bit. They sat and chatted through their meal, a most unusual occurrence for them. Many hours were spent in each other's company at home, but somehow Phyllis always spoiling it with her negativity about everything and Susan struggling to turn the conversations into something positive. She discreetly looked at her watch; the new lady must be arriving soon.

Chapter 12

At last, they heard the sound of the front door opening and Susan rushed out ahead of her mother to greet the new arrival. She took a step back as an elegant girl with a walk perfected by catwalk models on their five-inch stilettos stalked into the hall, a look of utter disdain on her face. Susan's glance took in the expensive outfit and the long flowing blond hair, a sinking feeling in her stomach. Looking down her nose at Susan the girl said, 'and you are?'

'Susan, and this is my mother Phyllis, have you had a good journey? I expect you are feeling as tired as we were yesterday; come and have a cup of tea, what was your name? I missed what you said.' Susan gabbled, shrinking under the arrogant gaze.

'India Thompson-Smythe and you,' she said turning to Hugh who was hovering in the doorway, 'take my bags up to my room for me, and be careful, they are worth a lot of money.'

Hugh, completely ignoring her turned to Susan and said he would see them in the morning and would she kindly explain everything to India, then he was gone; this time Susan could understand his reluctance to stay another minute.

'Come along India, let's go into the kitchen, we can sort your bedroom out after you've had something to eat. You have a lovely name, were you born in India? Come and tell us all about yourself, how far have you travelled? Have you been to Scotland before?'

'Susan for goodness sake stop rabbiting, let the girl get a word in edgeways.' Phyllis felt irritated listening to her daughter. The saying *Better to remain silent and be thought a fool, rather than to speak and remove all doubt,* popped into her mind. She realised guiltily that she shouldn't think about her daughter in that way, but she did have the habit of talking too much when she was nervous.

India totally ignored all the questions and instead asked, 'Is this it then? Am I expected to stay here with just you two? Isn't there any staff? That man wouldn't tell me anything about the place; I thought he was extremely rude.'

'It *takes one to know one.*' Susan heard her mother muttering again; and with a quick glare at Phyllis, turned to India and said, 'There are just us two at present, I'm afraid; this is it; it's a self catering holiday would you believe. There are some more women coming within the next few days; we were shocked too, when we arrived last night, weren't we Mum? But it's not that bad once you get used to it.' Susan gave India an encouraging smile.

India looked at them in horror. 'They don't expect me to stay here do they? I should have listened to Daddy, he was right all along.' India's high-pitched whine grated on Phyllis's ears. 'I am going to ring Daddy now to send someone to fetch me.'

'Daddy would send someone to fetch you would he, how posh,' Phyllis sneered, 'he must be important then, who is he anyway?'

'He's Sir Harold Thompson-Smythe of course, you must have heard of him, or seen him on TV.'

'No,' they both said, the name meant nothing to either of them.

India searched for her mobile.

'It's no good trying your mobile, there's no signal, I discovered that yesterday,' Susan said watching India rummage in her handbag.

'Well, there must be a land line then.' India's whining voice continued.

'Yes, but it is disconnected, please come and sit down, let's have a chat and do have something to eat, you've had a long journey.'

Seated in the kitchen after inspecting the chair for specks of dirt, India continued in the same whiny voice. 'Why has he left us here? He can't do that, what are we supposed to do? I'm starving, what's to eat? Who's cooking the meals?'

'I am at the moment, though I expect that to change; now what would you like to eat?' India was offered a choice of food, all of which she turned her nose up at, which did nothing to endear her to Phyllis. Standing up, India selected a banana from the fruit bowl, and turning to Susan said she would like to see her room.

As they reached the landing, Susan having been left to carry the bags, breathed heavily as she pointed to the rooms and said, 'Which one would you like India? Mum is in the Poppy room, I have the Rose room, there are Daffodil, Tulip, Iris and Peony left, which is your favourite flower?'

'For goodness sake, I don't have a favourite and what's wrong with this one?' India pointed, and then walked through the open door of the largest bedroom, which was positioned over the hall and front door, with a huge bay window and French doors opening onto the balcony. 'I'll take this one; make the bed up for me will you?'

'This room is not meant to be used; Edna told us we are only to use the made-up ones,' Susan replied, ushering India back out and shutting the door firmly.

'Hugh mentioned an Edna, the housekeeper I understand, why isn't she here? Can I speak to her about this room? I want this one.'

'Edna does not come very often apparently, and you cannot speak to her, the phones don't work remember, please just take one of the other rooms, they are all the same.'

India chose Tulip after much to-ing and fro-ing to see which was the largest, even though they were all the same size.

'I'll leave you to unpack, come back downstairs and have a hot chocolate or something before bed, a banana isn't enough, and we'll see you in a few minutes.'

Susan sighed as she ran back downstairs; now she had another difficult person to deal with as well as her mother. What had she done to deserve this? Taking a deep breath, she rejoined Phyllis in the kitchen, repeating the conversation with India who expected her to make up the bed as if she was a chambermaid. They were still discussing India's rudeness when they heard a loud wail coming from upstairs and rushed up to see what the problem was. India stood in the middle of the room holding a beautiful pale fuchsia evening gown against her and looking in the cheval mirror.

'What a beautiful dress.' Susan said enviously. 'It must be a designer one?'

'Oscar de la Renta,' India cried, 'I bought it specially to wear for the banquets I was sure they would be having, as it was supposed to be a castle, and now it's not even a castle; I'll never be able to wear it here in this horrible, dirty place. I won't be able to wear any of my lovely clothes, and I wouldn't be seen dead in clothes like yours.' She threw herself onto her bed sobbing.

Wondering how much more rudeness she could take from this girl, Susan shut the bedroom door with a bang and her and Phyllis made their way back downstairs.

'Well I never, have you ever met anyone like her? Such a spoilt brat, a good clip round the ear would sort her out. Are you going to let her keep talking to you like that?'

Susan sighed, ever the peace maker and said, 'let's just try and ignore it shall we, if she does stay she might get better, try not to be so unkind, it must be a shock for her coming here, it was for us too, remember last night how we felt; and she is obviously very spoilt. Her family must be extremely wealthy, judging by her clothes, that dress alone would have cost a fortune, and that luggage is Louis Vuitton.'

'*Spare the rod and spoil the child* I say.'

'You must admit she is very pretty though isn't she? I wonder why she got the letter; she comes from a totally different background to u...'

Phyllis had heard enough 'Huh, *Beauty is only skin deep.*'

India never made an appearance again that night, and Susan and Phyllis could hear no sound as they listened outside her door when they went to bed.

With a heavy heart, Susan climbed into bed and picked up her book. She had so looked forward to some pleasant company, but they had ended up with India, goodness knows what the rest of the guests would be like. She had just found her page when she heard a noise from above her room; she got out of bed so that she could hear more clearly and yes, there it was again, a sound like something heavy being dragged across the floor above. It wasn't the usual creaks and groans of an old house that disturbed her and her mother and kept them awake the night before. She shivered in fright, went out onto the landing and tapped lightly on her mother's door.

'What's going on?' Phyllis asked as she peeped round the door.

'Did you hear that noise on the next floor? I think there is someone up there; I am scared. You must have heard something, Mum; you are in the room next to mine.

'Sorry, Susan, but no, only the same as I heard last night, I didn't hear what you're describing.'

Their voices disturbed India, who poked her head out of her bedroom and seeing Susan's scared expression asked what was wrong.

'For goodness sake stop acting like a child, it's just birds or a squirrel; they get into houses you know. I can't hear anything anyway, go back to bed.' India closed her door again.

Phyllis thought Susan was imagining it too, but said, 'Leave your door open if you're worried and I'll leave mine open too, then if you hear anything again just give me a shout, now goodnight Susan, try and get some sleep.' She went back to her room surprised at Susan's reaction, she wasn't usually so frightened of anything, it must be this house, it was far too big for just a few of them.

Susan entered her bedroom, leaving her door wide open. Standing in the middle of the room, she listened for what seemed like hours, until shivering with cold, she crawled under the bedclothes, pulled the covers up over her head and tried to sleep. It was a long time coming, but eventually she fell into a fitful sleep, dreaming of ghosts and burglars.

Chapter 13

Sitting at the breakfast table, Susan and Phyllis were just finishing their second cup of tea, when they heard the tap, tap of India's stilettos as she crossed the stone floor in the hall. They stared at her open-mouthed as she sashayed into the room, a picture of elegance in her cream designer slacks, co-ordinating cream and brown cashmere sweater, and four-inch heels.

Sensing a caustic comment from her mother coming and desperately trying to steer the conversation away from it, Susan said in a panic, 'You're right about this place, Mum, are we going to tackle it ourselves today, give it a bit of a clean before anyone else arrives? It's such a shame to leave it in this state. It would be nice to get the dining and sitting rooms done, don't you think?'

Phyllis, not to be distracted, muttered, 'Well, someone over there doesn't intend doing any work I see.'

Glaring at her mother, Susan snapped, 'Mum please stop that.' Turning to India she said, 'Why are you dressed like that? Have you not brought anything casual with you, like jeans or T-shirts?'

'This *is* casual, why what's wrong with it?' India looked down at her outfit.

Deciding to ignore the question, Susan stood, placed her mug in the washing-up bowl and told India to help herself to breakfast, and would she mind washing up when she finished as they needed to get on with the cleaning.

'Wash the dishes, are you joking? We have a maid at home to do this sort of stuff. If you think I am washing up, you are in for a surprise; I am not ruining my nails for anyone. While you are standing there, stick a piece of toast in for me will you?'

Susan looked at her. 'If we are supposed to be self catering India, then we need to sort out who does what, that's only fair and you are quite capable of making your own toast.'

'That shiny gadget there is the toaster in case you don't know what one looks like.' Phyllis could not resist a dig.

'Well you can count me out, I am not self-catering. I am going home.' There was that awful nasal whine again!

'Now look here, young lady, we are getting a bit sick of your attitude.' Phyllis had heard enough. 'We are all in this together; none of us can leave, we all agreed to stay here for four weeks. How are we going to leave anyway if we can't contact anyone?'

'Why should I listen to you? you miserable old bag, don't tell me what to do.' India stormed out of the kitchen.

'That went well mother, what are we supposed to do with her?'

'Just ignore her, she's not our responsibility.'

Phyllis and Susan decided to tackle the dining room first while they waited for Hugh or Edna to arrive. Collecting dusters and mops, they made a start. Phyllis shook one of the curtains, and was immediately covered in a cloud of dust. Coughing and spluttering she said, 'We ought to take these down before we do anything else,' and frowned as she looked up at the huge floor to ceiling curtains. 'Have we got anything to stand on? We need a stepladder or something, these curtains are really heavy.'

Leaving the dining room to search for a stepladder, they saw India coming back down the stairs with a smile on her face.

'Don't you just love this staircase,' she said to them, 'these wide, shallow steps, so easy to walk up and down, and the carpet not reaching all the way to the sides, so it leaves the wood showing, and the brass stair rods,' she continued, as she walked slowly down. 'it's just as you'd imagine on a film set isn't it?' she turned to look at them with such an animated look on her face, they were quite taken aback.

'What?' She said, 'What have I said now?' Seeing them staring at her.

'We're shocked that's all,' said Phyllis, 'that's the first nice thing you have said since you arrived.'

'Why you horrible sarky old woman,' India screeched. 'I can't say anything without your nasty comments, how on earth does Susan put up with you? I won't bother speaking at all if that's your attitude,' and with that she tottered back up the stairs to her bedroom.

'Well done Mum, you've done it again. Will you please stop stirring things up and try to be a bit more tolerant, I'm getting fed up with this, it was supposed to be a holiday.'

'Well, if you're going to take her side, I'll leave you to your exploration, I'm going to have a cup of tea.' Off Phyllis went muttering to herself about not having any newspaper to read.

Sighing deeply, Susan carried on the search for a stepladder, but being unsuccessful, retraced her steps, struggling to carry a large mahogany coffee table from the small sitting room, and placing it in front of the first window. Lifting one of the heavy dining chairs and placing it on top of the coffee table, she climbed up carefully and unhooked one pair of the brocade curtains. Dropping them on the floor, she climbed back down and sat in a window seat to get her breath back. It was exhausting all this housework and dirty too, she would need another shower.

She roused from a daydream by the sound of Hugh's voice calling from the front door. Without giving him time to draw a breath, Susan rushed out and fired off a whole load of questions, about Edna, about when the others were arriving, whether they could go out of the grounds, and most important of all, why were those doors locked?

'Ah,' Hugh replied, backed up against the wall under Susan's bombardment, thinking he would answer the last question first; in fact, this was the only question he could remember. 'You've discovered the locked doors I see. I suppose one of us should have explained before. The locked doors are for your safety. That part of the house is in a state of disrepair. Dunnbray hasn't been looked after too well for the last few years, as you can see.'

'Then why was this place chosen as our holiday destination? It would be like going abroad and staying in an unfinished hotel. Should we be provided with hard hats for our safety?' Phyllis's voice was icy as she came out of the kitchen on hearing Hugh's voice. 'Are we fully insured?'

Hugh chose to ignore the questions as he handed Susan a basket of fresh bread, milk and vegetables.

'What about Edna?' Susan asked, 'where does she fit in to all this, because she obviously doesn't do a great deal around here, the place is so dusty, and we haven't seen her since we arrived either.'

'She's here in case there's a problem, but otherwise you won't be seeing much of her, she's only part-time, she works somewhere else, same as me.'

'This place hasn't seen a lot of her for months by the look of it,' Phyllis muttered under her breath.

Hugh tried to explain that Dunnbray was selected for a specific reason, which would become clear at the end of the four weeks. They could walk around the grounds, he went on, but they couldn't leave the premises. The gate was always locked and the wall was too high to climb.

'We would appreciate it if you stuck to the agreement and not try to leave,' he said.

'We? Who are we then? The solicitors who wrote or are they acting on behalf of someone else?' Susan said, quickly noticing what Hugh just said.

He immediately realised his mistake. 'They are acting on someone's behalf, but I cannot tell you who, or why, not yet anyway. You just have to trust me on this Susan; all will be revealed as soon as you have all spent a few weeks here.'

India joined them and interrupted the conversation. 'Hugh, I demand to go home. I want to call my father, arrange it for me if you will.'

Hugh looked her up and down as he answered.

'Sorry India, I can't do that, and do I have to keep repeating myself? You are here for the full four weeks as agreed by all of you. And by the way does the word "please" ever feature in your vocabulary?' He was looking at her outfit in disbelief; he could not believe anyone would dress so inappropriately. India dolled up to the nines and Susan looking like a bag woman, what a mixed group they were turning out to be.

'My father thought it was to do with a reality TV show; is that what it is? If it is, he will be furious. He is Sir Harry Thompson-Smythe don't you know.' She stamped her foot and her eyes filled with tears.

'No, I don't know,' countered Hugh, 'and frankly, I couldn't care less who he is, it makes absolutely no difference.'

'Come on India, calm down.' Susan took hold of her arm, hating all this confrontation. 'Why don't you give it a chance, you might enjoy it, come on, have a look round the house with me, you have not seen it properly yet.'

India reluctantly followed Susan up the stairs, all the while looking back and glaring at Hugh. 'I am going home.' She shouted at him, but he just shrugged his shoulders.

The two of them discovered several more bedrooms on the first floor, not made up of course, and an enormous cupboard full of spare bedding and pillows, which engulfed them in a strong musty smell as they opened the door.

'Ughh, for God's sake, shut the door, it stinks.' India held her nose. 'What a disgusting place this is.'

Phyllis, who had followed them up, said, 'Don't shut it up again, pull it all out and I'll give it a wash. I want to be able to put clean sheets on my bed even if no-one else does.'

An enormous pile ended up on the landing floor. Phyllis picked up the first bundle, tucked it under her arm and carried it downstairs. Susan, in the meantime, had spotted another door and said to India, 'I wonder what's behind there?' Turning the knob she realised it was locked, just as the other doors were. They were completely locked out of one-half of the house, the unsafe part according to Hugh.

'I am going to take a look outside later, see what condition that part is in, it didn't look dilapidated to me. Do you want to come too? This really is a strange place and Hugh won't tell us anything.' Susan was desperately trying to engage India in some sort of conversation. 'You know it might be fun when the others arrive, there might be someone your age, please stay.'

'No, I told you, I'm going home, I'm not interested. When is Hugh expected again? Because I am telling him, I don't like this place; I wish I had never come.'

'Can't you put up with it and stay for the four weeks, just to discover the outcome? Our letter said it could be very rewarding. Aren't you even a little bit curious?'

'Why should I wait; it can't be that rewarding can it? Just look at the state of the place.'

Susan gave up and went back down stairs, wondering whether India might be right, what outcome could possibly be rewarding here? India meanwhile went back into her bedroom and shut the door.

Phyllis was in the dining room when Susan caught up with her. She was searching for her glasses, which she felt sure she had left in this room earlier, before Hugh called. Susan joined in the search, but they couldn't find them, so giving up, she climbed precariously up on the chair and coffee table again and took the rest of the curtains down and between them they carried them, one by one, through the kitchen and out into the yard and gave each of them a good shake. They folded the curtains carefully and left them on one of the armchairs in the sitting room; a couple of them needed some repairs to the hems and Susan could not face climbing up to put the others back.

'I'll do it tomorrow Mum, I've had enough cleaning for one day I'm going for a wander round the garden before it gets dark. Are you going to fix the hems that are coming loose? I'm sure you have brought your sewing kit with you.'

'I'll have a look at them later; and yes, I did bring it with me.'

'I wonder what India's up to, she has been in her room most of the day.' Susan wondered whether they should go and see if she was all right.

'I need to find my glasses, so when I go upstairs, I'll give her a shout and see if she will condescend to join us for dinner tonight, she's hardly eaten a thing since she's been here. It's no wonder she is so skinny.'

'Being skinny is all the rage nowadays; all these young girls are on diets. I wish I was a bit slimmer.' Susan pulled a face. 'I feel like a sack of spuds next to her.'

'There's nothing wrong with your figure, it's the clothes you wear that make you look like a sack of spuds.'

'There's no need for you to be so rude, Mum.'

The three women ate together that night, with India making more of an effort now that her mind was made up about going home; she still refused to help with the meal preparation or with the washing up afterwards though. They were just enjoying a cup of coffee when Phyllis said to Susan, 'By the way what did Edna want this afternoon?'

'Edna hasn't been today, Hugh came remember.'

'Yes, she was here earlier, about half past three, I was just coming downstairs and saw her heading towards the library, I didn't want to speak to her, so I ducked back upstairs again. She didn't see me and I thought she would come looking for you.'

'Half past three? I must have been out in the garden then, India can you remember where you were?'

'I was in my room; in fact I haven't even met her yet.'

'She didn't pass me on the drive, so where did she come from?'

'I'm really sorry now I didn't speak to her, you'll think I am making it up, but I really don't like the look of her, she makes me nervous. I lost my glasses again this afternoon too, I was sure I had left them on my bedside table, but they were not there, then when I went back up later, they had reappeared. I must be going a bit loopy, it's this place.'

'Never mind Mum, I am sure you did see Edna, we'll ask her tomorrow if she turns up again.'

Susan had just snuggled down in bed, feeling warm and sleepy after writing her journal when, there it was again, the same noise as the night before. She sat up, listening intently; something was definitely being dragged across the floor above. Could there be someone up there? She must ask Hugh to check tomorrow.

The noise came again; her heart thumped loudly as she got out of bed, crossed the room, opened the door quietly and made her way down the corridor to the locked door. She tried the handle; it was still locked, then she lowered her eye to the keyhole and peeped through but could see nothing. Could someone be living next door?

Back in the bedroom once again, should she disturb her mother? No, let her sleep. Should she go down and make a drink? No, she was too scared. She climbed back in bed and sat with her knees tucked up to her chin, leaving the bedside light on, afraid to go back to sleep.

Chapter 14

Susan woke with a start, her legs aching; she stretched them out, realising she must have fallen asleep still sitting up with her legs tucked up to her chin and just fallen on to her side in the night. The bedside light was still on; she reached out and switched it off. She stretched again, got out of bed and crossed to the window, and the night's activities came flooding back into her mind. What was going on above her room?

Having a shower did nothing to wash away the tension. She pushed her still damp hair back off her face and went downstairs. Phyllis noticed her daughter's pale face and dark circles under her eyes, as she entered the kitchen, and asked, 'What's wrong with you this morning? You look like you haven't slept.'

'I haven't, not much any way; I heard those noises again after I went to bed and then couldn't get to sleep.'

'You must tell Hugh today and why didn't you give me a shout like I told you?'

'I didn't want to disturb you; you need your sleep too.'

'Are you still determined to leave, India?' Hugh asked, when he arrived a little later, making an effort to be nice to her. 'Why don't you give it a bit longer and see if you change your mind?'

'I've already had that conversation with Susan, I demand to leave today, I am already packed.'

'Then in that case, I need you to sign a consent form agreeing not to talk about this holiday until the four weeks are up, so the end result isn't spoilt for the rest of the girls, I'll just go and fetch the form and I'll be back within the hour to take you to Strathdown to catch the train.'

'I'm not signing any form and I want to phone my father and get him to arrange everything. He would get a car to pick me up from here and pay for me to fly home from Glasgow.'

'You will do as you are told; I will see you in a bit.'

India stormed upstairs and a half hour later was back down, with her case and holdall and sat in the hall, her long legs tucked back under her, hands folded in her lap, staring at the front door, turning down an offer of a cup of coffee before the journey and refusing to take part in any conversation.

Phyllis and Susan, both now feeling embarrassed and not quite knowing what to do, beat a hasty retreat to the dining room, to re-hang the rest of the curtains and keep out of the way. A little later, they heard her shout that Hugh was back and came out to join them. He had a piece of paper with him, which he handed to India along with a pen.

'You expect me to sign this? I don't think so,' she said reading it before attempting to pass it back.

'You will sign it, or you won't be allowed to leave.'

'Is this place a prison now? You can't keep me a prisoner you know.'

Susan could see the conversation was not going anywhere, so went over and asked if she could see the form, and glancing at it asked Hugh if it was necessary.

'This holiday was supposed to be four weeks without any contact, so if she refuses to stay then there can be no discussion until the four weeks are up, and the rest of you are made aware of what is to happen. It can only be discussed once we have given permission.'

'Just sign it for goodness sake, the sooner you do, the sooner you can leave and give us a bit of peace.'

'Mum, don't be so awful.'

'She is right, give it here, I will sign, I cannot wait to get away from that miserable old bat, you are welcome to her. I feel sorry for the others who are coming.'

Phyllis was about to answer back, but Susan put a restraining hand on her arm.

India quickly signed the form and shoved it back into Hugh's hands, picked up her handbag, leaving him to get the suitcase and holdall and walked out without a backward glance.

'Well, that's got rid of her then.' Phyllis said with a little smile.

Hugh poked his head back round the door, 'I'll leave her to stew for a couple of minutes before I take her to Strathdown,' he said, with a big grin on his face. 'I have to go back again tomorrow to pick another two up. I hope they will be nicer than this one has turned out to be, how on earth does she stay upright on those heels?'

They all laughed, and then looked at the door as India stood there, hands on her hips, glaring.

'Are you taking me or what?'

With a backward glance at Phyllis and Susan he said, 'All this to-ing and fro-ing, I don't know why you couldn't have all come together.'

'Before you go Hugh, I need to ask you, is there someone living next door? Only I have been hearing noises above my room, it's beginning to scare me; I don't know what it is.'

'There's no-one next door, I told you it's dilapidated, run down, perhaps it's a bird or something that has got in.'

'It sounds much bigger than a bird; will you go and look for me please?'

'If I get chance I will, but I told you it is not safe to go in there.'

'Please Hugh, it's scary, I can't sleep.'

Susan pulled a face as he shut the door. 'Did you see his expression? He thinks I'm stupid Mum, he must be sick of us women.'

'What with me seeing Edna, and losing my glasses, you hearing noises, do you think this house is haunted?'

'Don't even go there. Just forget it; we will get India's room tidied up and then we have the two other women to look forward to meeting, that will be nice won't it.'

'Huh.'

The rest of the day passed peacefully enough, the house beginning to look lived in once more. Susan picked some early daffodils and tulips from the garden and placed them in the cut crystal vases she found in a cupboard in the sitting room.

Susan completed her journal for that day and tucked it away under some underwear in a drawer in one of the bedside cabinets, then snuggled down in bed. She had just begun to drift off when, what was that? She sat up and listened, there it was again, a tapping sound coming from the window this time. Was a bird roosting on the ledge? Climbing out of bed, she crossed to the window and peeked behind the curtain, but it was too dark to see anything.

Telling herself firmly that it was nothing to be scared of, she climbed back into bed, pulled the covers over her head for another night, determined not to listen to anything else and soon fell into a deep sleep.

Chapter 15

Peace at last, Shelley Dyer thought as she sat at the breakfast table after Brian, Lily and Jane all left for work. Her shift at Sainsbury's didn't start until two o'clock, so she had a few hours on her own; then her gaze fell with dismay on the overflowing ironing basket, and letting out a big sigh, turned to the post which had arrived earlier.

There were a few letters for Brian, hopefully payments for some building work he was waiting to get paid for. He would accept work without taking any deposits, then trust people to pay him. Shelley repeatedly told him to get a deposit first; even a small one would help their own cash flow. However, he wouldn't. Money was always so tight, even with her job; they just managed to scrape by. The two girls of course never contributed a penny out of their wages, Brian would not hear of it. Taken by surprise she suddenly said, 'Oh, and one for me, Molly.' Shelley always confided in Molly and the cat always stared at her as if she understood; what secrets she could have told if she could have talked too!

As she opened up the elegant cream envelope, a train ticket fell out; and then she pulled out a letter with the instructions for the holiday. She should have realised. Her peace now shattered, thoughts in a turmoil once more, she paced about the small kitchen with the letter in her hands.

'What have I done? What am I going to tell Brian? What will I tell the girls? What will happen if they try to stop me going? Oh, listen to me Molly, I am a grown woman, and how can they possibly stop me?' In a daze, she made herself another cup of instant coffee, grabbed a couple of custard creams and sat down at the table again with Molly on her lap.

The first letter arrived about ten days ago; in all probability, it was a time-share company; there had to be a catch, no one offered a free, four-week holiday these days. Nevertheless, she had not been able to resist reading it. *An opportunity like this only comes along once in a lifetime.* She knew the wording of the first letter off by heart. What had possessed her to reply? How could she put it to the rest of the family that she was going?

The first class ticket was open-ended, but the letter said to come as soon as possible. A mobile number showed at the bottom, asking her to contact a Mr MacDonald to let him know which day she would be arriving, so that he could arrange for her to be met at Strathdown station. Picking up the telephone with shaking fingers, she dialled the number.

The rest of the morning was taken up with Shelley, absentmindedly, finishing the ironing and putting it all away neatly. Then she wandered from room to room not knowing quite what else to do before it was time to leave for work. Firstly, there was hers and Brian's bedroom; all neat and tidy, just as she liked it. The girls' rooms, a disgrace, both of them; if she didn't tidy them they never got done. Her own fault, she had always been too soft on them.

Downstairs again, Shelley entered the open plan lounge/dining room and looked around in despair. She was forever plumping up the cushions on the sofa and chairs, putting the magazines and TV controls away. She straightened the curtains, where Brian had just yanked them back that morning, and gazed out of the window. Looking around, but not really seeing the small front garden, with its tiny patch of grass and border of shrubs; the tarmac drive, just large enough for Brian's van and the small family car that she drove. There was no garage. The house was a semi-detached on a large sprawling estate in the suburbs of Derby. Having always lived in the area, she longed to move somewhere else, but Brian would not even consider it. 'Derby born and bred,' he'd say.' And. 'Here we'll stay.'

There was still another half hour before Shelley was to leave for work, so she went back upstairs and gazed into her wardrobe; what clothes should she take to Scotland? It was bound to be cold up there at this time of year. Her skirts and trousers were getting tight due to her comfort eating. She ate because she was fed up with her life, and then got depressed because her clothes did not fit. It was a never-ending circle. She had tried various slimming clubs, but somehow could never stick to the diets.

Tucked at the back of the wardrobe was a smart grey trouser suit which she had worn to a winter wedding a couple of years ago and she remembered it had been a bit on the large side then. She pulled it out, hoping that it would fit. Glancing at her watch, she thought there was just enough time to try it on.

Gosh, the trousers were a bit of a squeeze to do up, she was fatter than she thought. Next, the jacket, that would not button up, but did not look too bad if she wore a smart blouse underneath. Shelley decided that she would travel up to Scotland in the suit and if there was time before she left she would try and find a couple of larger skirts and she could do with a new pair of shoes. The rest of her clothes would have to do. Perhaps she could lose some weight on holiday, especially if there were many places to walk. On that note Shelley left for her afternoon shift. She would tell her supervisor that her ticket had arrived, so she would be finishing for the four weeks. Excitement began to kick in as she realised what a big step she was taking.

Plucking up the nerve to tell her family that night after their dinner took a lot of courage, but she took a deep breath and plunged straight in and announced, 'I have received a letter and a first class train ticket, the letter says I have been *chosen to spend a four week holiday of a lifetime in Scotland.* I have already accepted this opportunity, so I am leaving in two days time.' A stunned silence fell round the table, and then all hell broke loose.

'A holiday? A four-week holiday? On your own? And what about us then? You can't go away just like that,' said Brian with the irritated look on his face she recognised so well. He snatched the letter off her, '*a life changing experience,* what a load of rubbish; you won't be able to get the time off work, or you'll get the sack and we can't manage without your money and how will me and the girls cope?'

'There won't be a problem with my job, it's already been agreed with my supervisor, I have three weeks paid holiday due, and we haven't planned on going anywhere, we can't afford it can we? The fourth week, they have agreed I can take as unpaid leave, so we will only be one week short on money, I can work some extra shifts when I come back and anyway there'll only be three of you here.'

'You mean you have already talked about this to someone else? You should have discussed it with me first.'

A big mistake, she knew that.

Lily and Jane screeched at her, 'You can't go, what will we do, you are so selfish Mum.'

A look of disgust flitted over Shelley's face as she shouted, 'Call me selfish, how dare you, I think it's you three who are the selfish ones, you never lift a finger to help, I deserve this holiday. I am going and you can all manage without me so there.' That will teach them, she smiled to herself seeing their jaws drop as she left the room.

Shelley sneaked a sideways glance at Brian. The telltale sign of his jaw clenching and unclenching in anger was plain to see. They snapped at each other all the way to the station, with Brian letting her know that he was supposed to be starting a new job that morning, and they needed his money now more than ever didn't they? She stared out of the window wishing she had caught a taxi, her nerves were all on edge, what with the atmosphere at home, and the thought of the train journey, and having to change trains twice, once at Edinburgh and then again at Glasgow. It was all new to her, going off and doing something on her own and there was the worry about getting on the wrong train, but then again there would sure to be someone to ask.

'I've stocked up the freezer and the fridge. There is food in the cupboards. It will be good for you and the girls to spend some time together. A chance to practice your cooking skills too and make sure the girls do their own washing and ironing, and don't forget to feed Molly.' Shelley said trying her best to keep things light hearted as they pulled into the station car park.

'I still don't see why you need to go. You can't wait to get away can you?'

Little did he know what truth there was in those words.

They walked onto the platform in silence. Brian gave her a quick peck on the cheek as she boarded the train, then strode off without a backward glance. Why had she expected anything different? She lowered her hand which was about to wave to him. Neither of the girls had even mentioned her going when they left for work that morning. Well, bugger them all.

First class travel; that brought a smile to her face and she cheered up at the thought of the forthcoming adventure; it was the first time she had ever travelled first class anywhere and it was worth receiving the invitation just for that. Easing herself into a very comfortable seat, she slipped off the new shoes, with higher heels than she was used to and picking up the selection of magazines bought at the supermarket yesterday, she sat back to enjoy the journey.

The train gathered speed and left the outskirts of Derby. A thought suddenly popped into her mind, and she put down the magazine, what if... what if she didn't go back after the four weeks? What would happen if she could stay wherever it was she was going? Would it be possible? Was it what she wanted? Could she leave Brian and the girls? Where did such an idea come from? It shook her and it was several minutes before she stirred and picked up the magazine again

Chapter 16

Pulling the letter out of her handbag and reading it for the umpteenth time Marilyn Jones finally came to a decision, she would go to Scotland. Last night had been the final straw.

The meal with his new clients was not the success Ken was expecting, and Marilyn could feel her husband's disapproval emanating in waves across the table all through dinner, but refused to meet his eye.

'What sort of meal do you call that,' he shouted, as soon as the clients and their wives left the apartment, 'we could have got a meal like that round the corner at the Toby Inn; melon, steak and chips, what do you think you are playing at?'

'I have not felt quite myself the last few days; I was distracted, I did not go shopping, I'm sorry.'

'Distracted, I bet you weren't distracted enough to forget to meet your friends for lunch were you?' he sneered.

'Ken, I've said sorry, I'll do better next time.'

'You'd better; I expect more from you than that.'

'What more can I say? I'm going to bed.' She could not listen to him any more. Pig! She thought, how dare he speak to her as if she was a child. If only she had kept her job and independence, why had she let herself get into this situation? She had to find the strength from somewhere to do what she had to do.

Ken was coming home for lunch before a business meeting which would go on into the evening, so Marilyn knew telling him about the holiday could not be put off a moment longer.

'I have something to tell you,' she said, looking at him as he helped himself to a gin and tonic. He glanced at her warily; he had made an effort to be extra nice to her that morning, telling her to have a lie in and presenting her with a cup of tea and some toast and marmalade on a tray.

Just go for it, she told herself and taking a deep breath blurted out, 'I have been invited to go on a holiday of a lifetime in Scotland, it's only for four weeks and I am leaving tomorrow.'

As soon as the words were out, his expression changed, his eyes narrowed as he came and stood up close, towering over her.

'You've been invited, since when?' he snarled, looking down at her nervous face. 'Don't you think you should have discussed it with me first? Haven't I given you enough holidays of a lifetime? Why would you want to go to Scotland anyway? it always rains, it is cold and full of damn Scots people who you can't understand. You are not going, I won't allow it.'

Expecting this reaction, Marilyn silently passed him the letters and the train ticket. Just for an instant, she regretted it as she thought he was going to tear them up, but instead he said, 'You can't be taking this rubbish seriously can you? I thought you were brighter than that. *A once in a lifetime opportunity,* come on Marilyn even you cannot be that stupid. I credited you with more intelligence.'

Her eyes flashed in anger; she was about to say how dare he be so patronising, but realising that retaliating was not the right way to go about it, she spoke calmly and reasonably and looking him in the eye said, 'I am going Ken; I am leaving tomorrow, it's all arranged. You cannot stop me. It is something I want to do. I will only be gone a few weeks, so I am sure you can manage without me.'

Realizing she was serious, he backed off, turned on his heel leaving her alone, forgetting about the lunch he had come home for.

With a sigh of relief now that it was out in the open, Marilyn began choosing the outfits she would take from her extensive wardrobe of clothes. Ken was very generous with her clothing allowance and there were several designer dresses, but she decided against taking them. It was Scotland after all; castles could be draughty places, much better to be sensible. She selected a smart trouser suit to travel in, and then chose an assortment of trousers and tops. She could always go shopping up there if she did not have enough clothes. The hours passed quickly and pleasantly.

The following morning, loud banging and clattering from the kitchen let Marilyn know that Ken was still angry. A few minutes passed, and then the front door slammed shaking the apartment. She lay in bed a little longer, then got up and wandered out into the lounge. With a deep sigh, she knew he obviously was not going to forgive her for going away. There was no cup of tea in bed this morning; no offer of a lift to the station. She reached for the telephone and called a taxi.

Arriving at Euston station in plenty of time, she treated herself to a takeaway skinny latte and bought several of the latest fashion magazines before heading straight to the correct platform and boarding the train. She had made sure she knew where she was going before she left home.

Forward planning had been one of her talents, making her stand out and accelerating her rise in the banking business. Unfortunately, her well-deserved career had come to an abrupt end when she married Ken, who, she now realised only wanted a trophy wife not one with an independent, successful career.

Marilyn remembered clearly how the conversation went just after returning from their honeymoon in Mauritius.

'I want you to give up working, I need you to be available to attend business functions with me and act as hostess at the dinner parties I am expected to give now I have been promoted and of course, there will be no children,' she was told, 'I'm not having snivelling kids around. There's no room in our lives for them is there?'

Why hadn't they had that conversation before they got married? Why had she gone along with his plans? Whatever happened to a mind of her own? She might not have been quite so eager to marry this charismatic man, who was fifteen years older than she was, if they had discussed all this before their whirlwind marriage. How stupid could she have been?

They had several great holidays a year; their home in Kensington was a large beautiful apartment on the first floor, with three bedrooms, two bathrooms, huge hall and sitting room cum dining room and a modern, high gloss, chrome and granite kitchen to die for. She loved living in the city, but life was becoming a bit empty if she was honest. Ken's decision not to have children was beginning to eat away at her, her biological clock was ticking and she was broody.

A few minutes later the train started to move and Marilyn sat back just relieved to be on her way. The sick feeling in the bottom of her stomach was still there; nerves probably, from all the stress of the last few days. Right, there would be no more thoughts of that husband of hers, she was going to enjoy the holiday whatever it entailed. A whole four weeks away, it was going to be heaven. She sipped her coffee and opened up one of her magazines.

Chapter 17

What a beautiful sunny morning, Susan thought pulling back the curtains and gazing up at the wispy clouds drifting across a bright blue sky. The weather was great so far. A colleague at work, a regular visitor to Scotland, told her it always rained here, especially in the West. She opened the window a little and could hear the blackbirds singing in one of the nearby trees.

Thought of the arrival of the two women later that day lifted her spirits further, but please make them nicer than India she thought. Entering the kitchen, she was just about to speak to Phyllis when Edna appeared.

'Good morning ladies, hope you are well, I hear there are two more arriving today, shame about India not stopping, what a silly girl. Hugh said she was very spoilt.'

Susan looked at her in surprise. 'How did you get in Edna? We didn't hear the door bell.'

'I did ring it, I stood outside for ages then decided that you hadn't heard, so let myself in, that's alright isn't it?'

'Well, not really, if you aren't here to do any work, then I don't think you should just walk in like that, Hugh always rings the bell and we *always* hear him,' she emphasised, ' and by the way, what did you want yesterday? Only Mum said she saw you in the hall, but India and I certainly didn't.'

'I never came yesterday, this is the first time I have called.' Turning to Phyllis she said, 'You must be imagining it. I suppose that when you reach your age, your memory starts to play tricks on you. Never mind, I suppose it comes to all of us. I have just popped in to see if you need anything, if not I will be on my way then, I'll see myself out. Bye.'

Phyllis had been standing by the Aga, but sat down in the nearest chair with a bump. 'My age, my memory, who does she think she is talking to me like that? She *was* here, I *did* see her Susan, and you do believe me don't you?' Phyllis's hair usually set in a tight perm so popular with women of a certain age, stuck out at all angles as she ran her fingers through it in obvious distress.

Susan was not used to seeing her mother in such a state; she always looked as if she was dressed for a W.I. lunch, with not a hair out of place. 'Don't let her get to you Mum; I think we both know she was here. What I would like to know is how is she getting in? She definitely did not ring that bell; it makes enough noise to waken the dead. And have you noticed that smile of hers; it never quite reaches her eyes does it? I do not trust her one bit. In fact I am going to have a look and see if she drove here or walked.'

Susan rushed to the front door and pulling it open gazed up the drive. 'She isn't there Mum; she hasn't done either, unless she has come round from the back of the house.' Crossing the hall to the passage, which led to the other rooms and the locked door, she tried the handle, it was still locked.

'What are you doing?'

'Just checking, it occurred to me Edna might be coming in through this door, or the one upstairs, do you think that is possible?'

'I have no idea, and have you seen my glasses? I'm sure I left them on the hall table but they're not there now.'

'Get a piece of string and hang them round your neck for goodness sake, I'm fed up with you losing them all the time. I'm going outside to have another look round the back, see you in a bit.'

Susan wanted to check out the access to the back of the house and see if there was a way for Edna to get through. She had only had a cursory look the first day. Was it only three days they had been there? It felt longer.

The high stone wall showed how impossible it would be to get out of the grounds. Stretching round on either side of the house, she guessed it must have been built to keep deer out. It would be silly to think about climbing over. The grounds were large enough to wander round, but it would still be nice to have the freedom of going through the gates as well. She wished she knew why they were not allowed outside, or to have any contact with anyone; hopefully if they were patient, it would eventually become clear. There must be a good reason for all the mystery. Perhaps the arrival of the other guests would shed a bit more light on the situation.

Walking past the back door, she followed the wall to the rear of the property. The drive opened up into a courtyard and in front of her was a large old walled vegetable garden. Making her way through the long grass, she peeped through the opening. It would have originally been a gateway, but the gate had disappeared years ago and the old frame clung onto the wall, with rusting hinges. A few collapsing greenhouses with cracked or missing panes of glass stood at the far end and the once well cared for vegetable beds, still just about visible in their rectangular shapes, were covered in a carpet of weeds.

What a waste. She would give anything for a garden like this. Her small apartment in Poundbury had no garden at all. The only plants she had were indoor ones. Standing, looking over the neglected space, her imagination worked overtime; she would plant potatoes, carrots and onions and over there some runner beans and peas; tomatoes and cucumbers in the greenhouses, perhaps some courgettes. Susan shook her head, they were only here for four weeks, what was it with all these silly thoughts? She carried on with her search.

The remaining courtyard consisted of a few outbuildings, one of which housed some gardening equipment. Making a mental note of which tools would be useful, she reached in carefully, as it was extremely dark and cobwebby, and moved the tools she would need nearer the door, so that she would just be able to reach in and get them without actually entering the building, then closed the door quickly. Between the house and the outbuildings was a gravelled area large enough to park a few cars.

Finishing her look around, she stood and stared up at the rear of the house. With only a quick glance at the wing nearest, which was the utility and scullery, they had already explored, she turned her attention to a much larger one to the right, which was the part that was closed off to them. Several boarded up windows on the side facing her made it impossible to see in from where she was standing. It looked safe, but she supposed there could be subsidence or damp not visible from outside.

The wall from the main boundary to the end of this wing was much newer than the original wall. Wondering if this had also been built to keep people out, she walked over and touched the stonework, yes, definitely new, it was a lighter colour. It was much too high to see over, even standing on tiptoe; no-one was meant to see into that part of the house at all. There was no door in the wall, either, that would allow Edna to get into their side of the house. How was that woman getting in? Susan was very confused.

With a glance at her watch she realised there was only an hour before the new arrivals. She could not meet them dressed as she was, in dirty jeans and an old baggy top she had worn since she arrived; she just had time to nip upstairs and get washed and changed. Back in the kitchen, the aroma of freshly baked cakes made her sniff appreciatively.

'Those cakes smell delicious Mum; you really are getting the hang of the Aga aren't you? Isn't it great having a hot oven all the time? And running the central heating too, it certainly is an efficient system; run on oil, I wonder how often that has to be delivered? The house is not cold at all, considering how big the rooms are. I am just going to nip upstairs and get changed before the others arrive, are you going to change?'

'What's wrong with what I'm wearing?' Phyllis smoothed down her pleated skirt and fiddled with the collar of her jumper. 'I'll just remove my apron, that's good enough, they are not royalty.' Phyllis never wore trousers; it was always blouse and skirt or jumper and skirt.

Susan ran up to her bedroom and about to open the door, to her surprise discovered it already ajar; she was certain she closed it earlier. On entering, her eyes were immediately drawn to the bedspread, with the journal lying on top. What on earth? The last thing she did before going downstairs was tuck it away in a drawer. Was her mother secretly reading it? She had definitely put it away, hadn't she? Doubt crept into her mind; Phyllis's forgetfulness must be catching.

Opening up the wardrobe, she gazed in and sighed. Then grabbed a long dark blue denim skirt and a pink blouse, put them on, leaving the blouse hanging outside the skirt, and stared at herself in the full-length mirror, and then she twisted sideways and looked again. The outfit did nothing to show off her tiny waist; but then none of the other clothes did. Perhaps her mother was right. Oh well, she could not do anything about it, these were all she had brought.

The sound of the doorbell ringing and the door opening pushed all thoughts from her mind as she rushed down the stairs, desperate for some fresh company to fill the huge house.

A petite woman in a smart black trouser suit, high heels, perfectly made up with blonde hair in an immaculate bob appeared, followed by a short, plump mousey haired woman in too tight trousers and jacket, introducing themselves as Marilyn and Shelley.

'Come on in, welcome to Dunnbray, I am Susan and this is my Mum, Phyllis. We are so glad you have come, hope you are going to like it here. Has Hugh explained to you about the place on your way here?' Shelley looked like a woman after her own heart, with an open, friendly face, but her heart sank, taking in Marilyn's hair, face and clothes, please, not another India.

Entering the kitchen, Shelley said, 'Oh, an Aga, I've always wanted one of those.' She stood in front of it warming her hands. 'We heard it is self-catering here, which is a bit of a shock, there was no mention of that in the letters was there?' Shelley threw her handbag casually onto the table and removed her jacket, revealing a blouse, which strained dangerously over her ample bust threatening to burst the buttons. She threw the jacket over the back of one of the chairs. 'I'm dying for a cup of tea and I can't wait to take these shoes off, they're killing me.' She waved a foot in the air, to show how puffy it was.

Marilyn tutted at Shelley then went on to say, 'I was looking forward to a bit of pampering, I was hoping there were some spa facilities or a swimming pool, but apparently there's nothing here so Hugh tells us.' She glanced across at him. 'It's a bit of a dump isn't it?' She looked at Shelley's discarded jacket and wrinkled her nose, putting her own, obviously expensive handbag down on a chair.

'Are you staying for a drink Hugh?' Susan asked in desperation as he was about to make another of his quick get-aways.

'No, I'll be off thanks; you can fill these two in on anything else they need to know.' His glance at Susan was sympathetic as he beat his usual hasty retreat.

'Do you realise we were both on the same train from Glasgow and didn't know until Hugh picked us up.' Shelley said. 'We could have travelled together, got to know one another.'

Susan noticed the look of distaste on Marilyn's face. Oblivious to this, Shelley continued, 'So, what's going on then? What is the big secret? It all seems a bit strange doesn't it? I suppose we all received the same letters?'

'Yes, we did. India had the same letter too, but she was not prepared to try it; a bit of a spoilt brat, would not pitch in and do anything, then again, she was a lot younger than the rest of us. You didn't get on with her at all did you Mum?' Susan glanced at her mother, who shook her head in reply. 'India demanded to go home yesterday, so you are probably lucky not to have had the pleasure of her company. There is supposed to be one more woman coming, but I do not know what has happened to her. We will have to wait and see, as we do with everything else around here. In fact we were hoping that you two would have some more information.'

'Did Hugh tell you about Edna, the so-called housekeeper, who has done bugger all as far as I can see, she is a weird one, can't stand her.' Phyllis's lips met in a thin line as she spoke about Edna.

They had heard about Edna popping in occasionally along with Hugh just to see if they were all right, but not to do any work. And was it correct that the gate was kept locked? Shelley had asked. She was hoping to have gone into Strathdown for a bit of retail therapy.

'Yes it's a shame about us not being able to go out, we could have gone clothes shopping, I could have come with you and helped you choose some larger outfits, those trousers are a bit tight for you aren't they? Have you put on weight recently?' Marilyn asked, her glance then sliding to Susan's outfit; she did not say anything, but as far as Susan was concerned she did not have to, the look was enough.

Susan and Phyllis were taken aback by Marilyn's rudeness, but Shelley just raised an eyebrow and chose to ignore her.

'We can't go anywhere,' Susan continued, feeling uncomfortable, 'it's so weird, but if we say anything to Hugh he just reminds us that's what we signed up for, so other than do what India did, we are here for the four weeks and then hopefully find out why it will be to our benefit. It's like trying to get blood out of a stone, trying to get anything out of Hugh.'

'If it's just the four of us holed up here, what are we supposed to do with ourselves for four weeks?' Marilyn asked.

'Housework,' was the comment heard from Phyllis.

Later, Susan showed them upstairs and they each picked a bedroom. While the three of them were alone, Susan took the opportunity of explaining about the locked doors, due to the rest of the house being supposedly unsafe. Also, the sounds she had heard in the night and about things being moved, she didn't mention the journal by name, but said something had been moved in her room and her mother kept losing her glasses and book.

'Haven't you mentioned any of this to Hugh?' Marilyn snapped. Her head and stomach were beginning to ache, which she still put down to the stress of the last few days and the long tiring journey.

'Of course I have mentioned the noises from above but he reckons it's birds or squirrels. He promises to have a look, but somehow, I don't think he will if it is so dangerous next door.' She needn't speak to me like that Susan thought, but continued. 'Now there are more of us, perhaps we can start searching for a key for the locked door, or find another way in. I have not been able to do much with just Mum and me here, and I don't want to worry her. You don't know how glad I am to see you two.'

'You said supposedly unsafe, don't you think that is correct then? If it's that bad, surely we don't have to stay here, they will have to move us,' Marilyn snapped again; the longed for holiday was turning into a bit of a disaster and she could well understand how India had felt. Now this odd, scruffy woman with the freaked out hair was telling them they were staying in a house that was falling down round their ears.

'You sound a little bit scared Susan.' Shelley did not like the way Marilyn was speaking to Susan; it was not her fault.

'I suppose I am a bit, especially when I hear noises after everyone has gone to bed and it's only above my room for some reason, no-one else hears anything and I don't like the idea of half the house being uninhabitable if that really is true. In fact, I don't know what to think any more. I'll leave you to unpack now, come back down when you're ready and we'll have dinner, Mum's cooking and we can get to know each other.'

'Why don't you just move to a different bedroom then? There are plenty of them.'

Without answering Marilyn's question, Susan hurried back to the kitchen; she had considered changing rooms, so why hadn't she? Because something was telling her that the sounds would follow wherever she moved to.

Entering the kitchen, where Phyllis was preparing a roast chicken and vegetables for the evening meal, Susan flung herself into a chair and put her hands over her face.

'Bit of a mixed bag aren't they?' was Phyllis's first comment. 'Shelley seems like a nice person, but I'm not sure about Marilyn, she could be another India, a bit snobby, if you ask me. Why is it that women with a bit of money, think they can put on airs and graces and look down their noses at the likes of us. It's just like the W.I. at home.'

Susan let out a big sigh and said, 'Let's just try and keep it light and pleasant tonight shall we, they are probably both tired, we'll see what tomorrow brings.' Susan was always one for a quiet life, and so wanted everything to go well.

Over dinner that night, the four women covered many topics, such as marriages, children, and husbands. Marilyn and Shelley were both married and talked about the problems they had both faced in getting their other halves to accept them coming. They could all tell Marilyn was not altogether happy with the situation, but Susan was more interested in what Shelley was telling them. Now she had made the break from home, she was considering not going back after the four weeks; hoping to look around and see if there were any jobs in the area, but it was going to be impossible now they were locked in. Perhaps Hugh would let them have a local paper. 'By the way I have not noticed a TV, is there one?'

'There's nothing, no TV, no radio, no computer, no phone line, what a place.' Phyllis was on her favourite subject again.

'I bet you wished you had never been invited now Phyllis. Maybe I can have a look round once the four weeks are up, I don't have to go back straight away, I could stay in a Bed & Breakfast for a couple of weeks, I suppose they have those round here?'

Susan looked at Shelley in admiration; she liked a woman with a bit of spirit, able to stand up for herself and said so.

'Oh, I haven't always been like this,' said Shelley, 'this letter has got me all fired up and realising how I've always let the family rule my life, until now, anyway. My two daughters are now nineteen and twenty-one, and both working, so quite capable of looking after themselves and Brian, well, it will definitely do him good to be without me for a few weeks at least. He probably won't even notice I've gone unless it's a meal time.'

'What about you Marilyn, what did your husband say when you told him?' Susan thought she had better make an effort with Marilyn; her mother obviously was not going to.

'He was furious; hardly spoke today when I left. He is a lot older than I am, a bit set in his ways I suppose. Ken does not want me to work and likes me around to entertain his clients, but I had a good job before we married and I miss it and the people I worked with. We were always going out after work to a bar or a club. It was fun; I loved it. By coming here I feel as if I have made a bit of a stand too. What a pair of naughty girls we are.' She giggled.

Susan could totally understand how they felt, remembering how controlling her ex husband had been. She suddenly felt lucky to be in control of her own life, it had its benefits, apart from her mother of course!

Phyllis had been getting more and more fidgety as the conversation went on and suddenly jumped up and pointed out that the washing up needed doing and she was not doing it. The other three looked at her in astonishment, what was all that about?

'We need a rota,' she announced, 'I've been doing all the cooking and the cleaning so far, it's about time someone else took over, I'm off to bed, see you all in the morning, not too early, I like to have a nice quiet cuppa before everyone else appears.'

Susan's cheeks burned with anger and embarrassment. Pushing her hair out of her eyes she said, 'I am sorry about that, she has not really been doing it all on her own.'

'Is she always so unpleasant? She has such a miserable face,' Marilyn uttered. Shelley just felt uncomfortable, hoping that Phyllis had not really been serious.

'How old is she if you don't mind me asking? She looks about seventy,' Marilyn continued.

'God, Marilyn, I am glad you asked me and not her, she is fifty-nine this year.' Susan was appalled at her rudeness.

'Good grief, she looks older than that, sorry to be so blunt. I'm afraid to ask how old you are now; I'd guess between forty and forty-five, judging by the way you dress, have I got that right?' Marilyn smirked.

'I'm thirty eight and I suggest you give up on the guessing.' Susan felt quite miffed that this was the second woman to criticise her clothes, how rude could people be? What was it about her that attracted all this criticism from other women, including her own mother? She did not respond, but turned to Shelley and asked if she minded telling them how old she was.

'Me, I'm forty five, and look it I know, before you say anything.' Looking at Marilyn, she said, 'Go on then, how old are you? You are obviously dying to tell us.'

Marilyn said with a smug smile that she was twenty-eight, but was always being told she looked younger. 'Clothes make such a difference,' her pointed glance taking in Susan's clothes again, 'good quality clothes and a good fit always pays off and of course if you have a figure like mine then the clothes look even better.' She smoothed the tight fitting top over her slim waist.

'Your husband obviously gives you a large allowance to pay for your upkeep then, as you don't earn any money yourself. I expect you have Gym membership too as you must have to work hard at keeping that figure of yours. I bet you're one of those women who eats a lettuce leaf for lunch and complains about eating too much.' Shelley felt embarrassed on Susan's behalf and couldn't resist a dig at Marilyn.

Susan squirmed in her seat and wished the floor would open up and swallow her. Marilyn chose to ignore the comments and decided she would go to bed; she did not feel well, it must be all the upset of coming to Dunnbray and finding it wasn't a castle, or even a proper hotel, it was all a bit much, she said. She bade them goodnight and would see them in the morning.

The two women looked at each other while they listened in silence for her footsteps to disappear up the stairs before either of them spoke.

'Can you believe that? She was so rude to you Susan, and did you notice her stomach wasn't as flat as she was trying to make out?'

'Ooh, catty! Women can be so unkind though can't they, do they realise what they are saying do you think? India was the same, unkind about my clothes; Mum said to me earlier, what is it that gives these women, with a bit of money, not earned by them you notice, the right to criticise other people less wealthy. Thank you for standing up for me, but I must get more assertive if I am to survive in this place for the next few weeks.'

'I will let you into a little secret, some of my clothes come from charity shops, don't mention it to Marilyn though, she would be appalled and I would never hear the end of it.'

'I will let *you* into a secret too Shelley; some of mine do too. I shall have to find a better quality charity shop now won't I?'

They both laughed and knew that they would get on with each other. Staying up much later than planned and doing the washing up to keep Phyllis happy, Shelley gave Susan more information about Brian; and why the two of them never had enough money. Susan, in turn told Shelley about how difficult she found her mother and how she did not know how to deal with it any more. Just before Shelley headed up the stairs, she asked Susan about Hugh, what she knew about him. Susan had to admit that she knew very little, he would not talk about himself.

'He's rather cute isn't he? Can't we get him to hang around a bit longer next time he comes?'

'You've only been here a few hours and already eyeing someone up, we'll have to watch you.' Susan laughed as Shelley shrugged her shoulders and continued upstairs with a smile on her face.

Susan carried out the nightly ritual that she had taken on, which was to check all the doors were locked and the lights all switched off before going to bed.

A few minutes later, a scream echoed through the hall downstairs, followed by a dull thud, then silence. Phyllis and Shelley, followed a few seconds later by Marilyn, rushed out of their bedrooms in various degrees of undress.

'What was that?' Marilyn looked scared.

'It came from downstairs, it must be Susan,' said Shelley. Rushing down the stairs and coming to a sudden stop in the hall, she saw Susan lying on the floor, just putting a hand to her head.

'Oh my God Susan, what happened, are you alright, did you fall?'

Susan sat up carefully. 'I got a shock off that light switch and it threw me backwards and I banged my head on the floor. I'm alright I think.' She stood up shakily with Shelley's help. By then the others had gathered round. 'Does anyone know about electric shocks? What should we do?' Marilyn felt herself panicking.

'She seems more hurt by the bang to her head, so I don't think it was too powerful a shock, I don't think there is too much damage, but perhaps she should sleep in my room tonight so I can keep an eye on her,' Phyllis said, a worried expression on her face.

They all went and sat in the kitchen for a while and Phyllis found a pack of frozen peas for Susan to hold on the back of her head, to ease the bruise which was sure to appear by morning. Marilyn, deciding that the drama was over went back to bed, but the others wanted to make sure she really was alright, so Phyllis put the kettle on and it was hot chocolate all round.

When they finally went back to bed, Susan picked up her journal from her own room before joining her mother.

'Leave that until tomorrow.'

'No, Mum, it won't take me a minute, I like to write it every night in case I forget anything.'

'I shouldn't think you are likely to forget your accident tonight. Now what have I done with my book? I'm sure I left it here.'

Chapter 18

Phyllis looked over at her still sleeping daughter, and felt an overwhelming sense of concern for her. Poor Susan, what a shame, she was so excited about this holiday and already it was being spoiled. Phyllis hoped there would not be any more accidents. She slid out of bed, washed and dressed as quietly as she could and went downstairs.

The kitchen was warm and tidy. The others had listened to what she had said then. Good. They really must get something sorted with the cooking and the cleaning. She did feel a bit guilty about how she had reacted the night before, but felt so disappointed with the two women who turned up. This holiday was not turning out how she had expected. She sat in the old rocking chair in its usual place by the Aga, and began to draw up a rota with a pen and paper she had brought down from her bedroom. Early mornings were her favourite time of day, always were, even when Bill was around, and she jealously guarded these times alone. She sipped her tea gratefully; you could not beat that first cuppa in the morning.

Phyllis was still writing when Shelley wandered in a bit later, enquiring about Susan. When she finally made an appearance, they sat her down at the kitchen table with a cup of coffee and some toast, making sure she was alright and checking the back of her head which, by now had a rather large bump on it.

'It's not too bad,' Susan said rubbing it gingerly, 'I'll survive.'

'We must get Hugh to check that switch when he comes,' Phyllis told them. 'I have stuck a piece of paper over it to remind us all not to touch it and I have started writing out a rota too so that I don't end up doing all the cooking.'

'You don't need to worry about the meals,' Shelley told her, 'I enjoy cooking so I'll be happy to do it if that's all there is to do around here, and I'm sure Marilyn will help too. She told me how much she enjoyed preparing dinners for her husband and his clients, so there you are, we can take over the main meals, if you are happy to do the cleaning, how does that sound?'

'Well, if you're sure, thank you.' Phyllis was a bit taken aback, she had been expecting some opposition, and left the kitchen muttering about fetching her glasses.

'Well done, tactfully handled if I might say so, she's not the easiest person to get on with.'

Shelley grinned at Susan and said, 'I've worked with far worse than her, I've learnt to be extra nice and then it takes the wind out of their sails, and I meant what I said, I do enjoy cooking, it will be nice to cook for a more appreciative bunch than I have at home.'

As Shelley had not seen outside yet, Susan suggested a stroll around the grounds, it might clear her own head too. They wandered around quite happily, chatting. Susan's enthusiasm for gardening was apparent. Shelley's own garden was quite small, mainly lawn, which Brian cut under protest, and with just a border full of shrubs that looked after itself, it was easy to manage. She did not know what any of the plants were called, but Susan happily reeled off the names of ones she recognised.

'Come and have a look in here,' she said to Shelley, leading her towards the walled garden, 'isn't this wonderful; this place could be self sufficient if this garden could be re-stocked with veg. Look there's even horseradish growing over there. Have you ever tried making your own horseradish sauce, God, it doesn't half make your eyes wat...'

Susan let out a short scream as she stepped through the long grass, and they both heard a loud snap of metal on metal and a sudden movement in the grass to their right.

Jumping back quickly, Susan said fearfully, 'What on earth was that?'

Shelley bent down and looked carefully in amongst the grass then stood up, with a shocked expression. 'It's an animal trap, it was set, if you had stepped an inch or so nearer it would have got you, you must have just touched it.'

Backing away, looking carefully at the ground as they did so, Susan found a bit of crumbling wall and sat down, hand over her mouth, her eyes wide with shock, staring at the patch of grass where the trap was hidden, realising what a near miss it had been.

'Who would have set that, and what were they trying to catch?'

'I thought those things were banned now. Whoever set that doesn't care about cruelty to animals; what if it had caught you Susan, it's so rusty you could have got blood poisoning, you could have lost a foot, Oh my God, what sort of place is this?'

'I went into the walled garden yesterday, I walked about here and could have stepped on it then, I'm a walking disaster in this place; let's go back, I don't want to go anywhere else if you don't mind.'

'A nice cup of tea is what you need, come on. It's one shock after another here.' Arm in arm they walked back to the house, both thinking about what could have been.

Phyllis seeing Susan's pale face, asked if her head was still aching; but with what had just taken place, Susan had completely forgotten her shock and the bang on the head.

They told the other two women about Susan narrowly missing being caught in the trap.

'This place is not safe, tell Hugh to get things sorted or we'll all leave,' Phyllis announced.

The rest of the day passed slowly, none of the women knowing quite what to do with their time. Hugh popped in and wished he had not. He was told about Susan's shock from the light switch last night, and today her near miss with an animal trap. He went first to the walled garden to have a look at the trap for himself while it was still light; he could not understand how it could have got there. Who could have set it? It was very old, but someone must have known it was there. And why was everything happening to Susan, she was like a magnet for trouble. He could not wait for the four weeks to be up and get the plan out in the open. He picked up the rusty trap and put it in the back of his Land Rover.

Then, he rushed off to get his toolbox to fix the light switch and was back again within the hour. Turning the electricity off, he undid the metal plate on the light switch and discovered the earth wire was not connected properly. How was it possible for the wire to come loose? It was almost as if someone had taken the switch apart and not put it back together correctly.

'Has anyone taken the cover off this switch?' He asked.

'Now why would we do that?' said Susan, still rubbing the bump on her head. 'Do you think we are that stupid as to do something like that deliberately, so that I or someone else would electrocute ourselves?'

'Just asking,' Hugh said, realising how upset Susan was and deciding not to get into any more conversation about the lights, 'I'll go and put the power back on.'

The switch troubled him. There was no way that could have happened on its own. The switch had definitely been tampered with.

Susan followed him out when he had finished. He looked at her troubled expression as he climbed into his vehicle. She was very pretty, but her face was always covered by that hair; she could do a lot more for herself with her clothes too. He was no expert, but could recognise an attractive woman when he saw one. He felt an overwhelming urge to put his arms round her and tell her not to worry, he would protect her, but he daren't, what was he thinking?

It was almost as if she was reading his mind as he stared at her, she felt the colour rise in her cheeks and said, 'Stop staring at me like that. I have had enough; can you get us moved to somewhere decent please?'

'I can't Susan, I'm sorry, you must stay. There is a reason for you to stay here.'

'So you keep saying.' He noticed as she wiped a tear surreptitiously from her cheek.

He started the engine, turned the Land Rover around and headed towards the gate, glancing in his rear view mirror at the woman standing disconsolately on the drive. He wished he could do more for her, for all of them, but his hands were tied, he had made a promise to Angus.

Shelley was as good as her word and cooked a tasty meal of pasta for their evening meal. She had put the idea to Marilyn about helping prepare the main meal each night but Marilyn walked off in a huff telling Shelley not to volunteer her for anything, she was not a cook.

Dinner over, the rest of the evening was spent in idle chat or reading; all of them wondering what the next day would bring.

Chapter 19

'You're up early,' snapped Phyllis, unhappy that someone had beaten her to what she considered her kitchen in the mornings. She glared at Marilyn who was sitting in her favourite chair too. Filling the kettle, she banged about with cups, saucers, and breakfast dishes. Marilyn realised she had upset Phyllis in some way and trying to ignore her tight-lipped expression, smiled timidly and decided the best way was to strike up a conversation.

'Can I ask you something? I have not been feeling too good in the mornings just lately. You know that sort of sicky feeling. I don't know whether I want a cup of tea, or coffee or nothing. What could be the matter with me do you think? It started just before we came here.'

'Pregnant,' Phyllis said without a pause, 'you're pregnant aren't you?' And carried on with what she was doing without even looking at Marilyn.

'What did you say?' Marilyn looked at her in disbelief. Was she being nasty or what? 'I can't be, Ken doesn't want children, I can't possibly be pregnant.' She stood up and gripped the edge of the table in shock. 'What makes you say that, it could just be a stomach upset? What makes you the expert on these things?'

'I'm no expert, but I would bet any money you're pregnant my girl and there's no need to take that tone of voice with me. Take a cup of tea and a rich tea biscuit, which should settle the sickness and go back to bed for a while.'

Walking slowly back up the stairs to her room, Marilyn could not believe what Phyllis had just told her. It couldn't possibly be true could it? What was she going to do if the old bat was right; and of course, she was bound to gossip to the others, she looked the gossiping sort. They would all be laughing at her. Why had she come here? She climbed back into bed, tears of self-pity trickling down her cheeks.

Downstairs, Phyllis shook her head as she poured herself a much needed morning cuppa after that conversation with Marilyn. 'Stupid woman,' she grumbled, was Marilyn totally unaware of what was happening in her own body.

Shelley and Susan arrived in the kitchen together a little later and realising that Marilyn was not there, asked if Phyllis had seen her.

'I saw her earlier; she had not slept well, so she went back to bed for a bit,' Phyllis replied.

'Did you two have a chat Mum? Was she in a better mood this morning?'

'No, not much of a one, she was too tired, I think. A sleep will do her good hopefully.' Phyllis decided she would not mention Marilyn's suspected pregnancy just in case she was wrong and anyway it was Marilyn's place to tell them not hers.

Breakfast over, Susan and Shelley went on a tour of the house, to see if they could find any keys for the locked doors, and bumped into Marilyn who was coming out of her bedroom. They asked if she would like to join in the search but she declined, saying she was hungry and would go and have some breakfast and have a chat to Phyllis.

'What was that all about then?' Shelley asked.

'I'll ask mum later, perhaps they have fallen out, I wouldn't be surprised.' Susan sighed.

Marilyn found Phyllis in her usual place beside the Aga and said, 'I suppose you have told them about me and had a good laugh to yourselves.'

'Actually no, Marilyn, it's up to you to tell them, not me, I just said that you hadn't slept well and had gone back to bed.'

Marilyn was taken by surprise. She was so used to her friends gossiping; especially if they thought someone was pregnant; and thawing a little said, 'I think you may be right, with everything that has gone on the last few weeks, I haven't kept track of my dates, I missed my period last month and I am late again this month. That means I am over two months. I must admit I have been feeling a bit odd, but I put it all down to the excitement and the attitude of Ken to my coming here. Oh God, what will he say when I tell him. He will think I have done it deliberately. What if he wants me to get rid of it?' And upon that awful thought she burst into tears.

'I don't understand, why would he want you to get rid of the baby, he must expect you to have children at some point?' Phyllis wondered what all the fuss was.

'But that's just it, he doesn't want children and stupidly I didn't think to talk to him about it before we married. He is adamant Phyllis, no children.'

'I should have thought that would have been one of the main areas for discussion between couples before they got married. But by the time you leave here you will be at least three months pregnant. He would not be so cruel as to expect you to get rid of it would he?'

'I don't know. What am I going to do?' Marilyn was sobbing by this time.

'Don't upset yourself; it won't do you or the baby any good. You had better tell the others later, they are going to know something is wrong. Everything will work out for the best, you'll see.'

'Thank you Phyllis, you are so kind.' She went to Phyllis and gave her a big hug, thinking that she might have been too hasty in her thoughts last night. 'Have you got grandchildren?' Phyllis went quiet and said no and Marilyn, seeing the look on her face decided not to ask any more questions.

Noticing a softer side of Marilyn made Phyllis think that perhaps she might have misjudged her, and then Marilyn came out with the comment about losing her figure if she was pregnant and would end up wearing shapeless clothes like Susan. Oh, well, she thought, perhaps my first impression was right after all.

Later that day, Phyllis popped back upstairs to fetch her glasses, so that she could see to repair one of the curtains, and with a look of surprise saw her book on the bedside table. That definitely had not been there last night or this morning; a puzzled expression crossed her face as she realised the book had reappeared but her glasses were missing. Was she going senile? Her thoughts went to the old folk she helped at Age UK; was she going to end up like some of them? She became quite upset at the thought.

Both Susan and Shelley had found things to occupy them that kept them out of the way of the other two. Susan went out in the garden, but this time stayed on the pathways, and Shelley spent some time in the library looking for a book on gardening for Susan, to help her recognise many of the flowers and shrubs.

Marilyn surprised Shelley by reconsidering later that day, and offered her help with the evening meal, and they worked companionably, chatting while they cooked. The meal finished, Marilyn told them the news that she might be pregnant. There was a stunned silence, and then they all talked at once. How wonderful it was, what a lovely surprise and how thrilled her husband was going to be if it was true.

'Don't be so sure of that,' Marilyn groaned, 'he will not be happy at all.' She repeated what she had told Phyllis earlier. They could not imagine him not being thrilled by the baby.

Kindhearted Susan decided she would give Marilyn the benefit of the doubt about her rudeness the night before, perhaps it was to do with her hormones being all over the place. She knew from friends that women could go a bit moody when pregnant, but she had no experience of it of course; children somehow never happened while she and Steve were married. They never bothered to find out why, eventually drifted apart and here she was, five years later, single, no man on the horizon, so no children either and stuck with a domineering mother. This was why the sudden offer of a free holiday appealed so much.

'We must tell Hugh tomorrow and get him or Edna to buy a pregnancy testing kit, just to be sure,' Susan said before they all went to bed, 'and you will need to see a doctor at some stage, I wonder if Hugh would let you go into Strathdown for that?'

Marilyn lay in bed that night, with her hands resting protectively over her stomach. 'We are going to be okay, you and I, little one,' she whispered to her unborn child and then got scared as she thought of the accident that Susan experienced the night before; what if it had been her having a fall, she might have lost this little life. She was going to be very careful from now on, was her last thought as she drifted off to sleep.

Chapter 20

'Anyone fancy a stroll round the grounds?' Susan called out as she opened the front door and looked out. 'It's a bit blustery and overcast, but it will blow the cobwebs away.' Her head still ached a bit from the fall, but she felt much better. Marilyn was feeling better too now she knew what the problem could be, she was not sickening for anything. A pregnancy kit would confirm it; she was sure.

The atmosphere in the house was much improved. Phyllis and Marilyn seemed to be hitting it off reasonably well since the discussion on Marilyn being pregnant. Susan and Shelley felt as if they had known each other for much longer than a day or two.

They gathered outside, and stood on the steps, their eyes drawn firstly over the flowerbed that Susan had started weeding and then on down the drive to the gates.

'Just look at that view, isn't it magnificent.' Marilyn said gazing about her. 'It may not be what we expected, but it is rather special in its own way, isn't it?'

'We must be a couple of miles from the road, judging by how long it took us to get to the house from where we turned off,' Shelley remarked, 'and look at the countryside around, I bet its all part of the estate.'

'Any idea why there is a fence across the garden?' Marilyn asked.

'I think it's been put up as a temporary measure to stop us getting to look in the windows on that side.' It was the only reason that Susan could think of. 'There's a wall at the rear too to stop us seeing over into the back of the house.'

'The gardens are going to look a bit silly then aren't they, all tidy on this side if you keep working on them, and just a mess on that side.'

Marilyn was right, Susan thought, it would look a bit odd, but it was not going to stop her working on the flowerbeds. The grass definitely needed cutting though; she wondered whether anyone came in and did it. 'The outside looks as sad as the inside,' Susan said looking around, 'it would need at least two gardeners here I would think, to bring this garden back to its former glory, it must have been so beautiful at one time.' Her fingers itched to get stuck into the weeds again. The borders on either side of the drive were barely distinguishable as flowerbeds, with their thick carpet of buttercups and dandelions. Susan knew the sooner they could be pulled out the better, before they flowered and seeded even more.

On reaching the gates, they gazed up at the magnificent, decorative wrought iron, at least 10 feet at either side sweeping up to about 15 feet where the gates met in the centre. The two gates were fastened with a large padlock. In the centre of each gate was a large oval plaque with some sort of inscription, a bit worn but just about decipherable. Shelley reached up, ran her fingers over the lettering, and picked out the words *"MEMOR ESTO."* 'That sounds like Latin to me, we will have to have a look in the library later and see if there are any books that might help explain the meaning.'

'Oh for a computer, it would be so much easier to look things up on Google,' Shelley groaned, 'but I suppose it will do us good to do things the old fashioned way for a change. That is what we would have done before computers. It is not good to rely on new technology all the time, and it gives us something to do. How else are we going to pass the time? I might have a go at sorting the books out if no-one minds. They are all mixed up.'

'Don't you think it's weird that there are no TV's, no radio, and no computer? I must admit it makes a pleasant change though and makes us talk to each other in the evenings.' Marilyn replied.

Beyond the gates they could see a narrow lane disappearing into the distance through the avenue of beech trees; a strip of grass ran down the centre, indicating that it was not used a great deal.

They turned to look back at Dunnbray; which was not a castle at all, as Phyllis had pointed out on more than one occasion, but more of a mansion, with ideas of grandeur. They could all appreciate its beauty though; the majestic towering sandstone walls, a warm honey colour in the morning sunshine just beginning to break through the clouds; its four imposing pillars proudly supporting the stone and wrought iron balcony. A decorative parapet ran round the top, partially hiding the tiled roof.

'What a magnificent property it must have been in its heyday, it looks a bit careworn now though. I wonder what its history is. We will have to look for another book in the library perhaps?'

They leisurely strolled back to the house, each lost in their own thoughts. Susan's was about Edna, she kept thinking about the woman appearing from nowhere.

The sound of a vehicle interrupted their thoughts as they reached the front door, and turning to look, they saw it was Hugh. They waited and pounced on him as soon as he got out of the Land Rover, telling him they thought Marilyn was pregnant and could either he or Edna get a pregnancy testing kit, just to make sure. After a few minutes chat to see if they were coping and not needing anything else, he drove away again. He couldn't believe what he had just heard, what would Angus make of this latest news?

A little later in the day, Susan just happened to glance out of the window and spotted Edna pulling up on the drive in her small red car. It looked like a Rover, but her recognition of cars was very poor, like many women. Edna got out and strode purposely through the front door, and barked out, 'Which one of you is Marilyn?'

'Me.' Marilyn sheepishly raised her hand.

'You should have told us you were pregnant, stupid woman, coming all this way for a holiday that you knew nothing about, you could have been putting yourself at great risk. You haven't got the sense you were born with.'

'I didn't know I was pregnant, do you think I would have come if I had known? I have only just realised I might be. Did you bring the pregnancy testing kit?' Tears sprang into Marilyn's eyes, as she could not believe how nastily Edna was speaking to her. Susan was right about her, what an awful woman.

'Here, go and do it now, so we will know definitely.' Edna shoved the pregnancy testing kit into Marilyn's hands. 'I hope you realise how embarrassing it was to have to go and buy one of these kits.'

Marilyn quickly ran upstairs to her room and a few minutes later the pregnancy was confirmed. Marilyn did not know whether to laugh or cry. Susan gave her a quick hug and whispered to her not to worry.

'By the way, hope you are alright now Susan, Hugh told me about your little incidents,' was Edna's passing shot as she left.

'Incidents, she calls them incidents,' Susan said as soon as Edna left, 'all heart isn't she?'

'She's a real bundle of laughs; treats us as if we are school children, I can just imagine her as a headmistress. It is quite a relief not having her around here. Why do you think she dislikes us so much?' Phyllis asked, but did not get an answer.

The afternoon saw Susan at work in the garden again, which had become her favourite place. It kept her out of her mother's way and she still wasn't too sure about Marilyn. She was in her element pulling out weeds, seeing the garden emerging under her hard work. The sun was shining, the birds were singing, what more could she ask for. Straightening up, and stretching, her back beginning to twinge, she saw movement out of the corner of her eye at one of the bedroom windows. Was it one of the girls perhaps? No, it couldn't be, that particular window was at the other end of the house, in the closed off bit. She stared hard at the window, but did not see anything else; it must be her imagination playing tricks again. It was this house. It was so lovely and peaceful here and yet... Leaving the thought unfinished, she decided to pack up just as Phyllis approached. Couldn't her mother even leave her in peace out here?

'The weather has turned out so nice, I thought I would come and give you a hand, but I see you're packing up already.'

'I've been out here half an hour and I'm too hot.' She did not want to mention her feeling of being watched.

'Gardens are not made by sitting in the shade.'

'Will you just shut up with your stupid sayings?' Susan picked up her tools and disappeared round the back of the house. She felt unsettled and her mother's appearance hadn't helped her mood at all. She put the tools away, grabbed a drink on her way through the kitchen and headed to the library.

Phyllis watched her daughter as she walked away and regretted her words; she knew she kept coming out with a saying; perhaps that was why people did not like her? She had several books on proverbs, which she spent many an hour browsing for in the local charity shops and found great pleasure in finding sayings to suit any occasion, and never missed an opportunity to quote one. For some reason a proverb written by William Blake popped into her mind, it was quite apt for the moment. *'You never know what enough is until you know what is more than enough.'* How true, she must try and act on those words.

Reaching the library, Susan threw herself on to the chesterfield, trying to relax. Why was everything going wrong? It could have been such a lovely holiday; staying in a smart hotel, being looked after, looking round the countryside, Scotland was so beautiful she had been told, and instead they had ended up here.

Not one for allowing herself to wallow in self-pity, it was not in her nature; she got up again, went to the first bookshelf, and began a search for anything that might have Latin quotes or sayings in. She was intrigued now to find out what the words on the gates meant; there must be a book somewhere.

There was nothing on the first bookshelf, so she started on the second one; by this time, her hands were filthy from handling the dusty books, and her unruly hair flopped over her eyes; she pushed it away just as she spotted a book of Scottish clan names and heraldry. Excitement growing, she sat down and leafed through the pages; there were lists of clan names and along side, Latin sayings which could be found on the clan's shields and badges.

She had no idea what clan she was looking for, so scanned every page searching for the motto on the gates. Halfway through, she found it, *MEMOR ESTO – Be mindful (of thy Ancestors)* and with her finger she followed the line back across the page to the list of clan names, and discovered it belonged to the McPhail clan. McPhail, now that's the family that Dunnbray belonged to then, well, that solved one mystery. Now who were the McPhails? She knew she hadn't come across any other books so far and there were still several shelves to search through, but by this time she had had enough, so decided to leave that search for another day.

Shelley and Marilyn cooked dinner that night, producing a wonderful roast, with apple pie and custard to finish. The chat turned to families again as they worked. Marilyn had become friendlier since the news about the baby and wanted to know about Shelley's daughters. Shelley cynically thought it was because Marilyn would need all the friends she could get now she was pregnant, but she made an effort and told her about her two girls.

'I know they are grown up now and it's time they moved out into the real world, but it was so lovely when they were young. They brought so much joy into our lives. We were a happy family back then. Do you think your husband would change his mind if you told him how important children are to you?'

'I don't think so, he was so adamant about not having any.'

'That's really sad,' said Shelley, looking at Marilyn's strained expression. Her delicate features looked pinched and pale, she was a little doll compared to Shelley.

As soon as they all sat down that evening, Susan told them what she had found out about the motto on the gate, and which clan it belonged to and she was going to search again for more information on the McPhails. 'We could be mindful if we knew who the ancestors were, it's intriguing isn't it?'

'Your father thought he might have some Scottish ancestors somewhere,' Phyllis said, 'but he didn't know what their names were.'

It was a very enjoyable meal, washed down with a bottle of wine, which Marilyn had collected from the cellar earlier. She, of course, only had a tiny amount of wine mixed with lemonade, a spritzer. It was disappointing she thought as she had looked round the cellar, but she had a baby to think about now. For once Phyllis was in a more pleasant mood, a half empty schooner of sherry by her side and her glasses on, which she discovered back on her bedside table when she went to change before dinner. She could not believe she had missed them earlier; her memory was not that bad. Was it?

'That was fantastic, thank you girls; are you happy doing the cooking? Susan patted her stomach, 'because I am so happy to let you, it's not my favourite occupation.'

'Nor housework judging by the state of your flat sometimes, I have to go round and clean it for her,' Phyllis let the others know.

'You don't have to tell everybody Mum. It is embarrassing. I am absolutely stuffed now, I couldn't eat another mouthful, but I do fancy another glass of wine, how about you Shelley, shall I fetch another bottle? I know we can't do this every night or we'll turn into alcoholics, but what the hell, just this once.'

As she went down the steps she shouted, 'What shall I get, red, white, or both?'

'White please,' Shelley called back just as there was a cry and a crash from the cellar.

'Susan, what's happened?' Shelley was the first to get to the top of the cellar steps.

'I'm alright, I missed the last two steps, and fell down; I reached for the light, but the bulb must have gone, it's so dark down here. Anybody know where there are any spare bulbs?'

No-one did, so Shelley told her to forget about the wine. Susan came back up the steps rubbing the knee that had taken the brunt of her fall.

'That cellar floor is a bit hard. We'll have to keep a supply of bulbs down there from now on, just in case.'

Shelley made sure Susan was all right before saying, 'How about I make us some coffee instead and there are some games in a cupboard in the dining room, anybody fancy playing monopoly or scrabble?'

Later that night, Shelley lay in bed thinking that Susan must be accident-prone; everything happened to her. With a mother like that though, she wasn't surprised; poor Susan always had that stressed look about her and that hair, it was such a mop, she obviously couldn't do a thing with it. Shelley wanted to offer to cut it for her but was afraid that Susan would think that she was being as rude as Marilyn was.

Chapter 21

All the household jobs were being carried out quite happily, considering they were all supposed to be on holiday. Each of them took on their allotted tasks and there had been no need for Phyllis's rota after all. They all got their own breakfasts; Susan and Phyllis would wash up and do the housework and Marilyn and Shelley were quite happy to take over the role of cooks as both enjoyed cooking. Susan and Phyllis were just finishing tidying up the kitchen that morning when Edna suddenly appeared. The doorbell had not sounded or a knock heard on the door, but they let it go as it only seemed to antagonise Edna if they said anything. Instead, Susan told her about the bulb going in the cellar and her fall down the stairs.

'A bit accident prone, dear, aren't you?'

'No I am not. Just let us know where the spare bulbs are please.'

'If there aren't any in the scullery cupboards, then we have run out, I will get a supply today and get Hugh to drop them in later. Now is there anything else you need before I get off? No? Then I'll most likely see you tomorrow.'

Hugh came later with a selection of light bulbs. Edna had told him about Susan, and he asked if she was all right. Yes, she told him but suggested they really ought to have a phone, just in case of more accidents and why couldn't they have one.

'Honestly Hugh, we're very worried,' Phyllis said, 'we are so cut off from everything.'

'I'll see what I can do, but rest assured, if anything happens, you will be looked after, please don't worry. The reason for all the secrecy will become clear at the end of your stay, I promise.'

While Susan and Hugh were talking, Shelley took a supply of bulbs and went to replace the one in the cellar. They had found a torch in one of the scullery cupboards, so she took that down the steps and swung it round until it shone on the broken bulb, or rather the space where the bulb should have been. She stood, looking shocked for several seconds as it dawned on her that there was no bulb. She shone the torch on the floor in case it had dropped out, but there was nothing. She shone the torch uneasily around her. Had someone removed the bulb in the hope that there would be an accident? Surely not, but... she did not like to think about someone prowling around the house, she must let the others know.

She placed the new bulb in the holder and walked slowly back upstairs, her mind in a whirl.

'Hugh gone has he?' She was hoping he would have still been there when she told the others of the missing bulb.

'He's gone to try and get us a mobile phone, that's good isn't it?' Susan said feeling a lot happier about that.

'Can I tell you all something?'

'What is it? They all looked at Shelley's troubled expression.

'That bulb had not broken, there was no bulb there; someone had removed it.'

'What! But who would do that and why?' Phyllis demanded.

'Someone wanted one of us to fall maybe? This is exactly what happened.'

'Shelley you cannot believe that, are you accusing one of us of doing it, because if you are...'

'No Phyllis, I'm not accusing one of you, but who else could it be? There is only Edna or Hugh, and I can't imagine Hugh doing anything like that. He's the one who has to keep putting it right.'

'You think it was Edna then? But why would she? Surely we would know if she was going down to the cellar.'

'She keeps appearing from out of nowhere and I get the distinct impression she doesn't want us here, she is so unfriendly the little I have seen of her. You have had three quite serious accidents now Susan, you have to admit it is all a bit strange. Why do you think these things are happening?' Shelley was beginning to change her mind about the accidents being Susan's fault.

That afternoon Susan opened the door and stepped out into the garden. It was very overcast and a violent gust of wind sent her scurrying back indoors. She gave a little shiver and decided to give the gardening a miss, but still intrigued by the closed off wing of the house, grabbed her coat and went to have another look around the back of the building. She shouted to Phyllis, who was repairing yet more curtains, that she would not be long, left by the back door and walked round to the rear of the property.

She gazed at the boarded up windows, wondering if she could loosen some of the boards and peep in. If only there was a stepladder, she would just about be able to reach. Turning her gaze to all the outbuildings once more, she decided to have another search. Her first look had been brief because of all the cobwebs and who knew what else lurking in them.

Opening the door of the first one, she noticed it was quite small and must have been a coalhouse at one time; it did not contain anything of any use.

The second one had various gardening implements in. This was the one she used frequently; she had initially put all the useful tools near the door so as not to have to go in any further, but today, she decided to brave it. There was one grimy window at the back letting a small glimmer of light in. Shuddering, but telling herself to stop acting like a baby, she stepped inside and looked around. Various old crates and pieces of wood lay about and some old sacking, which she didn't touch for fear of something jumping out at her, and the rest was just junk. She came back out, closed the door and headed for the next one, which backed onto the perimeter wall at the rear of the property.

This was the stable block, a very large old stone building, with big double doors in the centre of the front. Susan struggled to open them, they were so stiff she had to pull and tug to get one of them to open wide enough. Because it was stuck, she had not opened it properly the first time, just peeped in through the door, but she was determined to get in. After a great deal of effort, the door opened slightly and she squeezed through into the stable. There were stalls down each side, which would have housed up to twelve horses in days gone by. A loft area was above, which would make a nice conversion into a flat for someone. 'Oh dear, here I go again,' she said, laughing at herself.

There was a nice feeling about the space, Susan noticed that immediately, and her imagination was off again. She pictured the horses eating their oats in their stalls; the stable lads grooming the animals' coats until they gleamed. She could almost smell the aroma of straw, and feel the warmth emanating from the horses' bodies and their soft noses nuzzling her hand in search of a tasty carrot or a Polo mint. It would be so good to bring these stables back to life. Her thoughts drifted to riding holidays, which would be a great activity for Dunnbray to offer. She had never ridden, never having had the opportunity, but it wasn't too late was it?

As if she would ever live here and see anything like that. She went deeper into the gloom, looking in each stall as she passed, for anything suitable to stand on to get to those windows outside. The sudden creak of the door made her turn. One of the others were coming to find her perhaps.

She called out, 'Yoo-hoo, I'm back here,' but got no reply. The door gave another groan and she was plunged into darkness. 'Hey,' she shouted, 'hey, Shelley, Marilyn is that you? Stop playing tricks, it is pitch black in here, I cannot see anything. Let me out, please.'

She fumbled her way back to the door and pushed on it, but it would not budge. She banged on it with her fists, and then stood listening. There was no sound from outside. She had expected to hear giggling from whoever had shut her in, but there was nothing. What on earth was going on?

If they were going to play games with her, she would just sit and wait until they got tired of their joke and let her out. Feeling her way in the dark back to the first stall, she took off her coat and placing it on the concrete floor, sat down with her back against the wooden support and waited, and waited. Nobody came. She stumbled back to the doors and banged and shouted until she was hoarse, then gave up and sat down again. Someone would miss her eventually. It was warm in the stable with the door closed; she felt sleepy all of a sudden and must have dozed off, because she was suddenly aroused by voices calling her from outside.

'Susan, Susan, where are you?'

Jumping to her feet and stumbling to the door, she banged on the wood as hard as she could and heard footsteps running towards the stables, then Shelley's voice.

'Susan, is that you in there? Hold on I'll just move this piece of wood then open the door.'

While she listened to the commotion on the other side of the door, Susan thought wood. What piece of wood?

Shelley started to tug on the door and glimpsing daylight through the crack between the two doors, Susan put her shoulder to it and started to push. With their combined efforts, the door flew open and she fell out.

'How on earth did you get yourself stuck in there? You've been gone hours.'

'Never mind that Shelley, you just said you had to move a piece of wood before you could open the door. Where is it?'

Shelley picked up a wedge and showed Susan where it had been pushed under the door, making it impossible for her to have opened it from the inside.

'Someone shut me in there, was it one of you? Because I don't think that was very funny,' she glared at Shelley.

'We wouldn't do something like that; you can't believe it was one of us can you?'

She refused to answer, but stormed back in to the kitchen, shouting that she wanted to speak to them all.

One by one they appeared and stared at Susan. Her hair which had been held back quite neatly for once underneath a headband, now stuck up all over the place with bits of straw lodged in it, her cheeks were red with anger and her eyes blazed as she shouted at them.

'Who shut me in the stables? I want to know which one of you did that. It was not funny; it was horrible, shut in the dark. How long have I been in there?'

'About three hours, I suppose,' Phyllis said carefully, she did not think she had ever seen Susan so angry. 'We were all doing different things and we each thought you were with one of the others. We are really sorry, but it wasn't one of us, honestly, you don't think we would do that to you, do you?'

'Mum, someone locked me in the stables and I will find out who it was. I am going to have a shower now, I'm filthy.'

She walked out of the kitchen and upstairs to her bedroom, slamming the door behind her.

'What on earth happened?' Phyllis asked Shelley.

'A piece of wood was wedged under the door so anyone inside would not be able to open it. Someone did it; it did not happen on its own. She is really angry isn't she?'

'So would you be if it happened to you,' Marilyn said looking at the others, 'what a childish trick to play, it wasn't one of you was it?'

'No it wasn't,' they both shouted.

'Then who else could it be? Hugh perhaps, or Edna, they are the only other ones I can think of.'

'I don't think much of their sense of humour then. I will go up and speak to Susan in a bit when she has had chance to calm down.' Phyllis was getting more and more concerned for her daughter, everything seemed to happen to her.

No-one felt like doing anything after that episode so they made their way to the smaller of the two sitting rooms, which Phyllis had cleaned, drank cups of tea and bounced ideas off each other as to why they were at Dunnbray; what was Edna's involvement? And why wouldn't Hugh tell them anything? Marilyn even suggested that it could be some sort of reality show and they were being filmed. Susan re-joined them as this conversation was taking place.

'They wouldn't do that would they?' Phyllis looked around her with wide eyes, imagining cameras lurking in every corner.

'Funnily enough India's father thought the same thing and didn't want her involved. I can't see it somehow.' Susan said.

'Experiments then, like rats in a laboratory.'

'Stop it Marilyn please, you are making us more scared than ever.' A shiver of fear ran down Susan's back. 'Just change the subject will you?' Susan was still angry over the stable affair. The others had suggested either Hugh or Edna could have done it, but she still thought it might be one of them, so was very cool with them all for the rest of the evening.

Susan heard the sound at the same time as the bed began to shake. She leapt out just as the ceiling of the four-poster bed began to tip at an alarming angle; it wavered then the whole top fell and lodged at a forty-five degree angle over the bed.

She froze to the spot. What could have happened if she had been asleep? What if it had fallen all the way down and crushed her? Shaking with fear, hands trembling she pulled on her bathrobe and rushed out to warn the others.

On the landing, she tapped on the doors and called to them to come out. Sleepy faces with tousled hair peeped out at her.

'What's going on, you're as white as a sheet, what's happened?' Phyllis put her arm round her daughter's shoulder; she could feel Susan trembling beneath the robe.

'Look in there, look at my bed.' She could not bring herself to enter the room again.

There were gasps of shock as they all stared at the bed.

'Oh my God, Susan you could have been killed. I wonder if it's just your bed or whether they are all unsafe. I'm not sleeping in there again tonight.' Marilyn indicated her own room. 'I suggest we take our duvets and sleep in the sitting room for the rest of the night.'

'I think we'll feel a lot safer, come on I'll make us some hot chocolate and put the central heating on again and we'll camp out downstairs.' Phyllis led the way, still holding on to Susan.

Mother and daughter shared the sofa between them and the other two took the armchairs, all huddled up in their duvets, sipping their drinks and talking in low voices as if they all thought someone might be listening. They gradually fell silent.

Chapter 22

One by one, they roused themselves and stretched their cramped limbs. What a night! The four of them had stayed awake for hours, all now feeling more and more apprehensive about the coming weeks and wondering what else was in store for them. Susan finally accepted that none of them had anything to do with her being locked in the stable, but someone had.

Phyllis was up and about first, making cups of tea and coffee. Marilyn felt nauseous again. The sickness was beginning to wear off the last couple of days since she realised she was pregnant, but the scare had brought it back. She wanted to go back to bed for a couple of hours but was too frightened to risk it.

Impatient for Hugh to make his morning call, they pounced on him as soon as he arrived, and all talked at once trying to tell him about Susan's bed and could he look at them all, and about Susan being locked in the stable. He held his hands up. 'One at a time please, what's this about the beds first?' He was totally fed up with all the problems. How could a group of women create such a catalogue of disasters?

'My bed almost collapsed on me last night. It's lucky it didn't fall all the way down; I could have been crushed. You must put it back together and check all the others as well otherwise we are not sleeping here tonight. We have had enough of these accidents and by the way, we did not tell you before, but the bulb was missing in the cellar, so they are not really accidents, someone is doing this deliberately. And someone locked me in the stables on purpose, so who do you think that was then?'

Susan stopped to draw breath and Hugh saw her stressed expression and the hint of tears in her eyes, as she ran her fingers through her tangled hair.

'I am so sorry you feel like that, but how could someone possibly be doing all these things deliberately? There are only you four here, and you don't know what you're here for so why would one of you be trying to frighten the others? I don't understand.'

'It isn't one of us, but there is someone who doesn't like us being here and that's Edna, she is rude and unpleasant, she walks in here as if she owns the place, never knocks or rings the bell first; we think she is getting in here somehow, but we haven't caught her yet. I suggest you tell her we do not want her round here again, tell her to just stay away.'

'I can't tell her that, because if I can't get here, she will need to come. I have got you a two way radio, a walkie talkie, though, if that will help, you will be able to get me or Edna in an emergency.'

If he was hoping that would placate them, he could not have been more wrong.

Phyllis just looked at the gadget in disgust. 'What do you take us for Hugh, kids? We might just as well have a couple of tin cans and some string.'

'Ladies, please, these walkie talkies can cover up to several miles. If anything happens, just call, look I will show you how. It is easy. One of us can be here in minutes if there is a real emergency.'

'Why couldn't we have a phone? Shelley asked.

'Because we couldn't trust you all enough to not use the phone to call your families, that's why. I'm sorry, but that's how it is.'

Susan was furious. 'We'll try not to bother you with that thing.' She pointed to the walkie-talkie, 'and have you checked upstairs like I asked you? What if there's someone else living on that side, squatters' maybe, have you considered that?'

'Susan, I have told you that side is dilapidated, no one could live the...'

'Oh, forget it. It is a waste of time talking to you. Just get the beds fixed please.' She turned on her heel and walked away.

Hugh left to collect Jamie the lad who helped on the estate, and said he would be back within the hour to fix the beds. As he drove away, a worried frown creased his brow, what on earth was going on? The noises Susan had heard, he could put down to a vivid imagination, but these other things, they were not imagination, they were real. Why would they think it was Edna though? And why was Edna being so unpleasant? It was her idea in the first place that all the women came and stayed. She might be coming through the adjoining door instead of driving round as they had agreed; he must ask her, but she would not be doing anything would she? Could there be someone else on the property? Especially with Susan being locked in the stable, someone had to be watching her to do that.

Hugh's mind was a whirl of unanswered questions. Why had he and Angus thought Edna's idea such a good one? Just look at the chaos it was causing, and there was still another woman to arrive yet. God help them; roll on the end of the four weeks. It could not come too soon as far as he was concerned.

'It's obvious Hugh is lying to us isn't it? Have you noticed he can't look you in the eye when he speaks?' Phyllis could not take it all in; it was just one thing after another.

Why don't we have another search of the place? And see if we have missed anything, perhaps there is a spare set of keys somewhere.' Susan asked.

'It's too late to go searching now and could we just have a quiet day tomorrow please, all this stress, it's just too much. I cannot cope with any more. If this carries on I shall be going home like India.' Marilyn turned her back on them and went up to her room. They heard the door slam.

'Does everyone else want a quiet day then? Susan asked again, disappointed with Marilyn's comment.

'It's not a bad idea is it? It will give us chance to decide what to do next.' Phyllis felt like Marilyn, that enough was enough.

Hugh eventually turned up with Jamie in tow and together they fixed Susan's bed. Again he couldn't understand how it had happened. And why did everything appear to happen to Susan. All the other four posters were fine. He would talk to Angus about all these mysterious happenings.

Chapter 23

Hugh turned up bright and early the next morning with a basketful of fresh fruit, mushrooms, peppers and butternut squash. He was determined to be pleasant and greeted Susan with a smile and a wave as he drove up, looking at her working in the garden.

'You're doing a great job here; I can see it changing every time I come. You enjoy it don't you? I bet your garden at home is immaculate.' He looked at the patch she had just weeded as he handed over the basket.

'I don't have any garden, just a window box; it's a second floor apartment you see. Mum's garden is tiny too and she doesn't want me messing about in it, so it's a real treat for me to do this.'

'I really am sorry there is not more to entertain you all, and I know I keep saying it and you don't believe me, but it will be worth all the waiting, I promise you.' Pointing to the basket he said, 'Edna has sent you these, she apologises if she has upset you in any way, she didn't mean to and hopes you'll accept them.'

'Thank her for us please, Hugh,' said Susan, 'but we would still rather she did not come here herself.'

'I can't tell her that, but I will try and use an excuse for me to come rather than her, that's the best I can offer.'

Susan had mixed feelings about Hugh, he had really annoyed her yesterday; she found him very attractive and wanted to trust him but she still had reservations. She felt her cheeks warming under his steady gaze and not knowing what else to say said, 'Do you want to come in for a drink, it is so warm today. Is this weather usual?'

'I won't stop thanks all the same, I'll take a rain check on the drink and the weather usually is good this time of year, it seems more settled in the spring, less rain. I'll maybe see you tomorrow, bye then.'

Susan watched him thoughtfully as he drove away and locked the gates. One of these days maybe he might forget to lock them or he could be distracted long enough for one of them to get out.

She had only been working in the garden for a few minutes, struggling with a particularly difficult weed; yanking at its roots, when it suddenly broke loose, coming out of the ground so fast she fell backwards, and as she did so, caught sight of movement at the same window as before. She blinked and looked again, but this time she could see nothing. There was somebody there, she was certain, she was definitely being watched; who could it be? She wondered whether it could be the person heard above her room. It was so unnerving, she could not settle to do any more. Picking up the basket, she walked round the back of the house, put the gardening equipment away in the outhouse, and entered the kitchen.

'You've packed up early, have you had enough?' her mother asked.

'I'm not in the mood for gardening, I think I'll go to my room and have a rest, I feel a bit tired.'

'Are you all right, you look a bit pale, you're not going down with anything are you?'

'No, Mum, I'm fine, don't fuss.' Susan put the basket of veg down on the table. 'Hugh brought these just now, Edna has sent them for us, can you put them away please, and I'll see you later.' She headed towards her bedroom. Lying down on the bed, she picked up the gardening book which Shelley had found for her and flipped through the pages, but she could not concentrate, she kept thinking about being watched. What should she do, tell the others? Or keep quiet? She did not want to put ideas into their heads if it was only her imagination.

She sighed as there was a light tap on the door and Shelley poked her head round.

'Is everything alright? Only your Mum thought you weren't looking too well, would you like a cup of tea or something?'

'No, a bit of a headache that's all, it's the bending down with the sun on my back that does it; I'll be alright in a bit, I'm going to have a doze.' Why couldn't they all leave her alone?

Susan must have slept, for she was awoken suddenly by Marilyn, whispering from the doorway, 'Susan, Susan, come quick.'

'What is it now?' Susan grumbled as she staggered out of bed half-asleep. Out on the landing Marilyn beckoned her, and tiptoed back downstairs with Susan close on her heels. Holding a finger to her lips as they reached the bottom, she said, 'Sshh, come and listen,' and she pointed to the locked door.

Susan put her ear to the door and listened, voices! She could hear voices; there *was* someone on that side. Phyllis and Shelley listened too. The voices were too indistinct to hear whether it was Hugh or Edna. Susan decided then to tell them about being watched in the garden from one of the windows next door.

'Let's go into the sitting room a minute, I've something to tell you.' They all sat down expectantly as Susan went on, 'I thought I imagined it the first time it happened, but today I definitely saw someone at one of the windows in the shut off part, someone was watching me out in the garden, it scared me, that's why I came in. I wasn't going to say anything in case you didn't believe me, but now this, we must try and get in there, let's do it tomorrow, please, I can't stand not knowing.'

They all reluctantly agreed that they needed to find out and would try and find a way through to the other part of the house the following day.

Susan and Phyllis stayed in the sitting room whilst Shelley and Marilyn started the evening meal.

'I'm so sorry that I have got you involved in all of this Mum, it's all my fault wanting to come on a free holiday. If I ever get such a stupid idea again, please stop me.'

'Don't be silly, if it's anyone's fault it's mine, saying you couldn't go without me; it was a joint decision to come, we could have both said no. We'll get to the bottom of it somehow.' Phyllis reached over and gently pushed her daughter's hair away from her face and smiled. 'It will all work out, you'll see.'

'Thanks Mum,' Susan smiled back. Her mother could be kind when she put her mind to it. 'Come on, do you fancy a small sherry before dinner?'

Helping themselves to a drink, they sat in companionable silence until called into the kitchen.

While they prepared the evening meal, Shelley and Marilyn continued their discussion about children and adoption. Shelley herself had been adopted as a young child and because she wanted her daughters to have a happier upbringing than her, she made the mistake of spoiling them and doing far too much for them. She explained to Marilyn that her adoptive parents told her both of her own parents were dead so there was no point in ever looking for them. They had wanted a little boy, but she was the only child available at the time.

Marilyn could see that Shelley still felt hurt by being told this right from an early age. They had never let her forget she was adopted and how much she owed them for rescuing her from a life in a children's home. As she grew older, Shelley often wondered whether her life would have been better if she had not been adopted at all. They never showed her any love.

From a young age, Shelley was expected to keep her bedroom clean and tidy. Every birthday, another task was given to her; soon it was vacuuming the whole house, cleaning the bathroom, cooking, ironing, the list grew and grew. Her father worked long hours so was hardly ever at home. Her mother belonged to so many committees, and clubs she was always out, leaving a list of things for Shelley to do. The older she became the more she resented the fact she was always expected to finish her allotted tasks for the day before she could go out, even after she left school and got her first job. She left home as soon as she was able, and married the first man who came along, Brian.

Surprised at how honest she had been to Marilyn she finished by saying, 'You don't know how lucky you are to be able to have a baby of your own. Don't let anyone talk you out of having it; you might regret it for the rest of your life.'

'I hope I still feel lucky when I get around to telling Ken about it.'

'You'll be fine. He will be a bit shocked I know, but it will all turn out okay in the end.'

Shelley was beginning to realise that Marilyn's rudeness was partly down to worry about her own life and the disappointment over the holiday at Dunnbray and she was taking it out on the rest of them. Her manner had certainly improved the last couple of days. Shelley knew that Susan was still wary of Marilyn, but felt that it would all come right.

Dinner finished, they were all relaxing in their usual places around the crackling fire in the sitting room when Phyllis suddenly complained of a bad stomach and rushed from the room. Coming back a bit later, she said that her stomach still did not feel right and that she was going to bed.

'Hope you feel better in the morning Mum,' Susan called after her.

'Do you know,' said Shelley suddenly, 'thinking about Phyllis has made me feel a bit queasy, so please excuse me as well?' And with that she disappeared sharpishly.

'What's going on, have we eaten something off?' Marilyn was concerned, thinking about what they had cooked. 'All we did was use the vegetables that Edna sent and made the casserole. There was no meat tonight; the potatoes were out of the same bag that we have used for a couple of days, and we didn't have any sweet. Those vegetables were so fresh, it couldn't be them.'

The first thing Phyllis spotted as she climbed into bed clutching her stomach was her glasses, lying clearly on top of the bedside table. They definitely were not there earlier. Was someone playing tricks on her?

Susan knocked and peeped into her mother's room on the way to bed.

'How are you feeling now Mum? My stomach's playing up too.'

'I'll be fine once I get to sleep.'

'Are those your missing glasses? Were they there all the time and you didn't see them?'

'Something like that, goodnight Susan,' Phyllis muttered, annoyed about the glasses.

Chapter 24

A very tired and jaded group met in the kitchen the following morning; the stomach upsets had settled down, but no one had slept very well apart from Marilyn. Shelley suggested some dry toast; which was supposed to help stomach upsets.

'I've been thinking,' she said, 'it must have been the mushrooms. I wonder where Edna got them from? Do you think she could have picked some poisonous ones by mistake?'

'Did you notice anything about them when you prepared them?' asked Susan.

'I washed and chopped them up,' said Marilyn, 'but I was chatting to Shelley so perhaps I missed something, I am so sorry, and if you remember, I didn't actually eat any of the mushrooms, I suddenly didn't fancy them once they were on my plate, so it must have been them, as I haven't been affected.'

'It's not your fault, it's very difficult to tell which mushrooms you can eat and which you can't, even the experts get it wrong sometimes. Do you remember seeing in the paper a few months back those two women who died from eating poisonous mushrooms?'

'The next question is, did she know they were poisonous or not?' Phyllis said. 'I wouldn't put it past that one.'

'Mum, she wouldn't do it deliberately would she?'

No one answered that question.

'Something else to mention to Hugh then?' asked Marilyn.

'I don't think so, let's just leave it.' Susan replied. 'And I suggest if any of us sees Edna, let's not mention feeling ill, then if she did do it deliberately, she won't know if they upset us or not, it will keep her guessing.'

Later that afternoon, Susan was out in the garden, when she heard the clang of the gates being unlocked and watched as Edna drove up to her.

'Just passing, so I thought I would pop in and see if everything's alright,' she called out as she wound the car window down.

Pushing her hair out of her eyes Susan said, 'Everything's just fine thank you, and thanks too for the fruit and vegetables, the girls made a delicious veggie casserole last night. Did you pick the mushrooms?' Susan watched Edna's face for any reaction as she said this and sure enough, Edna's eyes narrowed just slightly as she took in what Susan had said.

'No, no, I bought them from the local market same as the other veg. Glad you enjoyed them; I can always get plenty of vegetables, so I will bring you some more in a few days time. Well, if you are sure everything is all right I'll leave you to it. Oh, by the way, your Mum hasn't been seeing things again has she? And I understand you have been hearing noises too. Dunnbray doesn't appear to be doing you two much good, must be the Scottish air; do you think you will be able to stick it out here? I'm sure everyone would understand if you wanted to leave.'

'We are not going anywhere Edna; we are made of tougher stuff than that.'

'Well, see you tomorrow or the day after then, bye.'

'Bye, Edna, have a nice day.' Susan watched her turn her car round and head back through the gates and lock them behind her, then went back to the house absolutely seething with rage.

'Hey everyone, come here a minute,' she shouted as she entered the hall. Luckily, they were all close by so came hurrying up.

'We've just had a visit from Edna, checking to see if we are all okay,' she said through gritted teeth, 'and I could tell she was surprised when I thanked her for the fruit and veg. I am sure now she did it deliberately, just a few poisonous ones to make us feel ill, but nothing too serious. She said she bought the mushrooms from the market, but I do not believe her. She is bringing us some more veg, so I suggest we avoid the mushrooms, all agreed? And the cheeky cow asked if Mum had been seeing things again and made comments about me hearing noises, she says Dunnbray isn't doing us any good, and perhaps we would like to go home.'

'She really doesn't want us here does she? I suppose we can't ask Hugh, he would never believe us would he?' Shelley voiced her worries.

'Let's just be on our guard where she's concerned.'

'*Beware of Greeks bearing gifts.*' This was Phyllis's passing comment.

The girls spent a relaxed evening in the small sitting room, in front of a roaring fire, playing cards, and the conversation turned, as always to their thoughts on what each of them would like to do if Dunnbray was theirs.

'It would make a wonderful wedding venue, especially if the actual service could be held here.' This was Marilyn's idea, which they all thought a brilliant one. She seemed to be settling down and was much nicer than when she arrived.

'That's such a wonderful staircase.' Shelley sighed. 'Can't you just picture a bride gliding down those stairs in a beautiful white wedding dress, her long train flowing down behind her, with her bridegroom and guests waiting at the bottom.'

'Do you think that's the reason we are here, to see if we can look beyond the dust and decay and breathe some life into the place?' Susan found herself fantasising about walking down that staircase and into the arms of some mystery man, and Hugh's face flashed into her mind; so feeling a bit flustered, she rapidly came up with some alternative ideas such as riding holidays, fishing, walking, or bed and breakfast; ideas they could all picture taking place at Dunnbray. Their imagination ran wild.

Chapter 25

The next day dawned wet and blustery. The sort of day to sit in front of a blazing fire, but today of course, they were going to have a good search of the house. Susan checked her journal was safely tucked away in the new hiding place she had found and went downstairs. It crossed her mind that one of the others could be sneaking into her room and reading it, but she decided it was more likely to be Edna or someone else from the other part of the house. She was dying to catch them at it.

'I've got an idea,' Susan suggested as they met up for breakfast. 'Let's fool Hugh into thinking we believe whatever he tells us, then he won't even think about us trying to discover what is happening here, we'll play along with whatever excuse he comes up with today, how does that sound to everyone?'

They all thought it was a good idea. 'Silly man, thinking he can pull the wool over our eyes.' Phyllis replied.

Hugh came as usual, told them he'd already looked around next door, which no-one believed; he said they were definitely imagining things, the place was empty, not even any sign of birds or squirrels getting in.

'You're right Hugh of course, we must have imagined it. You know what us women are like, I think its being shut up here that's doing it; our minds are working overtime, probably too much time on our hands. I suppose there is no chance of us going out one day is there, to have a break from the house. No? Never mind, I shouldn't have asked that. Thank you for calling round, see you soon.'

Susan ushered him out, not even suggesting that he stayed for a coffee this time and firmly closed the door behind him. She turned and grinned at the others as Hugh left, with a puzzled expression on his face.

'Did you see his face; he wasn't expecting that was he?' she said. 'Us admitting we were wrong, that'll keep him guessing for a while.'

They were up to something, that bunch, agreeing with him so quickly. Hugh thought and considered popping back a bit later to see if he could catch them out with whatever it was they were planning.

What with sounds being heard from Angus's side, Edna constantly whinging and now this crafty lot plotting something, he had just about had enough of Dunnbray. Why he and Angus ever agreed to this plan in the first place he would never know, they must have been mad. Give me sheep any day he thought.

'Come on then, he will not be back, let us get on with the search, we will start in the cellar and work our way up. If there's no way in down there from the shut off part, look in every drawer and cupboard again on your way back through in case we have missed any keys which will fit the doors.' With that, Susan headed for the cellar steps and the others trouped after her.

'Ughh, I really don't like it down here,' Shelley wailed, 'there's too many cobwebs and its freezing and Oh! My God what's that?'

It was a large dead rat, just lying on the floor. 'I hate rats, someone move it please.' She shuddered with disgust.

'That's a big one,' said Phyllis peering at it, 'I wonder how it got down here.'

'I don't care, I'm going back up and I won't be coming down here again.' They all stared at the rat.

'Lets just leave it, we'll get Hugh to move it next time he comes and see what he says, that definitely isn't our imagination,' said Marilyn, who couldn't wait to get out of the cellar either.

'I don't think we are going to find anything here anyway, I did see a small door round the back the other day which should open up into the rear of the cellar, it must be hidden by the wine racks now,' said Susan when they had all had a quick look round, avoiding the rat. They climbed back up the cellar steps and spread out on the ground floor. Everywhere was searched; even places already searched before, then a shout from Shelley had them all rushing to the library.

'I've found some,' Shelley stood triumphantly holding up a bunch of rusty keys, 'they were tucked right at the back of one of the desk drawers; let's see if one of them works.'

They all squeezed into the narrow passageway leading up to the mystery doors and Shelley started going through the keys, trying one after another. Nothing fitted either door.

'Is it because they are rusty?' Phyllis asked.

'I don't think so.' Shelley looked disappointed. 'They just aren't the right keys. Oh! Well, let's keep looking.' A very disheartened group carried on with the search.

They drew a blank in the rest of the drawers, but took the keys with them, up to the next floor. They each went to their own bedroom to search again for any keys, but again drew a blank.

Finally reaching the end of the corridor, Shelley, who still had the keys in her pocket, pulled them out and tried them one by one. The keys were very rusty, but when she finally found the one that fitted, the lock turned easily and the door opened. Why hadn't they tried that first? Idiots, she banged her palm against her forehead, before calling the others.

Quietly checking the hinges, Susan could see they had been recently oiled. She didn't say anything to the others but this had to be one way that Edna was getting in.

'It doesn't look dilapidated to me,' Marilyn whispered, as they stared down a similar landing to their own, 'it's the same as this side. What are we going to do now?'

'We are going to explore of course.' Susan was excited.

'I'm scared, it could be dangerous.' Marilyn's voice trembled.

'If we all stick together, we'll be alright. Are we agreed? We'll go together and check out the rooms one by one.' Shelley could not wait to get started.

They discovered a couple more large bedrooms, complete with furniture, but no bedding and again everywhere looking as if it hadn't been touched for months. At the far end, the corridor opened up into a large landing, with a wide staircase, not as grand as theirs, leading down into a hall. A large picture window on the side showed the boundary wall, and beyond that, the forest and the distant hills. Peeping over the banister, they could see a large square hall and another door to the outside. To the right was another small staircase, which led up to the top floor and another corridor leading to several more bedrooms.

'This is part of the shut off wing,' Susan whispered, 'let's have a look.'

Their eyes opened in shock as they looked in the first bedroom, the bed was made up, and it was clean, but worst of all, there was a pair of men's shoes on the floor and a jacket hanging from the wardrobe door. They did not recognise the clothes as belonging to Hugh, so it was not him living here. Could it be that Jamie perhaps?

Another bedroom next door was obviously occupied by a woman; there were clothes in the wardrobe and cosmetics on the dressing table. It could be Edna's room maybe. Susan had a quick look at the clothes to see if she could see anything that Edna might have worn when she visited, but didn't recognise anything. A third bedroom was made up ready for occupation, but there were no signs of anyone using it.

'That's it,' Shelley said, not feeling half as confident as she had earlier, 'I'm off. There are at least two people here; they could be dangerous. Is anyone coming with me? I definitely think you should Marilyn, in your condition, you don't need any shocks.'

'If you want to go back that's fine,' Susan replied, 'and I think you are right about Marilyn and you should go back too Mum,' she said turning to her mother. 'I'm going to keep looking; I need to know what's going on.'

'Susan, no, please come back, you will get caught, and then what, we don't know who they are.'

'All of you, go back please, I'll be careful. If I'm not back in half an hour, then come back and find me.' Reluctant to leave Susan alone, they hovered about. 'Will you please go, I promise to be careful.' She watched as they slowly went back along the corridor, through the adjoining door and closed it behind them. Staring at the closed door she didn't feel quite so confident and almost changed her mind.

She went back to the landing window and looked down, a large black people carrier and a small red saloon were visible on the drive; she wasn't very good at recognising makes of car but the red one looked very similar to Edna's, and the people carrier like the one Hugh had picked them up in.

Was Edna living here? And if she was, why was she?

To the other side of the stairs was another large bedroom, and judging by the clothes, also occupied by a man. It had a window, which overlooked the garden. She was sure this was the one where she had seen movement. Spotting a yellow folder lying on the desk under the window, she went over and picked it up; there was a name written neatly on the front, *Linda Mason,* and inside it seemed to have all the woman's personal details listed. Who on earth was Linda Mason and why was there a file on her?

Deciding that she had spent long enough, Susan was about to go back, but could not resist a quick look up on the next floor. She wanted to find the room above hers if she could. Leaving the file on the desk she tiptoed upstairs; again there was a corridor, with rooms off to the left, which was obviously the end wing again and rooms stretching the length of the house. Peeping only in the rooms at the front of the house, they all appeared empty except for one, which had a large wooden chest in the middle of the floor. This had to be the room above hers; Susan gave the chest a shove and it grated across the wooden floorboards. She was sure that was what she had heard, and she needed to find out who was doing it. Suddenly looking at her watch, she realised the half hour was almost up; the others would be worried.

She crept back down to the first floor and looked over the banister. Men's voices could be heard, near the bottom of the stairs. One was deep, the other a higher voice, but definitely men's voices. Was the deeper one Hugh's voice? She could not be certain.

In a panic, she rushed back along the corridor, through the door, locking it quietly behind her and leant against it gasping with relief, before joining the others downstairs.

She told them about the upper floor, and the room with the chest in, which she was convinced someone was pushing across the floor after she went to bed. Now she knew what was making the noise she was not quite so worried about hearing it. Then she told them about the file in the large bedroom. Someone called Linda Mason, whoever she was; then the two men's voices. One of which could have been Hugh's but she couldn't swear to it.

'Shall we ask Hugh if it was him you heard and who Linda Mason is?'

'I don't think we should, not yet, no wait, we could ask him the other lady's name who he said is still coming, I suppose we could do that.' Susan was pre-occupied. Her mind was going round in circles. Could there be more files on the rest of them? Why should it be such a big secret? Should they try to find out who it was or just leave it. Would they be told at the end of the four weeks? 'I just don't know what to think any more.'

The doorbell rang jolting them out of their conversation.

'I'll go,' said Marilyn. 'I wonder who it can be.'

A minute later she walked back in followed by Hugh. They were all surprised to see him back. Susan especially was glad she had got back before he turned up.

'To what do we owe this pleasure, Hugh?' Phyllis asked him as she offered him a cup of tea, which he declined.

'I was a bit rude earlier about the things you have been hearing, I came to apologise. These old houses do creak and groan a bit; maybe that's what you have been hearing.'

'Don't worry about us Hugh; as we said it is a bit strange for us all shut up here. Now, we do have another problem we need your help with, you see there is a dead rat in the cellar, would you mind moving it for us please, poor old Shelley nearly had a heart attack this morning.'

Hugh looked at them shocked. 'A rat did you say, in the cellar?'

'Go down the steps, you can't miss it, please take it out the kitchen door, we do not want to see it again.' Shelley called after him.

A few minutes later, he reappeared. 'That was rather a large one, we haven't had any rats around here for months, especially that big. I haven't a clue how it got down there, you must have left the doors open and it came in from outside.'

'We never leave the cellar door open,' Susan replied, 'it's always kept shut.' Then realising they were supposed to be agreeing with Hugh said, 'but obviously one of us must have left it open, we will have to be more careful. Now was there anything else or shall we see you tomorrow?' Susan guilelessly asked him, and he gave her such a look, she almost laughed aloud.

'No, there's nothing else, I'll probably see you the day after tomorrow.'

'Before you go Hugh, have you heard from the other lady yet, what was her name? You know the last one of us, is she still coming?'

'Linda Mason you mean, no we are still waiting to hear.'

Marilyn couldn't show him out of the door quick enough. She rushed back saying, 'That's the file you saw, what do you make of that?'

'It gets weirder here by the day,' said Shelley, 'and poor Hugh, I feel a bit sorry for him, we have got him totally confused.'

'Serves him right, don't feel sorry for him.' Phyllis shook her head.

Although Hugh's impromptu visit lightened the mood somewhat, a feeling of anxiety enveloped the group for the rest of the day, and they found it difficult to settle to anything. The weather had improved slightly so Susan took the opportunity to go outside. She was itching to deal with a small patch of weeds left in one of the flowerbeds; and now she had seen the bedroom from the inside, she wanted to have another look from the outside.

Walking in the direction of the gates, she looked about her, and then slowly turned and walked towards the flower bed casually looking about and yes, there was someone at the window again, watching her. It was a good job they were not there earlier she thought, pushing her hair off her face which let her raise her head and have a good look. It was definitely a man; she could see him more clearly today.

Who was this mysterious person and why didn't he want them to know he was there? There were so many unanswered questions.

The meal that night was a half-hearted affair with nobody hungry. All of them wrapped up in their own private thoughts. Phyllis had mislaid her glasses again, but did not mention it to anyone. She was still waiting an opportunity to speak to Susan.

Suddenly Marilyn stood up and banged her fist on the table. 'Why are they doing this? Why would Hugh lie to us? Why are they trying to frighten us? I'm really scared; I want to go home.'

'Relax Marilyn; I'm sure everything will become clear.' As she spoke, Phyllis put her arm round Marilyn's shoulders and persuaded her to sit back down. 'So many whys, that is all we seem to ask, why this and why that, have any of you heard the saying *Every Why has a Wherefore?* It means that there is always an explanation for everything. I am sure we will all have an explanation in due course.'

Susan raised her eyebrows as she looked across at her mother. Perhaps she had a soft side to her after all. She liked the fact that Phyllis appeared to have taken Marilyn under her wing. 'We could do with taking a look round that side of the house from the outside; we might manage to see who is there. I know,' Susan continued, in her excitement, running her hands through her hair, which made it stick up all over the place, 'Hugh will be here again the day after tomorrow. We know he locks the gate every time he comes in and out, but what if we cause a distraction long enough for one of us to slip out the gate when he's not looking.'

'What a great idea.' Marilyn's voice dripped with sarcasm. 'How do you suggest that person gets back in again? Do you climb over the wall or the gate? And how do you know that whoever went out would be hidden from view on the other side of the wall. We don't know what's growing there do we?'

'I should imagine there are loads of trees by the looks of things. If no-one has got a better idea, I suggest we all sleep on it then, and talk again in the morning, and someone else can lock up tonight I'm going to bed.' With that, Susan left the room.

'Oh dear, I think you have upset her now.' Phyllis knew her daughter felt responsible for all of them only because they were the first to arrive, but it really wasn't her responsibility, they were all grown women; she felt a pang of pity for her. 'Come on, let's all turn in, we have had a tiring day.'

Now's my opportunity, Phyllis thought as she followed Susan up the stairs. Knocking quietly at the bedroom door, she poked her head round and said she wanted to talk about something.

Phyllis told her of the missing glasses and her book, and suggested that someone might be playing tricks on her, and Susan confided in her mother that her journal was being moved about, and how she had now found a safer place for it.

'Who do you think is responsible? I can't believe any of the others would do something like that, what would they be trying to achieve?'

'I don't know,' Susan said thoughtfully, 'the only person I can think of is Edna, she must be coming in when there's no-one around, but I don't understand why she would be doing it, unless she is trying to make both of us look stupid and forgetful in front of the others. When we opened the adjoining door, I noticed the hinges had been recently oiled, I did not say anything, but I think Edna is using that door to get into our bedrooms. That is why she told us to use these two rooms; they are nearest the door. Then she must sneak downstairs when she knows we are in the kitchen. I am surprised she has only been spotted the once, when you saw her and she denied it. She is a sly piece of work, no doubt about it. Tomorrow morning why don't we both make sure we know where your glasses and book are and my journal, and see if anything gets moved again.'

'I'll see you first thing then, before we go down to breakfast, goodnight Susan.'

'Goodnight Mum.'

Phyllis climbed into bed feeling a lot better than she had the last couple of days. She had been so worried her mind was going, but talking had put her at ease, as they were both experiencing the same thing. But why would Edna do it? She lay in the dark for quite awhile before gradually drifting off.

Chapter 26

Alone in his office, Angus was angry with himself as he gazed out of the window; he could tell by the woman's actions that he had been seen. Hugh told him that Susan was a keen gardener and he so wanted to catch a glimpse of her. It was careless of him, but he could not resist the temptation. Hugh and Edna were annoyed with him too, for almost giving the game away; now the women would know someone was living in the other half of the house. Hugh was desperately trying to put them off by telling them it was their imagination running away with them, but they were not going to fall for that any longer.

What now, he wondered; it was going to be extremely difficult to keep himself hidden away for another three weeks, what was going to happen? He was not ready. It wasn't time to meet them yet. Hugh kept him informed of the accidents happening to Susan and he felt very concerned about her. Edna reckoned she was just careless, but that business with the light switch, well, that could have been very unpleasant for everyone and how had it happened?

It was Edna's idea for them to stay in the first place, and be kept away from everyone, so they would not hear any stories about him or Dunnbray. He and Hugh had gone along with it, because they could not come up with a better plan, but now he was not so sure it was the right way to have gone about things. Edna was becoming extremely critical of them all, especially Susan. He could not understand why, as she was so keen in the beginning to get them all there. He wanted so much to see how they coped with the conditions and how adaptable they were, so he could see if his plan was possible or not. India, the young one, could not cope with it. Not surprising really, after the description Hugh had given him. India was an extremely spoilt young woman who did not have the stamina by all accounts. Never mind, there were still four ladies left that he was interested in. He was still hoping that Linda would change her mind and come too. The solicitors were in touch with her again and she was wavering.

He was getting concerned about Edna who had looked after him for a good many years; they always got on so well, but just lately, she was acting strangely. Perhaps she wanted to retire; maybe she was tired of taking care of him, or maybe it was that son of hers, she was always suggesting that he could do more around the estate, but Angus thought him a bit of an idle lad, and not too bright either. Hugh needed to watch him all the time.

A smile crossed his lips, what a feisty bunch of girls they seemed; just like his mother, keeping Hugh on his toes, poor man, so many problems to deal with.

Then he thought about the riddle written by his grandfather, and opening the centre drawer of his desk, he pulled out the single piece of paper on which the riddle was typed, now enclosed in a clear plastic sleeve to protect it.

The secret of Dunnbray is never far away.
Is it under ground? Where the secret can be found?
Find four legs and a tail and the secret will unveil
Security for Dunnbray, always, forever and a day!

Still unsolved after all these years, he could recite if off by heart, but had never managed to solve it. He and his mother spent hours wracking their brains over it, but never came up with an answer and Isobel decided that it must have been a joke to tease Archie, there never was any secret money. Still, it would be interesting to know what the girls made of it when they found out.

Not long now, then the truth could finally be revealed. He could not wait. However, he must be more careful at the window for the time being.

He leant back in his favourite chair and closed his eyes. A little nap would not go amiss. As he drifted into a light sleep, his dreams as always were of his mother, Isobel.

Chapter 27

Spring 1928

One night, Alan showed his mother, Isobel, the bottom of his shoes where a hole was appearing yet again. It was no good, something must be done, they could not carry on any longer with little or no money. She thought about the rhyme that Allister had left for Archie; they still hadn't been able to decipher it. Archie carried it with him constantly and it was getting so dog-eared that Isobel recently copied it and put it in a safe place. If they lost the only copy then no one would ever solve the mystery. She was beginning to think it was a joke.

Isobel decided to talk to the boys, so called to them and when they arrived, she sat them down at the kitchen table and explained honestly about the money situation; how their father wouldn't give her any more and asked if they had any ideas on how to raise some. Was there anything they could think of to make some money without their father finding out? otherwise he would take it.

'What about growing more vegetables to sell,' they suggested. Will, the gardener kept them supplied with their own needs, but the vegetable garden was big enough to grow more.

'What a brilliant idea boys.' She wondered why she had never thought of it herself. They would enlist the help of Will, in secret of course. In return for the boys helping him with his work, they would ask him to help them with the vegetable garden.

Will had no respect for his Master, but he would do anything for the Mistress and her boys. He was more than glad to help them out and would buy seeds and plants the next market day so they could get their plan under way.

Then Angus came up with another idea. 'Mum, you know you are good at sewing, well I overheard Mrs Johnson, our English teacher talking to one of the dinner ladies. She said that there was no one in the village to do any dressmaking now that old Mrs Finch has died. Do you think you could do dressmaking? Could I tell Mrs Johnson that you would make a dress for her?'

'Angus, you are a dear boy, such a wonderful idea. I have not sewed anything in ages. Yes, I could make her a dress. Would you care to ask her if she would like to come to tea the day after tomorrow and we could discuss her requirements? Oh! I am so excited; we might have money after all. Oh dear, I do not know what to charge, what do I charge boys?'

'Just ask her how much old Mrs Finch charged, then add a little bit on, that should do it,' said Alex practically.

'Yes, yes, that's what I'll do then.'

Isobel sat in her cosy sitting room after Mrs Johnson left, and hugged herself with pleasure; two dresses, she could not believe it. Mrs Johnson had asked her to make two dresses, one for daywear and one for evening. Mrs Johnson already had the fabrics, ribbons, and the patterns, so all Isobel needed to buy was the thread.

We are going to be so busy, she thought but we must manage for the next few weeks, until I get paid for the dresses, then hopefully that will keep our heads above water until we have some vegetables to sell.

Isobel got the boys to help her move her sewing machine up to the nursery so that she could work without being disturbed. Archie would allow no servants in the house, so no one was around to see what she was doing. Andrew had started school the previous September so she knew there were several hours each day when she could work undisturbed, before the boys came home from school, and even if Archie was home he would never come looking for her up there. She wondered if he really knew there was a nursery up there at all. If he wanted her, he would open his study door and yell.

She enjoyed sewing, it was such a pleasure working with beautiful material and it was so long since she had made herself a new dress. Within a week, much to Mrs Johnson's amazement, her day dress was ready; Mrs Finch had always taken three to four weeks. Angus passed on the message asking Mrs Johnson to come to the house to try the dress on.

The boys fetched a large cheval mirror from one of the guest bedrooms and with a screen that stood unused in the main sitting room; the nursery was turned into a changing room. She was sure Mrs Johnson would not mind climbing up two flights of stairs when she saw the finished dress, and she was not wrong. Angus's teacher was delighted with the finished product. She twirled this way and that, admiring herself in the full-length mirror.

'Mrs MacPhail, you are an excellent seamstress, I can't wait for my evening dress, and I will tell everyone who has made this dress for me.'

'Mrs Johnson, please, call me Isobel. I am thrilled that you are happy with the dress.'

'Alright, Isobel, then you must call me Mary, and I will pay you for this dress straight away. Here you are, let me know as soon as the other one is ready.'

Isobel wrapped the dress carefully in tissue paper and Mrs Johnson, sorry, Mary, went away a very satisfied lady.

That night, Isobel showed the boys the money she had earned and gave each of them some pocket money.

From that day on, Isobel became the dressmaker for the surrounding area. As soon as the boys went to school, she was up in the nursery sewing and stitching until her eyes and fingers ached. Dress after dress was produced, tried on and left under the arm of very satisfied ladies. Luckily, Archie never noticed all the comings and goings. He was so disliked in the surrounding areas; no one was going to tell him what Isobel was up to. They knew how short of money the McPhails were.

The garden was starting to produce enough vegetables to sell at market. The boys would set up their stall if they were not at school, and Will, the gardener, would do it on the days when they were. Angus and Alan gained a lot of knowledge from the old gardener, and he in turn found them to be very quick learners. Even little Andrew was becoming involved and knew the weeds from the plants, so would go and do his bit to help.

Isobel bought one or two new items of clothing and a pair of new shoes each for the boys, but she was very careful not to spend too much in case Archie noticed, and she never spent anything on herself. She saved as much as she could, tucking it away in a shoe box under one of the guest beds.

One day Archie came back from the village and stormed into the house, shouting, 'Isobel, Isobel, where are you? Get in here at once.'

Isobel hearing him ran down the stairs immediately and found him in his study.

'What is it Archie, what ever is the matter?'

'Angus, and Alan, what are they doing with a market stall? Someone saw them selling veg, where did they get it from? Why aren't they in school? How much money do they make doing that? Why haven't they handed the money over?'

'Calm down Archie,' said Isobel, her mind quickly coming up with an excuse. 'The stall belongs to the school, who are selling vegetables to raise some money for a trip for all the children, and Angus and Alan offered to run it for them today, so you see its not their money it's the school's, so stop making such a fuss. You are home nice and early today. Shall I get you some dinner; I have made a nice lamb stew, with dumplings, and it is your favourite. Come on Archie, come and sit down in the kitchen, have something to eat. Tell me what you have been doing today.'

Isobel headed towards the kitchen, breathing a sigh of relief that there actually was a stew for their tea that night. Archie did not always come back in time to eat a decent meal.

Archie looked at his wife out of the corner of his eye as he ate his dinner. She looked different somehow. Did she seem happier? He couldn't quite put his finger on it. Was she up to something? He wondered what it could be, but wasn't interested enough to try and find out, luckily for her, and the incident was soon forgotten as he went down in the cellar and brought up the last bottle of port and disappeared back into his study for the evening.

Chapter 28

March 2008

The view from Susan's bedroom window changed daily. Sometimes dull or wet; sometimes windy; the hills appearing and disappearing depending on how misty the horizon was, and the garden was changing daily too. She realised she still had not asked Hugh what hills they were. Her eyes fell on the flowers, which were popping up all over the place and such an amazing variety of shrubs. Marilyn had found her another book on gardening in the library, which she was avidly reading, causing great amusement as she exclaimed, 'Got that one, and that one.' The grass still awaited cutting; it would look so much nicer if it were a smooth green lawn.

Before she went downstairs, she and Phyllis checked that they each knew where all their belongings were.

Shelley poured herself another cup of tea, and said, 'I think some of us should go through the door again today. Hugh isn't due to come is he? It could be a good opportunity.'

Susan looked at her gratefully. 'I think that's probably the best idea, better than mine anyway.'

'Count me out,' Marilyn shuddered, 'it's too scary for me, my baby doesn't need any more frights thank you and I don't think Phyllis should go through either.'

'That leaves you and me then.' Shelley smiled at Susan.

Leaving the others in the kitchen, Susan and Shelley headed upstairs. Passing the unoccupied main bedroom, Shelley noticed the door, which was always kept shut, now stood ajar, a look of panic crossed her face as she tapped Susan's shoulder and pointed. They stood and listened, hearing some muffled sounds coming from the room.

Looking at Shelley, Susan put her finger to her lips, then suddenly pushed the door open wide, shouting, 'Who's there, we know you are in there.'

They rushed into the room and stopped in amazement, as who should be standing there but Edna looking quite shocked herself.

'What are you doing here? How did you get in?' Susan asked sharply.

'I did ring the bell, but you couldn't have heard me, so I let myself in, I didn't know where you all were and I wanted to look for something in this room. I'm sorry if I startled you.'

'We were in the kitchen Edna, you know we were and we would have heard the bell if you had rung it, we are not deaf, or stupid. You made it clear to us you are not doing any housekeeping while we are staying here so you have no right to come in uninvited. What's wrong with coming round to the back door? You have come into our house without asking again, please don't do it.' Susan was angry and fed up with this woman, what was she playing at. 'Have you found what you are looking for, because if you have would you mind leaving now please, thank you.'

They watched as Edna left, empty-handed and headed down stairs. They looked round the bedroom, which they had already searched and there was nothing in any of the drawers or cupboards.

'What do you think she was looking for?' asked Shelley.

'Whatever it was I don't think it was in this room, I think she heard us coming up the stairs and just hid in here. I think she has been in our bedrooms.'

'But why would she do that?'

Susan did not answer; she was looking out of the window. 'There is no sign of Edna's car on the drive; I am convinced she is coming through one of those doors. She has a key.'

Shelley was shocked. 'I think you may be right, why don't we put something in front of the door later to stop her coming through and see what happens.'

'We'll let the others know when we go back down, and we can either do that or let her think that we haven't realised and try to catch her again, meanwhile let's carry on with the original plan if you're still happy with that, and hope we don't bump into her on that side. That would be funny wouldn't it?'

It all looked the same the other side of the locked door as it had the first time. They decided to go up to the top floor to have one more look around. One of the rooms Susan had not looked in before had obviously been the nursery once upon a time; a well-worn old rocking horse stood forlornly in one corner and nursery rhyme character wallpaper was beginning to peel off two of the walls.

'I suppose all these rooms would have been occupied in its heyday, all the servants, the children and the nanny,' Shelley said, looking around, 'there would have been so many people living here.'

They found nothing else of interest on that floor so they crept back down the staircase, listening for any sounds as they went, checking in all the occupied bedrooms again.

'Are we ready for this?' Susan whispered to Shelley as they gazed over the banister into the hallway below. Hearing no voices and not seeing any cars outside this time, - Edna must have gone straight out - but still not certain whether anyone was there or not, they crept down the stairs, holding their breath every time a step creaked. They made it to the bottom and stood quietly listening. A faint hum coming from something electrical could be heard; it was probably a fridge or freezer so they did not think it was anything to worry about. They headed for the door at the back of the hallway, where the sound was coming from. It was a utility room, complete with washing machine, tumble dryer and large freezer; it was the freezer making the noise.

A door led from the utility room into a large, modern kitchen, in a glossy white finish, with granite worktops, bigger than theirs was, complete with integrated dishwasher, microwave and large oven and loads of workspace, including a large tiled island unit in the centre with breakfast bar to one side and three high stools. Peeking in the cupboards, they saw well-stocked shelves. The huge American fridge was full. Hugh obviously kept this side of the house supplied as well.

'They know how to look after themselves on this side, don't they?' Susan said quietly. 'So much for it being dilapidated and run down, give me dilapidated any day.'

'Hugh has been lying to us the whole time, hasn't he? Could it possibly be his family living here and he doesn't want anyone to know, or Edna's even?' Shelley felt quite disappointed with Hugh; she could not understand his behaviour.

Listening at the kitchen door and still hearing no sounds, they went back out into the hall and peeped round the next door. They discovered another dining room, very similar in style and furnishings to their own, with double doors leading to a sitting room, again very like theirs.

Another door took them back out to the hallway, and then they realised they had missed a room to the side of the front door. Opening it up, they discovered a small office cum library. Shelves of books filled two walls, floor to ceiling. A window overlooked the garden. A computer and keyboard stood on a desk under the window, a swivel chair in front. A light on the tower under the desk showed that the computer was switched on.

'Shall we?' whispered Shelley as her hands hovered over the keyboard. As she touched it the screen came to life, but it asked for a password. 'Oh, bum' she exclaimed, she had hoped to find some information.

Meanwhile, Susan spotted a filing cabinet in the corner and finding it unlocked, pulled open the top drawer.

'Hey! Look at this, there are files on all of us.' Pulling her own folder out, she glanced inside. It was similar to the one on Linda Mason, with loads of personal information about her, where she lived, where she worked, how old she was, her relationship to Phyllis. She was busily leafing through the pages, when they both froze in panic as they heard a car's tyres crunching on the gravel outside. Susan quickly shoved the file back in and closed the drawer and grabbing Shelley's hand pulled her out of the office and back up the stairs. They raced along the corridor and through the adjoining door, shutting it and locking it securely.

'Phew, that was close,' Susan gasped, as they got their breath back, 'my nerves are shot; I think we deserve a drink, a strong one at that.' Susan suddenly realised with horror that she was still holding the front sheet of her file in her hand.

'Oh God, now they will know we have been in there,' she exclaimed, looking at the paper, 'do you think I should take it back?'

'No, you can't go back in there now, perhaps they won't notice. Why would they want to look at our files now we are here?' Shelley touched Susan's shoulder reassuringly. 'It will be all right, don't worry.' They went back to the sitting room where Phyllis and Marilyn were waiting anxiously, and filled them in on what they had found, but only after they had mixed themselves a stiff gin and tonic each; purely for medicinal reasons of course.

Phyllis and Marilyn were amazed. All tried yet again, but failed to come up with any explanation.

'We were obviously not picked at random then,' Susan remarked, 'they chose us for a reason, but how did they know we would all reply, what if we hadn't? What if we had all binned that letter, and treated it as junk mail? Would they have picked a different group of women? I wish I understood. The longer we are here, the worse it is getting.'

'There is something else we haven't told you about yet,' Shelley said, 'guess who we found in the main bedroom upstairs?'

'Not Edna by any chance?'

'It was indeed, she told us she had rung the bell and getting no answer, let herself in and not knowing where we were, ha! ha!, went up to the bedroom.'

'The bell never rang, did it? We would have heard it.' Marilyn and Phyllis glanced at each other.

'We are certain now she is coming through one of the locked doors, she never left in her car, so what other explanation could there be?' murmured Shelley.

'Do you think she knows that we have been in that side?' Marilyn asked.

'Shelley suggested blocking the doorway so she can't get through, but if we do that, she will know that we are on to her and I don't know what she would do then. I think we should let her carry on coming in for a bit longer until we actually catch her doing something.'

'If you think that's the best, Susan, that's what we'll do, but everyone please stay on their guard,' Shelley said. 'We thought it would be really funny if we meet up with her creeping about when we are creeping about.'

'I wonder what she would do or say.'

'I've just had an idea, why don't we invite Hugh to dinner tomorrow night? Try to pick his brains. He told us his favourite meal was venison when he brought us some the other day,' Phyllis said, a smile lighting up her usually severe face. 'Shelley and Marilyn make such wonderful meals, I am sure they can come up trumps with the venison, we can have a starter and a sweet, the whole works and select some good wine, what do you think?'

'What a great idea, butter him up, you mean Mum, wine and dine him, flatter him and he'll tell us anything. If that's the plan, I'm all for it. You know what these men are like, flatter them and they'll do anything for you.'

'*Nothing ventured, nothing gained* – as the saying goes,' replied Phyllis, 'sorry, couldn't resist slipping that one in.'

'Let's do it in style, we'll eat in the dining room.' Marilyn was getting excited. They had always been too busy to set the table in there before, and congregated round the kitchen table for all their meals. The kitchen was a cosy comforting sort of place to sit and discuss all the worries they were getting over their so-called holiday with a difference, and so the dining room had been overlooked.

Plans were put into action for Hugh's visit the next day. It never entered anyone's head that he might just turn them down. Susan especially was thrilled to think she could spend more time in Hugh's company; she really did like him and wondered if he felt the same way about her.

Phyllis's glasses and book had both disappeared and reappeared. She no longer worried that she was going senile; she knew it was that stupid woman's doing. It was very tempting to write a rude message and attach it to the front of the book for Edna to find, but she resisted, knowing Susan would not be happy about it, which was a shame, she could have written something nasty.

Chapter 29

There was much pacing to and fro, waiting for Hugh to arrive the following morning and when he finally did, they gathered round and invited him to join them for dinner that night; they were having venison, they told him, his favourite and they hoped he would be able to come. He ummed and aaghed and at first they thought he was going to say no, but Susan told him he must come, they were all so looking forward to having some different company at dinner. Hugh realised this would be a good opportunity to see more of Susan too, and decided that he could manage it after all.

Did the invitation extend to Edna?' He asked.

'No, it did not,' was the collective shout. He left laughing and said he would see them later.

The rest of the day was spent in cleaning and polishing the dining room again, getting out the best damask tablecloth and matching napkins, laying the table with the best silver and china and generally killing time until Hugh arrived. Susan picked some fresh flowers from the garden and placed them in a beautiful crystal vase. The table looked magnificent.

One incident spoiled what was otherwise a perfect day. A huge, dead rat had been discovered, by Shelley in the scullery, a couple of hours before Hugh was due to arrive. They had all heard the screams and gone rushing out to find Shelley frozen to the spot in fear, pointing to the rat. There were squeals of disgust, but it was Phyllis, who bravely went over and kicked it to make sure it was dead. Susan got a spade out of the shed, lifted the rat up and carried it outside, taking it over to the walled garden and dropping it with a shudder, hoping something else would come along and eat it.

All the best clothes were rescued from the backs of wardrobes where they had been hung when the group realised there was nowhere to wear anything decent. Only the best for Hugh they all decided, poor man, he did not stand a chance. Marilyn lent Susan one of her skirts and a tight fitting top, which looked lovely on her. The skirt was a bit short as Susan was taller than Marilyn was, but showed off her slim legs to great advantage. Shelley had offered to style Susan's hair so, when a little later, she made her entrance at the top of the stairs, there were gasps of surprise and admiration from the others gathered in the hall. What an elegant, beautiful woman she was; what a waste to keep herself hidden under the usual frumpy clothes, and her hair, they couldn't believe what a difference it made piled high on her head with soft tendrils curling round her pretty face.

The others knew Susan had a soft spot for Hugh and pulled her leg unmercifully, saying she would knock him dead in that get-up. They told her she must go to the door to let him in when he arrived.

Susan blushed. 'He's probably married, or he's not interested in me, I can't allow myself to get too friendly with him.'

'I don't think he's married, so let's see what we can find out tonight; you obviously like him and he's always looking at you.' Shelley laughed mischievously.

'Please don't make it obvious, I would die of embarrassment. I'll offer to make coffee after our meal and go out into the kitchen, then if he offers to help, I shall know if he is interested in me or not and you lot can give us a few minutes alone, is that okay? Are you happy with that?'

'No problem.' They all chorused, laughing. Even Phyllis didn't seem to mind about Susan getting friendly with Hugh.

Hugh was due to arrive at seven for dinner at seven thirty and promptly on the chime of seven from the grandfather clock in the hall, there was a ring on the doorbell.

'Go on Susan, go for it,' Marilyn laughed, pushing her towards the door.

Hugh was standing on the doorstep with a bunch of flowers, which he thrust awkwardly into Susan's hand muttering that they were for all of them, his eyes travelling up and down in surprise as he took in Susan's changed appearance.

'Why thank you Hugh, they're lovely.' Susan buried her nose in the fragrant bouquet, hiding the smile at his surprised appraisal of her. 'Come on in, Shelley will get you a drink while I go and put these in water.'

The fire was burning brightly in the fireplace in the hall, drinks were passed around and conversation was kept casual with discussion about the weather, how good it was for this time of year, and what a good job Susan was making of the gardens.

'The grass badly needs cutting,' Susan said, 'who usually does that? Is there a gardener? I haven't seen a lawnmower anywhere either; if there's a sit on one I could do it if you want, but I am not pushing one that's for sure.'

They all waited in silence for Hugh's reply.

Hugh, suddenly aware of what he had been asked, took his time, and then replied carefully. 'There is a part-time gardener, but he has been off work with a bad back, which is why the gardens have been neglected recently. When he comes, he brings his own mower, which is why you haven't been able to find one.'

'Has Edna been off with a bad back as well?' Phyllis could not resist having another dig at the housekeeper, but was quickly hushed up with a glare from Susan.

Changing the subject quickly, Marilyn announced that dinner was ready, and would they all go into the dining room.

'Come on Hugh,' said Susan, taking his arm and leading him to the head of the table, while Shelley went into the kitchen to help Marilyn with the last minute preparations and carry the homemade soup through.

Marilyn and Shelley really had pulled out all the stops; the meal was superb. The venison cooked to perfection according to Hugh, and he followed this by having two helpings of apple crumble and custard, another of his favourites.

Conversation had deliberately been kept light, since Phyllis's awkward question. Hugh had extracted information from them all by continually asking questions and avoided giving anything away about himself. He was a harder nut to crack than they thought he would be. Their female wiles were not working on him at all.

When they all felt as if they would burst if they ate anything else, Susan announced she would go and make the coffee.

As Hugh offered to lend a hand and left the room, there were knowing smiles all round the table.

Susan was surprised to see how quickly Hugh had followed her. He had been asked so many times to stop and have coffee, but had always acted as if he was trying to avoid them.

'You look beautiful tonight; I love the outfit and your hair.'

'Thank you Hugh, it is not often anyone sees me like this, I don't usually have any need to dress up.'

'I shall have to take you out for a meal one night then, when the four weeks are up, so you can dress up again. Would you come out if I asked you?'

'That would be lovely, yes; I would love to go out for a meal with you.' Susan replied as she turned away to put the kettle on so that he would not see her blushing with excitement. Hugh got the cups and saucers out, his mind still on Susan. He knew he was falling for this woman, but would it be right? He filled a jug with milk, put sugar in a basin and placed everything on a large tray, which he fetched from one of the cupboards in the utility. Susan watched his familiarity with the place and she knew that she had to take this opportunity to ask him some questions.

'You know your way around here don't you? It's almost as if you have you lived here yourself,' she said.

'Given myself away, haven't I?' He spoke the words carefully, 'do you realise how difficult it is for me to keep things secret from you all? I would love to tell you everything, but that would just spoil it, but I will tell you this – my parents lived here for about ten years, ran it as a Bed & Breakfast. They retired only recently as the place got too much for them. They have bought a small bungalow in Inverness and are much happier now the worry of making ends meet has gone.' He told her he also lived here for a time with them, which is why he knew his way around. It also explained the run down appearance of the place, the lack of investment.

Susan didn't quite know what to say without giving too much away so innocently asked, 'What about the shut off bit of the house? Was it shut off when your parents were here? or was someone else living in that half at the time?'

As she saw the expression on his face, she knew the conversation had ended.

'How many times do I have to tell you that no-one lives there, it is run down and unsafe. It was in a poor state before my parents came here and there are no plans, or money even to do anything with it.' With that, he picked up the tray and carried it into the dining room.

Oops, that did not go well then thought Shelley as she saw Hugh's grim expression.

'I think I'll give the coffee a miss if you don't mind,' he said as Susan came in with the coffee pot, 'I have a lot on tomorrow and don't want to be too late getting back.'

He thanked them all, giving each one a quick peck on the cheek, lingering just that bit longer with Susan, and then was gone, closing the door quietly behind him.

'What happened? What did you say to him? He didn't look too happy.' Phyllis asked.

'You'll never guess what,' Susan replied, 'the way he was getting the cups and things, I could tell he knew his way round the kitchen; he didn't have to ask me where anything was. I asked how he knew and he said that his parents had run a bed and breakfast business and that he had stayed here with them, and unbelievably, they had only recently retired. Then I made the mistake of asking him about the shut off part of the house, and whether someone else lived there when his parents were here or was it really run down and unsafe and that's when he got angry and left.' She decided not to mention him asking her out, especially as he had gone off in a mood, he might have regretted asking her.

'Never mind, at least we have learnt something tonight. What's our next move?' Shelley asked.

'We could just wait until the four weeks are up, then we'll know everything, anyway,' Phyllis said, suddenly wondering if she really wanted to find out, if it looked like it was likely to be dangerous to carry on delving into things.

'I can't wait that long Mum, I don't know about the rest of you, but my curiosity is getting the better of me, I need to know more. Shall we have another look next door? It only needs one of us to watch from the top floor to see when any cars go out and I think we need to know if Hugh does go there as well. He isn't back here until the day after tomorrow, if we leave it 'til then we can watch and see if he does. We know roughly what time he comes now, if one of us can get up there about half an hour before he usually arrives then we should be able to see his Land Rover. And, that people carrier we were picked up from the station in, I'm sure that's the same one we saw parked next door.'

'I don't know what the registration was, but it certainly looked like the same vehicle.' Shelley replied. 'I'm with you Susan, I don't want to wait a few more weeks to find out, I vote we keep searching.'

'Count me out,' said Phyllis.

'Don't worry Mum, you don't need to get involved if you don't want to, and Marilyn we don't mind if you want to keep out of it too in your condition.'

'Thank you,' said Marilyn, 'I really am too stressed about it all, this isn't doing my baby any good.'

Phyllis and Marilyn left the other two sitting at the table discussing their plans and cleared away all the dinner things. Entering the kitchen, they decided to have another cup of coffee before tackling the washing up.

'I don't know what to make of this holiday.' Phyllis's face was a picture of concern, 'I have a funny feeling about it. I won't say I wish I hadn't come, because otherwise I wouldn't have met all of you.'

'I feel the same as you, that no matter what happens, we will all stay friends. The so called friends I have at home, they aren't really, they are girls that I meet up with and have lunch with, but I don't think any of them are genuine, they wouldn't be there for me in a crisis and I suppose they feel the same about me. I had a couple of good friends when I worked at the bank, but Ken didn't like me mixing with them once I left, so I haven't seen either of them for a few years now. I miss them.'

'I don't have any friends either Marilyn. You would think at my age, being retired and belonging to different groups that I would have plenty of friends, but I know none of the women like me. Since being here I have come to realise it's my own fault, you have all shown me that, I am too sarcastic and I never have a good word to say about anybody and I keep coming out with stupid sayings. I treated India the same. I have been unkind to my own daughter too; I don't know how you have all put up with such a miserable old woman.'

Marilyn noticed Phyllis's eyes filling up with tears, spilling over and trickling down her cheek, and went round the table and put her arms round her, giving Phyllis a quick hug.

'You have always been kind to me,' she said, 'especially when you told me I was pregnant. I must admit, if I am being totally honest, we were all a bit worried when we first met you and Susan. We felt sorry for her, you do have a sharp tongue, you know, but you have been so much nicer just lately. We have all noticed it Phyllis, this place must be doing you good, whatever is going on, and if you are aware of what you have been like, then that's half the battle, you don't need to be like it any more. Keep seeing the best in people not the worst and they will respond to that and be nice to you in return. I am trying to practice what I preach; I can be a bit snobbish too.'

'Yes, we had noticed. I will definitely try being kinder to Susan, she has been such a good daughter to me; I have relied on her too much in the past. She doesn't have a life of her own; she always has to do something with me. That will change when we go home.'

'Good for you, and perhaps I can come and stay with you sometime, I can bring the baby to show you if you'd like, and you and Susan can come down to London and stay with me.'

It was Marilyn's turn to look sad as she thought about the life she might be leading when she got home, a single mum, that's what she would probably end up as.

Guessing what was going through Marilyn's mind, Phyllis grasped Marilyn's hand and told her that she was sure her husband would be all right about the baby once the shock had worn off. 'He won't want to lose you,' she said, 'not if he loves you.'

They gave each other another hug, and then got on with the job of washing up and getting the kitchen sorted.

The others meanwhile were still making plans in the dining room.

They decided that Shelley would sneak into the shut off bit, the day after tomorrow; she would check on the vehicles coming and going and let Susan know as soon as the coast was clear. They would then go through the adjoining door and see if they could find out any more information. One of them would have another search of the bedrooms and the other one would go down to the ground floor.

The library would be a good place to start as it had the filing cabinet, which they had to abandon the other day.

During the day, Phyllis's glasses had disappeared and reappeared again; and Susan's bedside drawer had been opened and things inside disturbed, Edna obviously searching for the journal, but

Susan was hiding it somewhere she thought Edna would never think to look and so far, it was working.

Chapter 30

Angus searched through the filing cabinet again. He would have asked Hugh about the missing sheet of paper only he had been dashing off to have a meal with the girls.

He only realised it was missing himself when he went to replace Linda's folder which had been left in his bedroom, and noticed that the suspension files were disturbed. Susan's folder was not in its place. He carefully went through the files again and found it in with the folder on Shelley, and on taking it out and opening it he saw that the top piece of paper with some of the details was missing.

Could it have been them in the house the other day? He knew he had heard something, but thought it was Jamie, perhaps sneaking in for something to eat, which he sometimes did. If it was them, what could they have learnt?

This plan was worsening. They might know by now that there were files on all of them, and then they would know someone had been spying on them, and their plan was obviously to try and sweet talk Hugh over a meal. Goodness knows what information they would drag out of him. They would wrap him round their little fingers if he did not watch out, especially Susan; Hugh appeared to have a soft spot for her.

They got more and more like his mother every day, like dogs with a bone, never giving up. I don't think I will be able to keep this up for another two weeks, he thought, I can just picture them bursting in here one day demanding the truth. I have the strangest feeling they may be able to crack the riddle too when they see it. I cannot wait.

He closed the library door and walked slowly back to his sitting room where the fire burned brightly. Edna had left a cold supper for him before she left. He sat in his comfortable old chair, and lifted the tray from the coffee table onto his lap and looked at the food. He felt quite peckish. There was a ham sandwich, made from local ham and granary bread, with a salad garnish, followed by a piece of Dundee cake: all to be washed down with his favourite tipple; a small tot of Glenfiddich Single Malt Scotch Whisky. He ate, gazing dreamily into the flickering flames.

Chapter 31

1929

Rage came over Archie like a red mist. He was sitting in his usual place propping up the bar, in his father-in-law's inn, when Rev McDougal came over and innocently said that his wife was thrilled to bits with the latest dress Isobel had made for her.

'What did you say?' Archie asked him to repeat himself.

Suddenly, things began to drop into place in his befuddled mind. Isobel hadn't asked him for money for ages, but he'd noticed the boys were wearing new shoes and the food on the table was much improved recently. Isobel was earning money and not told him. How long had this been going on? How much was she hiding away? The deceitful little cow, he would go home and find out what she was up to.

Archie mounted his old horse, which plodded sedately to the inn and back every day, her days of racing just a dim and distant memory. However drunken Archie was, he always managed to stay in the saddle. This particular day, though, he leaped up on old Bess's back, gave her a hefty kick in her side, which terrified the horse and she took off at an unsteady gallop. He could not wait to get home and confront Isobel and those three thieving toe rags he guessed were involved as well. He wondered too whether Isobel had managed to unravel the mysterious riddle. She couldn't have, could she?

The first Isobel knew about it, was when the local constabulary, that is PC Gordon, came knocking at the door. Opening the door and seeing the serious expression on his face, she knew immediately that something had happened to Archie, she had been expecting this moment for years.

'May I come in Mrs McPhail, I am afraid I have some bad news, please sit down. Is there anyone who can get you a cup of tea?'

'There's no-one here now, the boys are still at school, just tell me what has happened.'

'Your husband has had an accident, his old horse must have stumbled, he was thrown off, died instantly, the fall must have broken his neck.'

PC Gordon hated this part of the job, giving sad news like this was always difficult, but he thought Mrs MacPhail was taking it very well.

Isobel, although shocked at the news, also felt such a feeling of relief washing over her, that when the tears finally came, they were not only tears of sadness that her children were now fatherless, but also tears of joy too, that this was the beginning of a new life for her and her boys.

Isobel never re-married, but remained on the estate until her death years later. She gave up the sewing; slowly replaced the stock of sheep and deer; the fields were planted, and with the help of her sons and Dougal, re-instated as farm manager; he had returned as soon as he heard of Archie's death, Dunnbray became once again a thriving business. Angus was the rightful heir, and as the eldest son, would one day become Laird, but Isobel never took it for granted that he or her other two sons would stay to run the place with her. There was life beyond Dunnbray and she wanted them to experience it, so when they were old enough, Angus joined the Navy, Alan joined the Army and Andrew went to Law School. She just enjoyed their company whenever they came back to visit her.

The brothers, realising that their aging mother would not be able to carry on indefinitely on her own, met up one day and decided between them that as Angus was the rightful Laird, it should be him that went back to help with Dunnbray. His retirement was imminent from the Navy, so as soon as he could, he returned home, much to his mother's delight.

Chapter 32

April 2008

Saturday dragged by; the rain lashed against the windows and the front door rattled as it withstood the howling wind. It definitely was a day to stay warm and dry indoors. Phyllis found some sewing to do, and Shelley and Marilyn spent the morning in the library. All the books were removed from the shelves, everything dusted and polished and now they were in the process of putting the books back in alphabetical and subject order. It was a mammoth task, but undertaken with great pleasure.

Lunch came and went, and as it was still raining, they all headed to the sitting room with cups of coffee, where they sat in front of the fire and chatted. They agreed not to talk about the following day; it was beginning to dominate their conversation, so instead they talked about their families, their homes and their dreams for the future, topics that had not already been exhausted, in the many conversations carried on during their days spent together.

Marilyn had planned to get a job, which was now to be put on hold because of the baby. Her future was unclear and she was not optimistic about Ken's reaction, though the others tried their hardest to reassure her. Dunnbray was obviously weaving its magic on her as her initial rudeness, which they had all put down to nerves was wearing off. Because of her slowly expanding waistline, she hoped she could borrow some looser fitting clothes for the next couple of weeks.

'I'm really sorry for what I said about your clothes Susan. I think I was so shocked at the state of this place, I had been expecting somewhere much grander and then you two appeared, well, what could I say? I know first impressions count, but with you I needed to look beyond the clothes and find the kind, caring person that you are, so would you mind lending me a couple of your baggy tops? You are the nearest in size to me.'

Susan, never one to bear a grudge laughed aloud at Marilyn's little speech.

'You are right of course; and pinching a quote from my mother, *we should never judge a book by its cover.* Perhaps we were guilty of that too with India and her with us. Of course I can lend you some clothes. I think I need a makeover when I get home, with the amount of criticism I get over how I dress. I have never laid much store on clothes before. Mum, we will have to go shopping when we get back. I think we both need a new wardrobe.'

'Leave me out of this, I am quite happy the way I am thank you very much. Anyway, *a monkey in silk is a monkey no less.*'

'That's a new saying Mum, haven't heard that one before, what does it mean?'

'*It doesn't matter what you wear, you are still the same person underneath.* Sorry, I have been trying to cut down on the sayings, but that one just slipped out.'

The conversation continued. Neither Susan nor Phyllis said much about their plans for the future, for fear of upsetting one another, but Shelley was quite open about her relationship with Brian. She was honest about her unhappiness and coming away emphasised the fact that she had not missed her husband or her daughters at all.

'Do you know,' she said, 'I have never talked so much in my whole life, there is always at least one of you around to have a conversation with, I love it so much. I cannot face going home to that lot, now that I have stayed here. I don't know what to do when the four weeks are up. I wish we could go out, I might be able to find work up here somewhere.'

'Why don't you ask Hugh?' Phyllis smiled at her, 'I'm sure he would help you find something. I know he was a bit funny the other night, but I am sure he would help if you asked him.'

Susan locked up that night as usual and went to her room. She had just started her journal, when she almost fell out of bed in fright. There was that noise again, coming from above her room. Calm down, she whispered to herself; you have seen the chest in the room above, you know it has to be Edna or whoever else is living next door. She wanted to go and have a look, but the key to the adjoining door was downstairs and someone might hear her creeping about. The dragging sound continued for a short while, then stopped. She wrote for a few minutes, then suddenly there was a tapping sound and it was coming from the window again, 'What now?'

Susan got out of bed and crept towards the window; she stopped, unsure of what to do next, if she opened the curtains what would she see? Did she want to see? What would she do if it weren't Edna after all? What if the tapping sound she could hear, was something else entirely? The tapping stopped. She climbed back into bed and lay with the light on for what felt like hours, before falling into a restless sleep.

Chapter 33

Leaping out of bed the following morning, Susan could not wait to start exploring again; she rushed downstairs only to find all the others had beaten her to it. Excitement was mounting at the prospect of doing something positive that day to try to find out why they were there. Shelley had already volunteered to watch out for the cars next door.

Just before ten, Shelley and Susan went upstairs to the adjoining door. Susan watched as Shelley slipped through the door, and with a quick wave, she was gone, down the corridor and up the stairs to the top floor. Susan shut the door hoping they were doing the right thing instead of waiting as they had been told. Too late, she thought, we have found out too much to give up now.

Half an hour later, the doorbell rang and Hugh was standing there. He was quite chatty as he followed Phyllis into the kitchen. Nothing was said about his quick departure the other night. All bad feeling apparently forgotten, and as they had already decided, none of them made any mention of next door.

'Where's Shelley?' Hugh asked as he realised she was missing.

'Having a lie-in, she didn't sleep very well last night,' was Phyllis's quick reply, before anyone else had the chance to speak.

Well done Mum, Susan mouthed behind Hugh's back as she gave her mum a grateful look.

As soon as he left, Marilyn offered to run up, tell Shelley, and find out what was happening. Ten minutes later, she re-appeared to say that they had both seen Hugh turn up next-door and go inside. Shelley was going to carry on watching to see when Hugh left and if anyone else was going out in the cars. They were just getting a bit concerned about her when she appeared at the top of the stairs.

'It looks like everyone has gone,' she said, 'Hugh's Land Rover left just now, and the other red car has gone. The people carrier is still there, but if Hugh drives that one as well, he can only take one vehicle at a time. I couldn't see who got in the car, it was parked too close to the house, but at least we know they have gone, so are we going to risk it? I'm dying to have another look.'

'Come on then,' said Susan, 'Mum, we'll see you and Marilyn in a bit. Have the kettle on for when we get back.'

'Be careful, both of you please, don't do anything silly,' Phyllis told them.

'Good luck,' called Marilyn.

They headed to the adjoining door and listened to make sure there were no voices, then made their way towards the occupied bedrooms once more. Susan said she would go downstairs to the library to have another look in the filing cabinet while Shelley had a good search of the bedrooms.

Susan quietly entered the library, she was careful not to make a noise, even though they knew the cars were not there.

She went straight to the filing cabinet, intent on a better look at the details in their folders inside; she quietly opened the top drawer and pulled out a folder, took a step back to look at it and bumped into a precariously balanced pile of books on one of the shelves. With an almighty crash, they fell onto the floor at her feet. Rooted to the spot in fear she stood listening, not daring to breathe. Suddenly, a man's voice called out.

'Who's there? Jamie is that you?'

Susan ran with the file clutched in her hand.

Shelley heard the crash and the man's voice and peered anxiously over the banister.

'Quick,' whispered Susan, racing up the stairs. 'Run.'

They burst through the adjoining door, locking it behind them and raced down the stairs and into the kitchen.

'What on...' Marilyn could not get her words out before Susan butted in, 'I knocked some books over, and someone was still in the house, we heard a man's voice calling, he heard me; what are we going to do?'

'Come and sit down all of you, the kettle has boiled, we'll all have a cup of tea and calm down. 'What are they going to do? Whoever they are, they cannot harm us. Four women can't just disappear; one of your families would soon notify the police.'

'Yes, but we have another two weeks before anyone would think of looking for us, who knows what could happen in that time.' Marilyn was almost in tears.

'Look, I managed to pull out the folder on you, let's see what we can find out before we do anything hasty,' Susan said as she placed the folder on the table in front of them.

They gathered round and all stared at the folder. It was identical to the file on the desk spotted by Susan on their first visit next door. The front page was full of personal details on Marilyn, her age, address, all her various places of employment, including her last one at the bank. There were details on her husband and his business. It mentioned there were no children. The restaurants where she met up with the girls were all named. The charity shop she volunteered at one day a week. The places she shopped for clothes and food. It was all there. In fact there was so much information about her, they concluded it could only have been gathered by her being followed.

'What an awful thing to do,' Marilyn said, horrified by the thought, 'why would anyone do that?' She sat down.

'Relax Marilyn, you're not doing your baby any good, getting stressed, there has to be a rational explanation for all this, there just has to be.' Susan turned the page over.

Suddenly realising that Susan had gone very quiet, they all said together, 'What? What have you found?'

Instead of answering them, Susan asked Marilyn, 'What was your mother's name?'

'Margaret, why do you ask?'

'And what about your grandparents, did you know them?'

'Susan, please, just tell me why you are asking me about my family.'

'Bear with me, Marilyn, it's important. Both your parents are dead aren't they? Did you know anything about your mother's family, who her parents were for instance?'

'All I know was that she was illegitimate and her mother, my grandmother was forced to give her up. She was brought up in a children's home. I don't know anything about my grandfather; stop asking me all these questions, what have you found?'

'I'll read what it says,' replied Susan, 'it says that someone called Alan McPhail, a brother of Angus McPhail, Laird of Dunnbray had two illegitimate daughters, by two different women. One of the daughters was called Mary and the other was called Margaret. Margaret married a man by the name of Sidney.'

'That was my Dad's name,' Marilyn gasped.

'And Margaret and Sidney had a daughter called Marilyn! – You are a McPhail, Marilyn; your grandfather is Alan McPhail. Angus

McPhail is your great uncle and you must have an aunt somewhere called Mary. And remember the motto on the gates, that belongs to the McPhail family, it is all beginning to fall into place. Marilyn this must be your ancestral home, isn't that wonderful news?'

They all fell silent, their minds churning over what they had just learnt and wondering what was in the other folders containing their details.

Lunch was forgotten as the four of them went over and over the information in the folder. It must be one of the McPhails living next door, probably Angus, if he was the Laird, but what was he after? Why was it all such a big secret? Why didn't he just introduce himself instead of going through all this rigmarole?

The biggest, most worrying question of all was, who had been following Marilyn and finding out so much about her life? And if all the other folders were the same as hers, that meant they had all been followed.

'Have any of you made any new friends recently, met anyone at work, or has anyone been asking questions about you?' asked Phyllis, 'I hardly go anywhere, so I can't imagine anyone has followed me; Age UK or Women's Institute, I can't see it happening somehow, but the rest of you, someone has spent a lot of time following you.'

'I met someone through work, you remember him Mum,' Susan said, 'a tall good looking man, David his name was, he said he was looking for business premises in the Dorchester area. He even asked me out and we went for a drink a couple of times, but I was so busy at work at that time and obviously, Mum takes up a lot of my spare time, I didn't take it further. He came in one day and said his business plans had changed and that was the last I saw of him. I didn't tell him much about myself though.'

'You are blaming me now aren't you for being on your own?'

Susan looked at Phyllis, 'Mum, I'm not blaming anyone; don't be so touchy, for goodness sake.'

Turning back to the others she said, 'I do have a photo in my bag; we drove down to Weymouth one evening and we got someone to take our photo leaning on the railings on the sea front. I will go and fetch it.. One of you might recognise him.' She was back a few minutes later, and handed the photo to Shelley and said, 'This is David.'

Taken aback, Shelley gazed at the photo. 'Did you say David? His name's not David, that's John, the man I got chatting to in the supermarket. I quite fancied him, I thought he liked me too as he always came to my check-out, but he just stopped coming in one day and I haven't seen him since.' It quite upset her to think that Susan managed to go out with him; why hadn't he asked her out. Forgetting of course that she was married and if he were collecting information on her, he would have known that.

'What on earth is going on?' Susan said. 'Do you know this man Marilyn?' The photo was passed around, Phyllis, of course, recognised him from when he came to pick Susan up the one night.

'That's Keith, a possible new client of my husband's,' said Marilyn in disbelief. 'I met him once at Ken's office.'

'So, we have all met this man, and he seems to have a different identity each time. He's the one who has been getting all the information. He has to be a private detective.'

The hours passed without them noticing, they were all too wrapped up in the latest discovery and it was beginning to get dark.

'It's dinner time,' said Shelley, 'anyone hungry? Shall I rustle up something quick? Then I suggest we come up with a plan for tomorrow, it's too late to do anything now.'

'I think that's the best thing to do,' Susan replied, 'we'll have something to eat, make a pot of coffee and go into the sitting room, then decide what to do. Hugh won't be coming tomorrow unless they have guessed it was us next door today, in which case he will be on the doorstep first thing, I have been half expecting him this afternoon to be honest.'

Chapter 34

The two women tiptoed quietly along the corridor, looked out of the landing window to check there were no cars around and crept down the stairs. Marilyn insisted on coming with Susan this time, as it had been her file read out, and she felt that if Angus McPhail or even her grandfather were there, she should be one of the first to see him. The others argued with her last night, as they were deciding what to do, they were concerned she did not get any more shocks, but she was adamant. So it was that she found herself outside the library with Susan.

There was the sound of a radio coming from somewhere close. Somebody must still be in the house again, was it the same person as before?

'Let's go this way,' Susan whispered, 'that's where the sitting room is and where I think the voice came from yesterday.'

The door to the sitting room was ajar and the radio was a bit louder now. The gap between the door and the architrave was just wide enough to see through. What they saw made them gasp in amazement. Marilyn stepped back suddenly and stood on Susan's toe and in the ensuing kerfuffle they realised they were making far too much noise.

'Who's out there?' said a gruff voice. 'Is that you again Jamie? Stop lurking boy, come in here, and show yourself.'

Shaking with trepidation, Susan and Marilyn pushed the door open and entered a sitting room, which felt cosy and warm, with a roaring log fire. Sitting in the corner, with a blanket over his knees they saw an elderly man, with a full head of white hair hanging over his collar, and glasses perched on the end of his nose, which he peered over and stared hard at them.

'Who are you and what are you doing here?' He demanded.

'Um, well, we are staying next door and we heard voices and I am sure I saw someone at one of the upstairs windows, so we wanted to find out what was going on,' Susan stuttered out an explanation, while Marilyn just stared.

'You're curious, eh? We wondered how long it would take you to realise someone was on this side of the house. I am impressed; it has only taken just over two weeks. The others thought it would take you a lot longer, and to be honest I wish it had taken longer, you have caught us on the hop.'

'Others, how many others?' asked Marilyn.

'You will find out soon enough.' The old man replied. 'Susan, I recognise you, it was me you spotted at the window, but who is this?'

'This is Marilyn and there are two more of us, Phyllis – my mother, and Shelley.'

'Ah yes, Marilyn, you are the pregnant one, are you keeping well my dear?'

'I suppose Hugh has been telling you all about us.' Marilyn's tone was sharp, as she knew now that their lives were being discussed by Hugh and this old man. 'And exactly who might you be?'

'Me? I am Angus McPhail, the Laird of Dunnbray. This is my family home. Unfortunately, I am, or was the only one left. I have a housekeeper, Edna, who you know, who lives in and looks after me and the house, and of course Hugh who is the estate manager.'

'We've seen the file on me,' Marilyn blurted out. They had agreed not to say anything yet, but she could not help it. 'You are my great uncle, I want to know more about my grandfather; I want you to tell me what is going on. You have been spying on me and the rest of the girls; you can't go around doing things like that, it's not right.' And with that she burst into tears.

'I am really sorry my dear, we didn't mean to cause you any distress; we did plan to tell you, but didn't expect you to find out in this way, and so quickly; this is not how we wanted to tell you. Now ladies, if you don't mind, I am rather tired and would like to take a nap, having been so rudely interrupted.' Angus replied, trying desperately to buy himself some more time before he was forced to explain, and in doing so, came across as uncaring of their situation.

Marilyn was not happy. 'But we need to know the truth, why are we here?' She spluttered through her tears. 'Why can't you tell us now?'

'Hugh will come and see you first thing in the morning and tell you what my plans are, as they have obviously changed and I need to give them some thought. So I suggest for now you go back to your side of the house and I will see you tomorrow.' With that, he turned away from them and drew nearer the fire, holding his gnarled hands out to the flames.

They felt dismissed, like naughty children and in silence they slowly went back along the passage, up the stairs, through the door and went to pass on the amazing news to the others.

When they left, Angus felt so guilty, he knew how concerned they all were, and he really had not wanted to upset Marilyn, but he was not expecting any of them to just turn up in that way, and had not handled the situation very well.

His original plan was for Hugh to keep a watchful eye on them, find out whether they were able to discover anything about this side of the house, and what their plans for the house would be if they owned it, but more importantly, how well they all got on together. The first week was extremely difficult, according to Hugh, but they soon settled down into a team working together, which thrilled Angus no end. His plans were coming together nicely.

Susan and Marilyn were immediately bombarded with questions, as soon as they reached the kitchen door. 'I need a sit down,' Marilyn looked quite pale and they could see she had been crying.

'What happened? What did you see? We were getting worried about you,' Phyllis asked as she put very welcome cups of tea in front of them.

'We met Angus McPhail.' Marilyn and Susan spoke in unison.

They told them of the old man who they discovered in the sitting room, and what he had divulged so far, but that there was much more to come, hopefully tomorrow.

Susan could tell that Shelley was dying to interrupt, a look of excitement on her face.

'What is it Shelley?'

Shelley blurted out that while they waited, she had gone through the pile of papers left in one of the desk drawers in the library, and at the bottom of the pile discovered a newspaper article, which she snatched up off the table.

'Just listen to this.'

What does the future hold for Dunnbray Castle?

Dougal MacPhail, the great, great, great grandfather of Angus MacPhail, the present Laird bought the land and built Dunnbray Castle on the proceeds of a very successful but distasteful slavery business, so his past has been mainly erased from the family history. The property has been in the MacPhail family ever since.

Dunnbray Castle is a fine example of Georgian Manor Houses built in the nineteenth century. It was designed by major architect, Archibald Simpson, who was well known for his many architectural designs in the city of Aberdeen. He was a contact of a friend of Dougal's and of course only the best was good enough. Dougal would have liked a genuine castle, but decided the upkeep of such a property was prohibitive so instead called his mansion a castle. 'An English man's home is his castle' so the saying goes, so why not a Scottish man's also. Dougal McPhail was heard quoting this saying on numerous occasions. Dunnbray Castle stands in over 800 acres of woodland and grazing pastures, which have been farmed with great success over the years. There is a lake fed by the river Bray, in which trout can still be found.

The property went into a decline in the nineteen twenties, when Angus's grandfather died and his only son, Angus's father Archie, became Laird. Archie was a heavy drinker and drank away all the money his father amassed. He let the farm go to rack and ruin, tried running a business arranging shooting parties, but this eventually failed. Angus's mother Isobel struggled to make ends meet. Secretly, and with the help of her three sons she built up a fruit and vegetable business, supplying the local area by selling produce at the weekly market. At the same time, Isobel began a very successful dressmaking business. All these activities kept secret from Archie. She was an extremely clever woman and managed to put money away.

The story goes that one day Archie found out what his wife and children were up to behind his back and riding home from the Inn in a great rage, fell from his horse and broke his neck. Isobel, with the help of her sons, gradually re-stocked the farm with sheep, hired a farm manager and went back into crop growing. She didn't expect her sons to remain working at Dunnbray, so allowed them all to follow their chosen careers. Isobel continued to run the estate with just her manager until Angus, the rightful Laird, returned in the nineteen *sixties and took over the reins. His mother died at the grand old age of ninety-three.*

Angus himself is now eighty-two and has an estate manager to take care of the land with the help of some casual labour. In the house, Angus has a live in housekeeper to take care of him as he has difficulty in walking. He still has a good business mind and wants Dunnbray to continue after he has gone. The house has been divided into two separate properties for the last ten years, with tenants running a bed and breakfast business. They have now retired and a question mark hangs over the future of the property as Angus has never married and has no known heirs.

'How old is the article? Is it dated? It must be fairly recent after what Hugh said about his parents,' Susan said.

'No, there's no date, but it can't be that old and Angus is the one that you have just met and Edna is his housekeeper, so she *is* living next door. Shelley still couldn't contain her excitement.

'I can't wait to meet up with him tomorrow. I am sure we will get the whole story then,' Phyllis said. 'Isn't it exciting?'

What a strange day this was turning into, no one could settle to do anything. They drifted in and out of the kitchen, making cups of tea. Phyllis could not believe how much tea they seemed to get through. They needed more to do. Marilyn did some baking; there was a lot of talking, but all they seemed to do was go round and round in circles. Neither Hugh nor Edna made an appearance or even contacted them on the walkie-talkie.

'I can just imagine the conversation that is going on next door,' Shelley said later, 'it's a wonder our ears aren't burning, I bet theirs are too.'

Bedtime finally arrived and they all went up one by one, what was to come the next morning on all their minds. Susan was the last to go up as usual; she went round and checked the doors to make sure they were all locked and secure; even the downstairs locked adjoining door. Upstairs, she opened and shut her bedroom door, so everyone would think she was in her room; but instead of entering, continued along the corridor, took the key from her pocket, which she had picked up earlier, unlocked the adjoining door and slipped through, locking it behind her. More determined than ever to discover the truth, she ran quietly along the next landing and up the stairs to the top floor, deciding to hide in the first empty room and leave the door slightly ajar, so she could see through the gap, and lie in wait.

She was just beginning to think it had been a stupid idea, when voices could be heard down below calling goodnight to each other and footsteps coming up the stairs. She recognised Angus's and Edna's, but the other male voice she could not make out. It wasn't Hugh's; she didn't think he lived here any way. Doors closed, and then she heard the sound of someone creeping up the stairs towards her. Holding her breath, she strained her eyes to see in the darkness. Torchlight came into view and as the person passed the door, she could just make out Edna's shape. It *was* her making the noises above her room. Should she go out and confront her? What should she do? Susan was in a quandary.

She waited a few seconds, and then carefully poking her head round the door, saw the torchlight disappearing into a room farther along. It was the one above her room. Her decision now made, she crept out and ran down the stairs, opened the bedroom door she now knew was Edna's, and snatched the make-up bag from her dressing table, and left the room, quietly closing the door behind her and rushed back unlocking the door, then re-locking it again once she was safe on the other side.

She opened her bedroom door with care so as not to disturb either Edna above or any one else, and as she entered she could hear the usual sounds from above. Smiling, she thought what a stupid woman Edna was, didn't she realise that her strange behaviour would become known when they talked to Angus, and obviously Angus himself had not mentioned meeting Marilyn and her, otherwise she would not have bothered to go up there tonight.

Tossing Edna's make up bag onto the dressing table, she had a slight moment of panic, what had she done that for? What was she going to do with it now? Nothing, she decided, it was time to write her journal, she would make a decision in the morning. It gave her a sense of satisfaction to turn the tables on Edna for once.

Chapter 35

Linda Mason looked across at the office junior in despair. How many times had she told her how to answer the telephone properly? What was the matter with the girl? Chantelle, what sort of name was that? Didn't girls have ordinary names any more? She felt sure all those reality shows were to blame.

Chantelle had joined them just over a month ago. Her father was a drinking pal of Jim, the boss of the timber merchants where Linda was the office manager. To help out his friend's unemployed daughter and because he thought Linda was looking a bit tired lately, he decided to take Chantelle on to be trained up in office management. Linda was so used to having the office to herself that she resented the girl's arrival, and her total lack of interest in the job made it worse. Linda was at her wit's end. The offer of a free holiday was becoming more and more tempting.

The letter and train ticket had been tucked away in her handbag for a week. First she had written to the solicitor and said she wasn't interested, and then she changed her mind and said she would go, so the ticket was sent. She was still dithering, not knowing whether to accept the holiday or not, but looking at Chantelle again made up her mind. She would do it, and before she changed her mind yet again, she popped out of the office so she could telephone the solicitor's office in private.

A few minutes later, she was back in the office. She had done it, now all she had to do was speak to Jim, and tell him about the holiday and could he manage without her for three weeks.

Her boss was a kind man and very fond of Linda; he could see the excitement in her face as she explained about the holiday and said he was sure they could cope, as the trainee seemed to be settling in well. Linda doubted that, but refrained from commenting.

Phoning her son, Tim, at University was the next step.

'Go for it Mum, you deserve it,' was his reply, 'it sounds brilliant, *a holiday of a lifetime*, a *life changing experience*, don't you go doing anything I wouldn't do and see you when you get back.'

Putting the phone down, a sigh of relief escaped through Tim's lips as he realised that his mother suddenly had something else to think about, instead of continuously dwelling on him. He had no idea how this invitation to her had come about, but he did not care, whoever it was, he was eternally grateful to them; he looked forward to his few weeks of peace and quiet.

Linda was a tall, well-built woman in her late forties, with long legs and enormous bust, which she displayed proudly in low cut tops. Outwardly, she appeared a confident and somewhat brash woman, not afraid to speak her mind, some would say blunt to the point of being rude, but underneath, like so many women of this type she suffered the same insecurities. She worried herself into a right state over whether she had packed the right clothes. The spare bedroom of her three bed semi-detached near Exeter city centre was strewn with piles of discarded skirts and trousers, jumpers and blouses. She knew it would be cold in Scotland so finally picked the warmest outfits she had. If there weren't any decent shops in Strathdown, and she'd packed the wrong clothes, then she would be stuck for weeks. Oh God, what had she done?

    After a frantic three days, getting everything sorted and leaving Chantelle with a list of instructions, Linda caught the overnight train from Exeter to Strathdown. Jim offered to take her to the station, and saw her safely on to the train. There was no need Linda told him, but he insisted. She enjoyed the bear hug he gave her and he waited on the platform until the train pulled out, waving until she couldn't see him any more; she was more grateful for his company than she would admit; the nerves were beginning to kick in.

    She tried to lighten her mood by looking forward to the journey; this would be the furthest she had ever travelled on a train. Then she got herself all wound up again, with a load of questions: Would she like her holiday companions? Would they like her? Was it all a huge mistake? But, worst of all; would bloody Chantelle have pushed her out of a job when she got back?

Chapter 36

From the time of Tim's birth, Linda Mason swore that the best and only the best would be good enough for her son. All she wanted was a child, preferably a boy that she could devote all her time to.

There were never any plans to find a man; get married and settle down, but there were plans to find a man, get pregnant, and then take him for every penny, to give her and her child a life of ease. Unfortunately, that plan did not turn out quite how she expected. At the age of twenty-eight, she found her ideal target. A wealthy property developer appeared on the scene, with a team of builders who bought various items from the builders' merchants where she worked.

The name of her target was Milek Kowalski, a migrant from his homeland of Poland, who arrived in England in the 1960's when his building apprenticeship finished. He was a hard man and a hard worker and gradually built up a business and a reputation as an excellent builder, with pride both in his own and his employees' work. However, unbeknown to Linda, Milek was a womaniser, with his mind always on his next victim. When he clapped eyes on the tall, buxom brunette at the builders' merchants, who gave him the eye, he knew he had made yet another conquest and wasted no time in asking her out.

Linda was thrilled to be dating this very good-looking man. Taller than her, thank goodness, she towered over many men in her high heels. His dark crew-cut hair, deep-set brown eyes and a cute dimple in his chin, always drew admiring looks. He always wore black polo necks, or crisp white shirts with the sleeves rolled up, the top four buttons always undone to expose a chest covered in a thick mat of dark curly hair. The look completed with tight denim jeans and a heavy gold chain around his neck.

They enjoyed dining out at expensive restaurants and Milek being a gentleman, always insisted on paying. He was recognised everywhere and offered the best seats. They went to bars and clubs. Linda, who was thrilled to be seen on his arm, made every effort to impress him. With his undoubted wealth, he was just the right man to be the father of her planned baby. She stopped taking the pill, made herself irresistible to him and within a very short time became pregnant.

This was Linda's undoing. Milek did not intend to be tied to some woman, because of a child; and especially an English woman. He knew that when the time was right for him to settle down he would return to Poland and find a wife from his own country to marry. He made this very clear to Linda, the night she told him she was three months pregnant. He was not her meal ticket for the future and if she pursued him for child support, he would just return to Poland where English jurisdiction would count for nothing.

The relationship ended there and then. Shocked to the core by his behaviour, she was blind to the fact that her own actions were just as cold and calculating, and vowed then never to get involved with another man. She would bestow all the love she had on the little baby, be it a boy or a girl.

Six months later, Linda gave birth to a healthy seven-pound baby boy. She named him Timothy, Tim for short and from that day on her life revolved around little Tim.

Returning to work after maternity leave, she left him firstly with child minders, then a nursery as soon as he was old enough. It broke her heart to leave him every day, but he was a good child and never seemed to mind being left. Weekends were crammed full with trips to the park to feed the ducks and join other children in the play area; she would read to him, play with him and talk to him non-stop.

Tim flourished under this bombardment of mother love until he started school and gained friends outside of the home. He was a very intelligent little boy and soon recognised the difference between his mother and the other boys' mothers. When he did manage to escape out of her clutches for any length of time, Linda would smother him in hugs and kisses on his return; question him on what he had been doing, who he played with, and what someone's mother was like. As he grew older he fought against this over-powering, stifling love; he tried to tell her that it was embarrassing, but he was ignored and she would tell him how wonderful he was, how bright, how clever, and what a future he was going to have.

Receiving excellent grades in his 'A' Levels, Tim gained a place at Leeds University, studying Maths, Physics and English, which he needed in order to pursue his planned career in engineering.

Relieved to be out of the relentless clutches of his mother, he found the furthest University away from home that he could.

Linda went up to Leeds with him to inspect the hall of residence where he would be staying until he made friends and hopefully find someone to share digs. She left him loaded up with food and drinks, and reluctantly drove back home. He heaved a huge sigh of relief as he watched his mother pull out of the car park, and waved until she disappeared round the corner. He was free at last.

Heartbroken at her only son leaving home, Linda made him promise to come home every chance he got. She phoned him at least twice a week to see how he was doing and would leave messages on the answer phone if he did not pick up the calls. Tim, in turn would not answer the phone, but instead listen to her sad words, and wish that she could find a man in her life to take the pressure off him.

Chapter 37

No-one knew what would happen today; Hugh was supposed to come and fetch them at some point. They all tried to occupy themselves with different chores just to keep their minds off things. Susan popped upstairs to collect some dirty laundry and as she walked out of her bathroom, she was confronted by Edna, with the make-up bag in her hand.

Startled, Susan said, 'What on earth are you doing?'

'I might ask you the same thing. You had to interfere didn't you, had to keep poking your nose in. I tried to scare you off but you would not leave. You were a bit stupid taking this weren't you? Did you think I wouldn't come looking for it?' She shook the make-up bag in Susan's face. 'This place belongs to my son and me, we should be the ones living here, he has much more right to be here than you.' Edna was shaking with rage, eyes staring; face flushed a horrible purple colour.

Susan backed away from the onslaught. 'What do you mean? I don't understand. We don't even know why we are here except for the fact that Marilyn is Angus's grand niece; why do you think you have rights, are you related as well?' Susan knew she had to try to keep Edna talking, to buy herself more time, but Edna continued.

'Angus's father had another child before Angus and his brothers were born. Before he married Isobel, but it was all hushed up and Angus's grandfather paid the girl's family to take her away. Unbeknown to Angus's family, when the child grew up, she came back to the village and began working at Dunnbray as a maid. She married a local blacksmith and they had a daughter – me! And I in turn came to work here. She told me the history of our family; how poorly we had been treated and the inheritance that should have been mine. I have cared for Angus all these years, biding my time. Jack, my husband wouldn't ever let me say anything, but now he's gone, I want what is ours, mine and Jamie's.'

'But what's to stop you talking to Angus, I'm sure he would understand, and make sure you received your inheritance if he knew who you were. Why don't you just talk to him, and end all this craziness. We are going to see him today; come with us if that will help. Come on Edna, please calm down.'

Edna was past calming down and listening to reason and carried on. 'Because of those bloody solicitors chasing him to make his will, he had to go digging for relatives didn't he? He could not leave well alone. When I knew that he wanted to meet you all, it was my idea to get you here, and make sure you did not have any contact with anyone. I didn't want you finding out anything about Dunnbray; then I planned on scaring you off so that Angus lost interest in such a useless bunch of women. He wanted so much for you to be like his blessed mother, God, I am sick to death of hearing about Isobel. But it hasn't worked has it, so now you are going to pay for it, you have to disappear.'

'You are out of your mind, Edna, how are you going to make us disappear?'

'You already know too much; your accidents, the dead rats, the disappearing glasses and stuff, and I think you have guessed that I have read your journal. I have been practicing your handwriting, Susan, I will leave a note saying that you have all had enough, made your escape and gone back home and none of you want any more to do with Dunnbray. That should put Angus off you all. Then I can tell him about Jamie.'

Susan could see the crazed look in Edna's eyes and realised how dangerous the situation was becoming; she had to be very careful or Edna would not hesitate to harm her.

With more courage than she felt, and keeping her voice as calm as she was able, Susan asked, 'How do you plan on getting rid of us?' She desperately tried to keep the conversation going while she looked for a means of escape, and considered throwing the armful of dirty washing at her, but Edna realised what Susan was thinking.

'I've got a knife here,' she said pulling a large kitchen knife out of her coat pocket, 'and I am not afraid to use it, get downstairs to the others, quick. Jamie is coming in a bit with a big vehicle and we'll take you away and hide you somewhere until we decide what to do with you. Now move.'

Edna pushed and shoved Susan down the stairs and into the kitchen.

Shelley was just about to ask Susan where she'd been, she was waiting to put the washing machine on when she saw Edna standing behind her.

'What's she do…'

'Shut up all of you and sit down.'

'Do as she says,' Susan whispered; eyes wide with fear for their safety.

'Edna, what are you doing with that kni.?'

Marilyn cowered and stopped speaking under Edna's stare as she said, 'Will you all shut up, while I wait for Jamie.'

They sat round the kitchen table, Marilyn with both hands clasped round her stomach, her face white as a sheet. Edna repeated what she had told Susan.

'Edna, please, can't we just talk about this, you are obviously upset, can't you just tell us what you want, and I'm sure…'

'Shut up, just shut up all of you,' she screamed at them, eyes bulging, veins sticking out on her forehead, 'I can't think with you all talking.'

Phyllis squeezed Susan's hand under the table, Susan squeezed back, but her mother gave her hand a little tug and when Susan looked at her, Phyllis's eyes went to the vase of flowers in the centre of the table. She gave an imperceptible nod and Susan winked; she got what her mother meant. A weapon, if she got the opportunity.

A second later, everything seemed to happen in slow motion, Phyllis went to stand up, trying to create a distraction for Susan, Edna stepped forward and just as Susan's hand snaked out to grab the vase, the doorbell rang and the front door opened. Edna swung round to see who was there and in that instant Susan hit her with the vase on the back of the head and Edna crashed to the floor.

'Quick, sit on her, hold her still, while I get the knife,' shouted Susan desperately.

'What the hell is going on here, what are you doing to Edna?'

Hugh's shocked expression took in the sight before him as he stood in the kitchen doorway, and a woman they did not recognise, was peeking over his shoulder in alarm.

'There's no other weapon,' Susan said, and climbing off Edna's back, she showed Hugh the knife.

Edna struggled to her feet holding her head.

'A knife, for God's sake Edna what's going on?' Hugh helped her up and she sank into a chair. Her eyes had a faraway look in them, she did not answer.

'You had better call a doctor to her,' Susan pointed at Edna's slumped figure. 'She's either concussed or lost it completely. You had better call the police as well.'

She quickly filled Hugh in with the details that Edna had told her in the bedroom. 'She seems to think that Jamie has more rights here than us, what could she mean? What is Angus going to talk to us about?'

'He will explain it all, but he needs to know about Edna first,' said Hugh as he pulled out his mobile phone. He walked out into the hall as he spoke first to the police, then the local surgery.

While Hugh was making his calls, Linda came further into the kitchen and looked around.

'My letter said *the outcome could be quite unexpected*, it wasn't wrong was it? Is it always like this here? Hi, I am Linda Mason by the way, I've come to stay too, but at the moment I'm not sure whether I want to or not.'

She held out her hand.

'You must be the Linda Mason that we saw a file on the other day.'

'File, what file? What are you talking about? Have I arrived at the funny farm or something?'

'It will all be explained later; hopefully we are all going to find out, and before the four weeks is up too, thank God, I've had enough shocks to last me a lifetime.' Phyllis placed her hand over her wildly thumping heart.

'Sit down Mum, it's all over, we will see Angus in a bit, then we'll find out the truth.'

Hugh re-entered the kitchen saying the doctor was on his way and the police were coming out to Dunnbray as fast as they could, and had arranged for Jamie to be picked up. He then spoke to Edna, encouraging her to stand up and go with him.

'I'll take her through to Angus's side; I don't think she is capable of any more threats. The police will want to come and take statements, so I suggest you all stay here for the time being. I've spoken to Angus; as you can imagine he is deeply shocked and sends his apologies; he will speak to you all later.'

'Oh well, I suppose another hour or two won't hurt. I think a stiff drink is called for, my nerves are shot, we can fill you in on the story so far, Linda, and then I'll show you your room.' Susan said.

As Susan and Linda walked upstairs a little later, the other three huddled round the table.

'What do you make of her then?' Phyllis had made one of her quick judgements again. 'She talks a lot about herself doesn't she, not a bit interested in what we have had to put up with.'

'I noticed, it's all Tim, Tim, Tim or her job, the jury is out on her I think,' Shelley replied. 'Hey Phyllis, how about one of your sayings, we will let you just this once, you must have one?'

'*Every ass likes to hear himself bray*, that is a good one don't you think?'

'Phyllis you are so funny.' Shelley and Marilyn could not stop laughing and somehow it eased the tension. Susan of course, was totally unaware of what had been said as she strolled back in saying she thought Linda was a nice woman, and couldn't understand the laughter breaking out again.

Two police officers showed up an hour later, and took their statements. Linda did not have much to tell them, but the rest explained about the so-called accidents and the noises above Susan's room, and Edna's plan to get rid of them all. The police officers were amazed at what they were told; things like this did not happen around Strathdown, it was a quiet, peaceful place. Edna's family were well known in the area having lived here on and off for generations and neither police officer had ever heard any rumours of Edna's link with the McPhails; obviously a very well kept secret. The girls were informed that Jamie had been picked up for questioning and he and Edna were now at the police station.

The statements completed, Hugh came to take them to meet Angus.

'He's very shocked about all this and obviously very tired too, so he mustn't over-do it today. How are you feeling Phyllis, are you sure you are up to this?' He tucked his hand under her elbow and they all started walking towards the front door, but Hugh pointed to the adjoining door and said, 'You can come through this way now you know Angus lives on the other side,' and with that he took a key from his pocket and unlocked the adjoining door.

'Welcome to the dilapidated side ladies, though I wish it could have been in better circumstances. I'm sorry for all the lies I have told you, but you will soon find out why I had to.'

He led them along the corridor and into the sitting room, where Susan and Marilyn had already met Angus, and introductions made all round.

'Linda,' Angus said, 'on reflection, you probably made the right decision, coming up here last minute, I should have suggested this for all of you, got you up here and explained straight away, instead of acting like a silly old fool.'

'How are you feeling now Uncle, it must have been such a shock for you, finding out about Edna?' Marilyn said.

'That's a strange word, Uncle, I've never been called that before, I'm still a bit shaky, thank you for asking. That woman has been with me for years, I can't believe she would do such a thing, I suppose in her warped mind, she was trying to get security for her only son, but she was totally deranged and she went about it in completely the wrong way I'm afraid, and is now going to pay the price for that. She should have been honest with me from the start. It doesn't bear thinking about what she could have done to you all. I am so sorry.'

Angus asked them all to sit down, and explained that he was never aware of Edna's connection to the McPhails until a short time ago, when he managed to get some sense out of her while awaiting the arrival of the police.

'But that's enough about her for the time being.'

'Yes, but why the secrecy in the first place, who is the man who has been following the girls around, why all this cloak and dagger stuff, I can't be doing with it.'

Susan could see her mother was quite stressed about the whole thing. 'Mum, please just listen to Angus, I'm sure we will get the whole story soon enough, though why we had to be kept here under lock and key, is something I would like the answer to.'

'You can ask questions when I have finished,' Angus replied. And he did his best to explain. It was a long story.

Chapter 38

Angus never married. He enlisted in the navy at eighteen and enjoyed a wonderful career, which took him all over the world, and when he finally came home, being the eldest and heir to Dunnbray, he felt it his duty to remain with his mother. When Isobel passed away, he continued to live in the family home alone. He had several affairs throughout his naval career, but nothing became of any of them. His career was always more important. This left Dunnbray with no direct heirs of which he was aware at the time.

His solicitors were getting concerned about the absence of a will and considering his age, were afraid he might die without leaving instructions on what was to happen to the estate. So it was their suggestion that he start looking to see if there were any relatives from his brothers' side still alive. He recalled that his younger brother Andrew had been married years ago and had two daughters that he had lost touch with, but they were the only ones he knew about.

That was when Douglas, the man they all knew, but under different names, came on the scene; he was recommended by the firm of solicitors and been despatched to see what, if anything, he could unearth. Angus said he was amazed at what Douglas eventually uncovered. It was eighteen months of hard work, but what a story.

'Marilyn, as you already know that you and I are related, we will start with you, if the rest of you don't mind.'

He continued.

Douglas discovered that Alan, the middle one of the sons,, who was in the Army, had two illegitimate daughters, by two different women, which Alan himself was aware of but never told the rest of the family, and never supported either of them. He was too ashamed and embarrassed to admit to anyone that he had children, so their existence was brushed under the carpet. Both of these women were now dead unfortunately, but each left a daughter. Angus looked at Marilyn.

'Did your mother, Margaret, ever tell you anything about her past?

'The only thing she told me was that my father wouldn't have anything to do with us when I was born. I have never met him and don't ever want to. He wanted her to have an abortion but she refused.

So she brought me up alone. Are we really related? I cannot believe it. Are you telling me that my grandfather was Alan MacPhail? You said his other daughter had a child too, have you found her, have I got a cousin?'

'You have indeed; unfortunately she decided not to stay; India, my dear is your cousin.'

Marilyn stared at him in disbelief.

'India's mother, Mary, died when she was a baby,' said Angus. 'so she never knew very much about her.'

'I am sure we haven't heard the rest of the story yet.' Shelley said looking at Angus; she could not wait for him to continue, to find out where the rest of them fitted in.

Angus took his time sipping his coffee, while they waited with baited breath until he continued. His younger brother, Andrew, already mentioned, was married with two daughters, who he had lost contact with, due to his ex-wife turning his daughters against him and not allowing him access once the divorce was finalised. She moved away with the two girls, and Andrew passed away quite recently never having seen his daughters again.

Douglas managed to find out that Andrew's daughters were taken into care about a year after he lost touch with them. The mother turned to drink and drugs and the girls were taken away from her. Some years later she took an overdose and died without ever telling the authorities about the girls' father, so no-one ever tried to find him. They were fostered and subsequently adopted, but by two different families. Both grew up not knowing each had a sister and not knowing their father was still alive for so many years.

He paused for breath and they all waited expectantly for the next startling piece of news. He then turned to Linda and Shelley and said, 'I am so sorry that you have found out about your father in this way and that you never got to see him again, but, you two are my brother's daughters. He would have been so proud of you. You are sisters and I am your Uncle.'

There was utter silence, while Linda and Shelley stared at each other. They did not look at all alike; no-one would ever have known they were related.

'Sister? You're telling me I have a little sister?' Linda said with tears in her eyes. 'I always felt like a part of me was missing, but

I didn't know why; my adoptive parents must have known, but they never mentioned it. They told me both my parents were dead so there was no point in looking for them.'

Shelley just stood, speechless for a moment, trying to absorb the news, and then she said, 'Mine said the same thing, that my parents were dead. It never occurred to me that I had a sister. All those years lost.'

With arms opened, Linda moved towards Shelley. 'I am so glad I have met you, there is so much to catch up on, I don't know where to start. I can't believe I didn't want to come, and look what I have found out in the space of a few hours.'

'That makes you, Linda and Shelley my aunts, is that right?' asked Marilyn, 'Hi Auntie Linda, Auntie Shelley.' She rushed over and hugged them both. My family is getting bigger by the minute, wait until India finds out. When are we going to tell her? Do you have her number? Can we ring her?'

'Not just yet. I haven't quite decided the best way of dealing with the situation,' said Angus, smiling at their enthusiasm. This was going so much better than he expected.

Susan and Phyllis by this time were utterly confused. Neither could work out what their connection to all this news was. All their holiday companions related to Angus; what on earth did it all mean? They just looked at each other.

'Shall we continue?' Angus said. 'There will be time for questions later, but I must continue with the story, there is so much more to come and I am getting tired. Now ladies, what I am about to tell you has been the biggest surprise, no biggest shock of all.'

He carried on. 'The most amazing discovery of all that Douglas made whilst going back through birth certificates and archives was that I had a son. A son I knew nothing about. One of my brief affairs led to a pregnancy, but the woman decided not to tell me, even though my name was on the birth certificate. She ended the affair shortly after she knew she was pregnant, with no intention of telling me and becoming a naval wife, and her family supported her in this decision. They didn't want their only daughter following her husband all over the world. I can never understand how families can be so cruel. To deny me my only son was heartless and I was totally shocked by this discovery; and to make matters worse, I discovered that my son had passed away about ten years ago, but my daughter-in-law is still alive and their only daughter, my granddaughter.'

Angus said he had taken several months to come to terms with all this information and he was at a loss as to what was the best way to meet them all. After some deliberation, and the input from Edna and Hugh, they came up with a plan. A very silly, even dangerous one, he now admitted.

They waited again, while Angus drained his coffee cup, before placing it carefully on the table beside him; then he leant forward.

'Phyllis?' Angus asked, reaching out his hand to her, 'Phyllis, did your husband ever tell you anything about his background?'

'Only what his mother told him, that his father never wanted a baby, and definitely didn't want to marry his mother; he was in the navy and wanted her to have an abortion, which was illegal at the time and very dangerous if she had gone to a back street abortionist. She refused; he would have nothing more to do with her so she brought him up alone. Why? What are you saying? She paused for breath. Are you telling me that you are Bill's father? That you didn't know anything about him, that his mother lied to him?'

'Phyllis, you will never know how sorry I am, that I didn't get to know Bill while he was alive and that I have a granddaughter I never knew I had, but at least I can try and make up for lost time now if she'll have me.' He turned to Susan with outstretched arms. 'Susan, will you make an old man very happy and accept me as your grandfather after all these years?' His eyes glistened with unshed tears.

Wordlessly, Susan went up and gave the old man a hug, but Phyllis hung back, too shocked to move. Then she said, 'Let me get this straight, if I can, you are telling me Susan has a grandfather, two aunties and two cousins. Linda and Shelley are my cousins and Marilyn and India are my nieces by marriage; my family has grown from two to seven in just over an hour. After all that's happened, I can't take all this in, I need to have a lie down, please excuse me.' She brushed Susan's hand away and walked out of the room. Susan went to follow her, but Angus stopped her.

'Leave her, it has been such a shock to all of you, I can understand how she feels, and she will come round, just give her time.'

A stunned silence descended. The coffee stood untouched and Susan felt all eyes on her, she still had not spoken, she was speechless; at the age of thirty-eight, she had discovered a grandfather, it was all too much.

'I'll just finish for now by telling you Edna's involvement in all this shall I? Then you can all have a break, I definitely want a rest. If you don't mind, could we continue this tomorrow morning, say about eleven o'clock, when we have all had chance to let the news sink in.' He then went on.

Edna had apparently been so angry when she found out Angus's plans and all these women were discovered. It was her idea that they all came to stay; then she could prove to Angus what an unsuitable group of women they were and not fit to benefit from his will. She set about causing little accidents to happen to Susan, knowing she would be the main beneficiary, hoping that they would leave as quickly as they could and never come back. She wanted Angus to feel so disappointed in them that he would never contact them again and then it would leave the way clear for Jamie to become Laird of Dunnbray. What she had planned on doing with them all when they would not leave did not bear thinking about. Dragging poor unsuspecting Jamie into her dreadful plans was the worst thing of all. Obviously, in her disturbed mind, her plan would work perfectly. She never considered the consequences of her actions.

'I don't know how involved Jamie is; I expect the police will find out shortly. Edna's mental state is obviously under question, so I am not sure what will happen to her, locked up somewhere secure I should think.'

They all nodded at this latest piece of news, then seeing how tired Angus looked, they said they would leave him to rest.

'I'll come for you in the morning if you like,' called Hugh as the women walked slowly down the corridor.

When they got back to their kitchen, they went about making cups of tea, going through the motions, acting like robots, each lost in thought at the news they had received and not knowing what to say to each other. At last sitting down, Susan realised her mother wasn't with them.

'I'll just pop up to see how Mum is,' she said.

As she walked up the stairs she could hear muffled sobs from her mother's room, she opened the door quietly, went up to the bed where her mother was sitting with her head in her hands, and put her arms round her.

'I hate him, all these years he has been living here and poor Bill didn't know, the bastard, I hate him.'

'Don't say that Mum, he really didn't know, he told you that. Imagine finding out you have a son, only to be told he was dead; just be grateful that he has found us, before it is too late; what if you had found out after he had died, that Dad's father was living up here all this time. You should be angry with Grandma, for not telling him about his father. I will never understand how some women can be so selfish when it comes to their children. Even if Dad had seen his birth certificate, he would not have tried to find his father if he was told he was dead.'

In fact, the whole McPhail history was full of illegitimate children or children and fathers who had been denied access to each other. What a sorry state of affairs, but hopefully the past could be put behind them now and they could become one big happy family. This was Susan's dearest wish. She held Phyllis's hand tightly as they made their way back downstairs to join the rest.

A great many tears were shed that day, tears of sadness at what could have been and tears of happiness for the future. They suddenly all started talking at once. These six women, from different walks of life, from different parts of the country were all related. What a wonderful discovery. Linda and Shelley had so much to catch up on; they took themselves off to the small sitting room and talked for hours.

The one thing they still could not get their heads around was the way they had been brought to Dunnbray, and kept as virtual prisoners. What possessed Hugh and Angus to go along with such a stupid idea? Edna must have been very convincing in her arguments.

Dinner was just being discussed; something easy being the consensus, when the doorbell jangled making them jump. Linda answered it and immediately recognised the man standing on the doorstep with Hugh.

'Barry? What on earth are you doing here?' She asked in astonishment.

'Hi,' Hugh said, 'sorry to bother you but we just wanted to make sure you were all okay, it's been a difficult day for all of you and I thought now would be a good idea to introduce you to Douglas.'

Linda stared at Douglas. 'So you are the mystery detective. How many times did you come to the builders' merchants? Calling yourself Barry and I never realised what you were up to. You'd better come in,' she said leading them into the kitchen, where Marilyn and Shelley had started to prepare the meal.

They all stared as Hugh introduced Douglas.

'It's nice to meet you Douglas.' Phyllis emphasised his name with a touch of sarcasm in her voice.

'I am so sorry that I got to know all about you under false pretences. I was so excited at what I discovered about you all that I could not wait to tell Angus what a lovely family he was gaining. It is a wonderful story, and I know you have lots more questions for him, but he did all this with the right intentions, it is just so awful that Edna did what she did. I hope you will all accept my apologies.'

No one said anything, just stared at Douglas until, feeling very uncomfortable under their gaze he said, 'We'll leave you in peace now and hopefully see you in the morning.'

The two men were almost at the door, when Phyllis suddenly said, 'would you like to stay for dinner with us? It's not much, you'll have to make do, but I'm sure the others won't mind.' She looked at the others for confirmation.

'Are you sure? That is so kind of you, I would really like that,' Douglas said. Hugh agreed but said that he and Douglas would check on Angus first, as he was so tired after the day's traumatic events. Once they were happy that Angus was settled, they would return.

'Use the adjoining door Hugh, you can come and go that way now, we don't mind.' Susan called to him as he neared the front door. 'What are you playing at Mum?' she whispered.

'I thought we could all do with the company and hopefully make it an easier evening for the rest of us, that's all, it's been such a strange day.'

The two men were back in a few minutes and Susan suggested they choose some wine from the cellar.

A relaxed atmosphere fell round the kitchen table that night. Susan thought to herself that it had been a good idea of her mother's to invite the two men, it was very pleasant to have some male company for a change, especially that of Hugh. Marilyn wasn't too happy about missing out on a celebratory drink when Hugh raised a glass and toasted the MacPhail family, but she made do with fruit juice.

Susan looked round the table at them all and laughed.

'Thank you for staying for a meal with us, it has certainly helped, there has been so much to come to terms with. I can't believe my family has grown so quickly in such a short time. Has it sunk in yet? Marilyn, you and India are my cousins. My Mum is your Aunt and Linda and Shelley are our Aunties too. I don't know about you but I am getting very confused. Would you like some coffee Auntie Shelley?'

'It's wonderful to have nieces and cousins I didn't know I had, but shall we drop the titles?' Shelley said. 'Have you noticed it is all females in the family?'

'Don't forget my Tim, he's just as important you know,' Linda interrupted, 'he's your cousin too Susan and Marilyn.'

'Yes, how could we forget your Tim.' Susan heard her mother muttering and gave her a warning look.

'There's no need to be rude Phyllis, in fact I would like to know why Tim wasn't invited.' Linda unfortunately heard Phyllis's comments. 'He is family too. Can you answer that Hugh or Douglas? Or do I go and ask Angus now?'

'Please don't bother Angus, he is extremely tired,' said Hugh, 'I think it was decided that it would be better if it was just you six women as you would all be living together. Angus has his reasons for that decision which he will discuss with you tomorrow. Also Tim is in university and wouldn't be able to drop his studies for a four week holiday. So it was decided not to involve him at this stage I hope that answers your question for now Linda.'

Linda did not look very happy with the answer, but decided not to push it any more tonight. The others obviously felt a bit uncomfortable about it as silence fell round the table for a few minutes, then Douglas picked up the conversation once more and soon had them laughing at the way he had found out information about them.

They remained around the table and talked for hours. Douglas then apologised to Susan for asking her out, he didn't know why, it was just on impulse, explaining that he had been divorced for years and intended staying that way.

Just like me, Susan thought to herself as she surreptitiously looked at him with a twinge of disappointment, he was rather nice.

Linda, unable to miss an opportunity for a dig said Douglas would definitely have asked her out, but she obviously gave him the impression that she was not interested. 'Who knows where it would have led. He probably asked you out because he felt sorry for you.'

There were a few audible gasps heard around the table.

'Yes, but Douglas has already said that he does not want to get involved with anyone, so one or two drinks weren't going to lead anywhere were they? I think it was rather a nice thing for him to do.' Susan kept her temper somehow.

Hugh sensing how embarrassing this was becoming for Douglas changed the subject by mentioning that the family solicitor was coming the following morning. Douglas smiled at him in relief and suggested it was time they left. He was staying the night next door at Angus's and Hugh was going to stay because he was worried about Angus's state of health, especially now he was without a housekeeper.

As soon as they left, Phyllis turned to Linda and said, 'That wasn't a very kind thing to say to Susan, I think you ought to apologise.' She felt extremely angry on her daughter's behalf.

'Nothing to apologise for, I was just being honest. Most men fancy me, they like women with big boobs and slim legs like mine.' As she spoke, she ran her hands over her large bust and narrow hips. 'I'm off to bed; see you all in the morning, goodnight.'

Susan looked at her mother's flushed cheeks and clenched fists.

'It's alright Mum, I'm getting used to people being rude to me when they arrive here, it must be something in the air.' As she said this, she looked at Marilyn, who had the decency to blush remembering how rude she had been.

Changing the subject quickly Marilyn said, 'I've just realised, the adjoining door is unlocked now but what about the other locked door, we have forgotten that one, maybe there are more secrets to uncover.'

'We'll ask Hugh tomorrow,' Shelley replied. 'When do you think we will be able to talk to our families, surely they will not make us wait until the full four weeks are up now, will they?'

'I should think after we speak to Angus tomorrow, we will be able to phone everyone,' said Susan, 'and the gate can be left open, we can escape at last ladies, who's for a trip into Strathdown as soon as we can arrange it?'

'I could do with some retail therapy after all that's happened,' Marilyn replied, 'I'll need some new clothes to cover my expanding waistline, and sign on with a doctor too'

They all drifted off to their respective bedrooms and Susan joined Phyllis in her room just to check that she was happier about everything now.

'It has been a very strange couple of days Mum, who would have thought it a couple of weeks ago, when we were deciding whether to come or not. What do you think of our new found family?'

'You can choose your friends, but you can't choose your family springs to mind.' Phyllis muttered. 'Do you think we are going to get along, we are all so different? Shelley is all right I think and Marilyn is much better than she was, but Linda, well, you would think the sun shone out of her son's backside the way she goes on about him. She wasn't happy that he hadn't been invited was she?'

'I can understand it though, he's a relative as well, but I suppose Hugh was right, we might not have got on so well if there was a man living here with us and of course he is at university. He will be able to join us once we have the phone connected.'

Chapter 39

A sleepless night was had by all, except for Susan, who slept solidly, without waking once. Her mind at rest now she knew there would be no more strange noises and tapping when she went to bed. The morning found them drifting downstairs one by one and congregating in their favourite place, the warm cosy kitchen. The atmosphere was a bit cool, after Linda's comments the night before, but she appeared oblivious to it all, asking many questions about Hugh, which began to wind Susan up, who was impatient to find out the rest of Angus's story.

It was a long wait until eleven o'clock again; many cups of coffee were drunk and a lot of wandering aimlessly around took place before they were summoned.

'Hello Grandfather, hello Uncle,' a chorus of voices could be heard, and they all laughed as they met Angus in his sitting room later that morning. 'Are you feeling rested?'

'Yes, thank you ladies, and I am so pleased you have accepted the strange situation so easily. It must have been extremely difficult for you all.'

'Grandfather,' Susan said, 'I think I can speak for all of us when I say it was such a wonderful surprise. When we first realised there was someone living on this side of the house and spying on us, we were getting quite scared, and the episode with Edna was terrifying, but it was almost worth it now we know the truth. But did it really have to be such a secret? What was the point of it all? No phones, no TV, no radio, locked gates, that is what we find so difficult to come to terms with.'

Angus was spared from answering the question, because at that moment, there was a knock on the door and a rotund middle-aged man entered.

'Come in Charles. This is Mr Charles MacDonald of MacDonald, Scott & MacDonald,' Angus said. They saw a neat dapper little man, with the look of a bank manager about him in his pin-stripe suit. He was introduced to them all. 'He has been my solicitor for many years and wants to be present while I explain my plans to you.'

'It is so good to meet you at last,' Mr MacDonald said with a big smile on his face as he shook their hands. 'I have heard so much about you all, I feel as if I know you already. This is the oddest set of circumstances I have come across in all my years as a solicitor, but I can assure you that if you can put Edna's actions behind you there are some exciting times ahead for you all, so I'll hand you back to Angus to explain a bit more.'

Angus then proceeded to tell them his plans and hoped they would all be part of it. He was getting on in years and needed to decide what to do with Dunnbray. Originally thinking that there were no heirs, he considered leaving it to the Scottish National Trust, but then suddenly remembered the two daughters his brother had lost touch with; Charles suggested he hire a private detective to do a bit of digging and see what he could find out, before any firm decisions were made.

'Well,' he said, 'the rest is history so they say; once Douglas got his teeth into the project, there was no holding him; he did a grand job and what he unearthed left me absolutely stunned. As I said yesterday, all these family members kept appearing, who I never knew existed and none of them knew each other, apart from you Phyllis and Susan.'

He continued. 'Douglas found out as much as he could, and then Charles and I sat down to discuss whether Dunnbray would still be bequeathed to the National Trust, and any money divided between my relatives. You would know nothing about me until after my death, when Charles would contact you, and I would never have the opportunity of meeting you. To me, this was totally unacceptable. Our talk then turned to how to let you all know of your extended family, and whether to come and meet you and tell you in person, but that didn't seem right either. In the end, it was Edna's suggestion that you all come and stay. I, of course, thought it a brilliant idea not knowing Edna's ulterior motive.'

The story continued to unfold. To make matters more complicated at the time, Angus also decided that he would like to see how the women coped with all the problems Dunnbray threw at them before he met them. He wanted to know how resourceful they could be, how inventive, how curious, because by then he had settled on the plan for the future of his home. This explained why they were all invited to take part in a holiday with a difference. If they were all genuine McPhail women, in his opinion, they would turn out just as resourceful as his mother.

He knew his plan would be difficult to arrange and if he was honest, in retrospect, perhaps he had been a bit naïve, especially with the decision not to allow any contact with their families, and not allow phones, TV or radio, because he didn't want any information on him to come out before he had the opportunity to explain. He realised this part would be hardest of all for them to accept. The only ones, who had caused him some concern in the end, were India, and of course, Marilyn, her pregnancy had come out of the blue, but she had coped remarkably well.

As he paused for breath, Susan spoke.

'To tell you the truth, Grandfather, we were all scared and wanted to leave, but at the same time were curious. All the incidents that happened and my so-called accidents, got to us, but we were all becoming attached to Dunnbray; there is something magical about this place, it is our family home isn't it? It has to mean something to us all, even India; it will probably take her a bit longer to accept things, but I think she will come to feel the same as the rest of us. I do wonder what you would have done if one or other of us had just thrown the letter away and not bothered to contact the solicitors; what would you have done?'

'We would have had to tell you then, but we decided to give you all a few weeks to make up your minds and five of you agreed to come quite quickly so it made the decision easier. And I am so pleased that you can accept Dunnbray as your family home, you don't know how happy that makes me feel, and it makes it so much easier to explain my plans to you. I do hope you like them.'

Angus took a deep breath and with a smile on his face continued. 'I understand you all have commitments and three of you have family to take into consideration, but I would really love you all to come and live here if that's possible, either now or at some time in the future, your families as well if they wish, the place is big enough. As Susan says, it is your family home as much as mine and I would love to see you taking on Dunnbray and running it as a going concern of some sort again, a family business, whatever you would like to do. What do you think?' His face was anxious as he watched their expressions changing. 'Take as long as you like to think about it, there's no pressure, we'll get the telephone re-instated so you can talk to your families.'

The women were speechless, just sitting in stunned silence. Then he announced the biggest surprise of all, his plans for Susan. As his nearest relative, after his death, Susan would become Lady of Dunnbray – the female equivalent of Laird – and automatically inherit the house and the estate.

As Angus paused to get his breath, the news of inheriting Dunnbray seemed to pass Susan by; she was more concerned about Jamie's future within the family. He was a relative after all.

'What are you going to do about Jamie? You haven't mentioned him and he is still your nephew, have you any plans for him after the police have finished their enquiries?'

'Good question, I don't feel I have any responsibility to Edna after what she has done, she could have been honest from the start and told me who she was, and it would have been a different story then. Jamie, I think was coerced into helping his mother, he is not the brightest of lads and would not have understood the consequences, so I will set up a small trust fund for him, he can then do what he likes as long as he never sets foot on Dunnbray soil again. I think that is fair. Charles here will set the wheels in motion for that.'

'I think that's very kind of you, and you say there's no pressure for us to make our minds up what we want to do, to take as long as we like, but you must have some timescale in mind. Susan's heart was racing, could she live here? She need not ask herself twice, the answer was a resounding yes, but of course, there was her mother to consider as usual.

'Well, the sooner the better as far as I'm concerned. Now, going back to Dunnbray Susan, did you understand what I said about inheriting it? I know it has come as a huge shock and you will need time to adjust. One day this *will* be all yours and you will need to decide what to do with it, which is why I have suggested some sort of business, which can involve the other members of the family. It is a big responsibility but you needn't be on your own, and anyway I will be around for many years yet I hope.'

'Of course you will, Grandfather, and you are right I just can't take it in yet. I need time to think.'

'I will leave you to your thoughts for the rest of the day then, and I will come and visit you tomorrow and see what, if any, ideas you have. Until then, enjoy the rest of your day ladies.'

The girls left Angus and sat in the garden on the seats that Susan had found in one of the sheds. The sun shone in a clear blue sky, it was pleasantly warm and silence enveloped them for a few moments, then Susan said, 'I really can't take it all in, the next Lady of Dunnbray, the outcome certainly is unexpected. What do you make of it Mum?'

'*Don't count your chickens before they're hatched,* I say.'

'Auntie Phyllis, you have a saying for everything, you do make me smile,' Marilyn said with a mischievous look on her face.

'You can cut that out for a start; I'm not going to be an Auntie to anyone at my time of life, thank you very much.' Her curt tone belied the happiness she felt inside at her suddenly extended family. She was slowly coming to terms with the situation and a happy smile spread across her usually stern features.

'Angus was very fond of his mother wasn't he?' Marilyn said. 'The way he talks about her, she must have been an amazing woman; that's a lot for us to live up to, especially you Susan, he really is counting on you taking over.'

They sat quietly again until, 'What about a wedding venue?' Susan said to start the conversation again and looking at the others for agreement. 'That's the most popular idea we came up with the other night. Dunnbray just lends itself to weddings don't you think? To start off with, it would have to be receptions and accommodation only, and then we could perhaps apply for a licence and hold the ceremony here as well.'

'That's good, I missed out on that discussion but I like that idea, anything else?' Linda said.

'What about wildlife watching. There are so many opportunities, we are spoilt for choice.' Shelley joined in.

'Horse riding, we have the stables, as Susan knows very well.' Marilyn laughed as she said this.

'That's not funny.' Susan remembered her imprisonment in them, but it was a good idea, one that she herself had thought.

All eyes turned to Hugh as his footsteps crunched across the gravel. He greeted them all with a beaming smile, a smile, which lingered just that bit longer on Susan and she could feel her cheeks redden under his gaze. Phyllis did not miss this connection between the two of them. But Linda was up on her feet and giving him a quick peck on the cheek, before anyone else realised what was happening, least of all Hugh.

'I'm sorry Hugh, did I startle you?' Linda smiled coquettishly, fluttering her eyelashes, 'I always greet people with a kiss.'

'You didn't greet any of us or Angus like that.' Phyllis could not help herself.

'Well, who would want to kiss a face like yours? Have you been sucking on a lemon again or do you always look like that Phyllis.'

'Will you all stop it?' Susan thumped the table with her fist, her eyes blazing. 'We are family now, and you are going to act nicely towards one another, or you can go home, is that understood. I won't put up with it, do you all hear me?' She stood up and marched back to the house, trembling with anger, but shock too at her outburst, which was totally out of character. But she had a responsibility to Angus now, her grandfather; she would eventually be in charge of Dunnbray, and had to start taking her position seriously and there was no time like the present.

The others watched her stride off across the grass, then not quite knowing what to do, began a conversation about the weather and the garden to hide their embarrassment.

Susan grabbed a cold drink from the fridge, and then headed to the library; she shut the door and sat at the desk. Her hands were shaking; that outburst was not like her at all, but she would not be able to put up with bickering amongst the rest of them. They just had to get on. There were huge adjustments to be made in her life, was she up to it physically and mentally? Would they be able to run a business from here like her grandfather wanted? She could tell he was so proud of them all and did not want to let him down, but could they, and especially her, live up to his expectations?

She knew she wanted to stay here, but what about the others, could she live and work with them? Shelley, most definitely; Marilyn? Maybe, she had improved over the days, but Linda. No, she did not think she could live with her unless she changed her ways drastically.

Then what about her mother, she couldn't imagine she would want to stay here, what was she to do about her?

There was so much to think about; all her wishes could come true with this place. Then the doubts began to creep in; there wasn't a catch was there, that Angus hadn't mentioned? Luck like this did not happen to people like her. Her head began to ache and she closed her eyes for a moment.

A gentle tap on the door interrupted her thoughts. She frowned, was there never any peace in this place? Calling out, 'Come in,' she was surprised when Douglas poked his head round the door.

He had two cups of tea with him. 'Your mum guessed you might be in here, can I join you? Do you mind?'

Susan really needed some time on her own, but seeing Douglas's smiling face, she couldn't say so. 'Of course, come and sit down and she indicated the small leather sofa by the window. They sat sipping their tea for a few minutes in silence, then Douglas cleared his throat with a nervous cough and said he had come to apologise.

'Apologise?' Susan had no idea what he was apologising for.

'For mentioning asking you out and then saying I was a confirmed bachelor, that wasn't a very nice thing to say and I suppose I am apologising for Linda too as she didn't.'

'Don't worry about it; we can be friends can't we? Nothing wrong in that, friends can go out for a drink.' Now that Hugh had come into her life, it was easy for her to suggest friendship. For a few weeks, she had wondered what if with Douglas, but not since coming here. Hugh was the one for her, she had no idea how to go about it but a man in her life would be very welcome now with all the responsibilities she would have.

Drawing herself back to the present and seeing Douglas watching her she said, 'What are you going to do with yourself, now that you aren't following us around any more? What do you usually do?'

'Originally, I was in the police force in Edinburgh, then when I retired I became a private investigator, nothing very exciting, following husbands or wives around for suspicious other halves, missing persons, things like that. Your case was something I could really get my teeth into, I thoroughly enjoyed it. I suppose its back to the mundane stuff again now.'

'Would you be interested in working here at Dunnbray?' She heard herself asking, what was she doing? Engaging mouth before brain, why had she said that? Then she knew instinctively that here was a man she could trust. She watched his expression as she repeated the question.

'Would you be interested? You do not have to answer straight away, and I have no idea what job I am offering you; it is all up in the air now as you might have guessed. We are toying with several suggestions, but it's far too soon to make any decisions and I need to talk to Grandfather first of course, so think about it, let me know in a couple of days.'

'I must say I am very interested, thank you Susan, I will definitely give it some thought. I'll leave you in peace now, your mother has invited Hugh and I for dinner again tonight, and Angus if he is up to it, so hopefully I will see you later.'

'Mum seems to be very good at inviting people to dinner, especially as she won't be the one cooking it; I hope Shelley and Marilyn are alright about it.'

'They're fine; it's not a problem apparently, so see you in a bit.'

After he had gone, Susan sat for ages, gazing blankly out of the window, then realising Shelley was beckoning to her from the garden, she went back out to join the others on the lawn, her outburst forgotten.

'Come on Susan,' Shelley called to her. 'Hugh was just asking if anyone would like a trip into Strathdown this afternoon. We can escape at last, the gate is unlocked.'

The afternoon trip to Strathdown sped by. Firstly, there was the beautiful countryside on the drive there. They had not seen anything of this on their arrival in the dark. They enjoyed a browse round the shops and popped into a little café for tea and scones served on matching dainty china. The tables covered with embroidered tablecloths with matching napkins and small vases of fresh flowers. Susan suddenly realised she was looking at everything with a different eye; she was already looking for ideas for Dunnbray.

Phyllis asked Hugh how long it would take to have the landline re-connected, as the others needed to phone family, friends and workplaces.

It was all in hand, he said, but would take a few days and Angus would rather they all take some time to let the news sink in before they rang their families, and not to do anything in a rush. 'He wants you to have a few days of proper holiday and come to terms with your life changes if you don't mind.'

'Are you taking it all in girls?' Susan said grinning happily, as she gazed about her. 'We will need all the ideas we can pick up if we are to start a family business. How do you all feel about coming to live here, have you given it any thought? What about you Linda?' Susan secretly hoped Linda would turn it down, and felt a stab of disappointment when she said she was definitely thinking about it, she quite liked the idea.

Shelley was very noncommittal, muttering something about having a husband, a family, and she just could not up and move to Scotland just like that. It crossed Susan's mind that Shelley had become rather negative about the whole thing and in fact had not said much at all since they found out the news. She thought Shelley would have been the first to jump at the opportunity because of her unhappy life, what was wrong with her? Was she having second thoughts?

'What about you Marilyn?'

'I need to find out what Ken thinks of the baby before I can make any decision. Of course I would love to live at Dunnbray and be part of the family, but if he is happy about the baby I suppose I will have to go home.'

'But Marilyn, Dunnbray is part of yours and your baby's life now, your heritage; you must decide what is best for you, husband or no husband.'

'I hear what you are saying, but I must talk to him first, it will all be such a shock to him.'

Turning to Susan, Hugh asked her if she would like to go for a walk with him before they went back, he wanted to show her a little art shop he was fond of visiting. She jumped at the chance to spend some time alone with him.

'That's a budding romance if ever I saw one,' Phyllis said as she watched them walk away, not touching, but very close together.

'Do you really think so? Marilyn had noticed the looks that had passed between Hugh and Susan.

'I don't think Susan is Hugh's type and have you noticed the way he keeps looking at me?'

'Linda, just because you are divorced, it doesn't mean every man is after you, you know. Don't spoil it for them please, there are plenty more fish in the sea.'

'You're right Phyllis, there's always Douglas, he's free and single too isn't he?' As she said this Linda gave Shelley a cunning look from beneath her eyelashes.

Marilyn could see how upset Shelley was, two patches of red had appeared on her cheeks. That is how the land lies is it she thought, two budding romances, well, well. She went on to say, 'Let us watch this space, as they say, see what develops. We could have our first family wedding at Dunnbray, what about that?'

'You're getting ahead of yourself Marilyn; we haven't even decided whether we are going to stay here or not.' Phyllis rose and made her way to the ladies' cloakroom.

'What a misery that woman can be,' Linda remarked. 'Imagine living with that every day.'

'She's not that bad once you make the effort to get to know her, and it must have been such a shock for her.' Marilyn knew how kind and caring Phyllis was underneath her stern façade.

The afternoon soon passed and Hugh and Susan rejoined them ready to go home. As they walked back to the vehicle, Hugh and Phyllis taking the lead, Marilyn and Linda turned to Susan and asked what her own plans were.

Pushing her hair back off her face with both hands again, her eyes troubled, she told them that she would give anything to stay, she loved the place, but didn't know what to do about her mother; what if she didn't want to live here? Could she leave her mother in Dorchester on her own after all these years? Was she selfish to think about it?

'Phyllis might like to live here too you know, have you asked her yet?'

'No, Marilyn I have been a bit frightened to, to be honest.'

'Hey, Phyllis has got me at it now, I have come up with one of her sayings: *Better late than never.*' Linda laughed.

'You're right of course; I will have a chat when we get back if I get the chance.'

Later that afternoon, Susan caught hold of her mother's arm and suggested a walk round the garden before dinner. They donned their coats as the temperature had dropped considerably from the afternoon.

When they were a little way from the house, Susan said that she wanted to talk about their future.

'Your future is settled, you'll have to come and live here at some stage, when you become Lady of Dunnbray, but you don't know how long that will be, it could be years away, do you want to give up your home and your job and move up here now?'

'Mum, I won't make any decision that you are not happy with. I couldn't come up here and live and leave you in Dorchester.'

'Of course you could. I am perfectly capable of managing on my own. I love having you around, but if I am honest with myself, I don't need you. I have been a very selfish old woman since your Dad died, expecting you to be at my beck and call, I haven't given you the opportunity of a life of your own. I cannot expect you always to be there for me. It's taken until now for me to realise that.'

'But, Mum…'

'No, hear me out. I want you to make a decision that will make *you* happy, what do you want to do, live here, or go back to Dorchester even if it's just for a few years?'

'I would really love to come and live here. There is just no comparison, my pokey flat and no garden compared to this huge house and beautiful grounds. I want to move here if you really don't mind Mum.'

'I'm glad we have had a chat about things, I will go back to Dorchester, I can always come up for holidays can't I?'

'Of course you can, but I have just had a much better idea, why don't you move here as well? You have nothing to keep you in Dorchester, and look how much happier you have become just by being here for a few weeks. It has done you the world of good and anyway, Grandfather needs someone to become his housekeeper now that Edna has gone, that would suit you down to the ground, wouldn't it?'

'Are you sure that is what *you* want? Because I think I could be happy here too and I would love to look after Angus, he's such a lovely old man and he does need someone doesn't he?'

'That's settled then, we are both staying. We will have to go home to sort my flat and your house out, but the sooner we can move here the better. We'll tell Grandfather, he will be so pleased.'

Shelley was unusually quiet over dinner, but with Hugh and Douglas there, Susan could not ask her what the problem was. Coffee was just being served when Shelley announced she had a headache and was going to bed. As soon as the men left, the conversation turned to her attitude.

'She's been acting a bit odd since Angus told us the news, what could be bothering her do you think?' Susan asked.

'She's jealous.'

'Mum, what do you mean? Who is she jealous of?'

'Why, you of course.'

Susan could not understand why Shelley would be jealous and Phyllis would not expand on what she had said, but it put a dampener on the rest of the evening.

Chapter 40

The next morning, Susan was impatient for Angus to arrive. She paced up and down the hall, until she heard the adjoining door open, and he and Hugh appeared.

Leaving Hugh to go about his work, she tucked her hand under Angus's arm and escorted him to the small sitting room, where he looked about him appreciatively.

'I always loved this little room, you have made it very welcoming my dear,' he said, making himself comfortable in one of the easy chairs, as Susan fluffed up some cushions behind his back. Phyllis soon joined them.

'I know I shouldn't expect any decisions yet, it is early days, but have you had any thoughts? What about you Susan, do you think you could live here? And take over the reins? I know I am still around, but I really don't want the responsibility any more. It would mean giving up your flat and your job, in fact, your independence which I know is important to you.'

'On one level, it would be a backward step, moving back in with family, but at the same time, I think this place is big enough for all of us, we won't have to live on top of each other, and if it all gets too much, I shall disappear into the garden.' Susan laughed. 'I think it would be ideal for Mum too, so yes I want to live here and get the place up and running again, even though I don't know the first thing about running a business. I will need lots of help.'

'That is music to my ears, I am so happy, and don't worry about the business side, we can take our time and I'm sure we can get you plenty of help and advice. Now Phyllis how do you feel about moving up here?'

'I wasn't sure how I felt yesterday, but Susan and I had a long chat and I would love to live here with you, and now you don't have a housekeeper, someone has to look after you and keep the place clean, so if you don't mind I am volunteering for the job.'

'Marvellous, Phyllis, marvellous, but you do not need to volunteer, it will be a paid position; housekeeper, that is an important job in a place like this. I have Charles looking at all the ins and outs of salaries etc. as we speak.'

Phyllis surreptitiously pinched herself, to make sure she was not dreaming. A proper job, after all these years, she was being offered a job, and an important one too according to Angus. Thank you Bill, she whispered under her breath, for having such a lovely father. She smiled to herself at the thought of being able to tell the stuck up W.I ladies that her daughter was inheriting Dunnbray castle; they didn't need to know it wasn't a real castle, and it would certainly wipe the smug looks off their faces. She could not wait to go home and let them all know.

'What are you smiling at Mum?'

'Oh, nothing; just thinking.'

Linda, Shelley and Marilyn joined them a little later and Susan excitedly told them that she and her mother were definitely going to live at Dunnbray.

'I am going to need lots of help,' she said looking around at the other girls, 'how about it, has anyone had any more thoughts, does anyone want to run this wedding venue with me?'

'Are you absolutely sure you want us to stay, I mean this will be your home, not ours.' Linda was the first to break the silence that had descended.

'Grandfather said yesterday that he would like as many of us as possible to stay, there is plenty of room for us all to live here, this is the McPhail family home and you are all family, say you'll at least think about it, please,'

'Well, I don't have any ties, Tim is at university, so it won't matter to him where I live, so yes I think I would like to come and live and work here if you'll have me.'

'Brilliant, Linda, thank you,' Susan said, thinking she had to find a way of coping with this woman. Turning to the others she said, 'I suppose we will have to wait until you've told your other halves.'

'Ken wouldn't move here, I know that, but if he doesn't accept the baby, then I am going to need somewhere to live, as I said it all depends on Ken.'

'I am sure it will all work out for the best Marilyn. Even if you don't live here, it will be an ideal place for holidays. You will be welcome at any time you know that. Shelley, what about you? You are not happy with Brian; perhaps staying here with us would solve the problem.'

'It's alright for you; you don't have anybody else to think about do you? No ties, it's great for some isn't it. I have family to think about. I suppose I will be going home, but thanks for the offer. I'll go and start lunch shall I?' and she rose from her chair and left without even a goodbye to Angus.

'What the hell's got into her?' Linda could not believe what had just happened. 'After all that's taken place, I can't believe she's acting like that. She has told all of us she is not happy with Brian and thought about leaving him, now she has the opportunity to do something with her life, she is chucking it away. She might be my sister, but I do not understand her at all. I'll try and have a chat with her after lunch, see if I can find out what the problem is.'

'That was a bit of a shock I must admit, I wonder what's brought that on?'

'I told you Susan, she is jealous of you.'

'But why Mum? I do not understand. We are all in the same boat; just because I am going to be the Lady here at some point in the future should not be a problem for anyone should it? Susan looked at the others for confirmation.

'It doesn't make any difference, we are just both happy for you, and just goes to show you never really know anyone do you?' Marilyn was very honest in her comments. Linda voiced the same comment as Marilyn, but underneath her thoughts were far from happy; what about her Tim? Where did he fit into all these plans? She would have to keep her true feelings in check for the time being, no use showing how she felt at this stage; she would only antagonise everyone, especially Angus.

Out of the three of them, Susan thought she'd had the best relationship with Shelley and was counting on her to stay; it would be so much harder without her.

Angus suggested it had all been a bit much for Shelley to take in and she needed more time to think things over. And it was all well and good to talk about leaving her husband, but when the opportunity arose it wasn't always so easy to see it through.

'The voice of reason, thank you Grandfather, we'll give her some time and hope she will agree to stay.'

'It's almost lunchtime, if we are finished here for the time being, would you like me to bring you some lunch Angus?' asked

Phyllis, thinking it would be fun to start her duties as housekeeper straight away; no time like the present.

'Come on then,' said Susan, 'let's get lunch on the go, I for one am starving.'

Phyllis tucked her hand under Susan's arm and as they all headed towards the kitchen she said, 'As I will be the mother of the Lady of Dunnbray some day, and the new housekeeper, I expect you all to start treating me with the respect I think I am entitled to.'

They all stared at her because Phyllis being Phyllis, they were not sure whether she was joking or not, then seeing the broad smile spreading across her face, they realised she was thoroughly enjoying the moment and laughed with her.

'Come on then future Lady of Dunnbray's mother, let us all treat you with the respect you don't deserve.' Susan could not have been more pleased at the way things were working out.

Their laughter rang out again as they all headed for their favourite place, the warm, cosy kitchen.

After the lunchtime snack of sandwiches and soup were cleared away, Linda asked Shelley to join her in the small sitting room for a sisterly chat. They must have been in there a good hour and when they came out Shelley looking decidedly unhappy said she was going to her room, she had another headache.

'What did she have to say? Did you find out anything?' Phyllis demanded to know as soon as Shelley was out of earshot.

'She just said that she didn't think she would fit in here and wouldn't be able to manage financially on her own, and that she had more family responsibilities than the rest of us and couldn't just walk away from them. That's all she would say, but I felt she wasn't being totally honest; still I tried.'

'Thank you Linda. If she doesn't want to stay, we can't force her,' Susan replied, thinking about what her mother had said about her being jealous. If that was the real problem, then why was she jealous?

Chapter 41

Much of the next day was spent in conversation, each of them getting to know about one another's families. They went round to Angus's for coffee and got him to talk about his past and about Isobel, his mother of whom they could tell he had been extremely close to.

Hugh suddenly appeared at Angus's door and called out, 'Come on then you lot, you didn't remind me about the other locked door did you? Do you want to see what is behind it or not?'

The last mystery door had been totally forgotten in all the comings and goings of the last couple of days, and Angus laughed as there was a sudden stampede of feet and the girls all rushed to where Hugh was standing, waving the key in his hand.

Hugh turned the key, and threw open the door. 'Ta Dah.'

Five pairs of eyes gazed into the room awestruck. A double height room, met their gaze, it stretched the full length of the large extension, a ballroom, no less, with a gallery running round the top.

'How about this for a party,' he said, 'or a wedding reception?' and with that he grabbed hold of Susan's hand and pulled her into the room and began dancing around with her.

'This is absolutely wonderful,' Susan said, catching her breath, 'so that's why we had no access to this part of the house upstairs, that's why there is only one corridor with bedrooms in the extension, I couldn't work it out, now I understand. Definitely the cherry on the cake. This place just has to become a wedding venue. Can't you just picture it; bride coming down the stairs, service in the dining room, reception in the hall and disco in here.'

They all agreed it was a beautiful room and could Hugh please remove all the boards from the windows to let in some light and could he do it now please. Obeying his orders with a laugh, he went off to find a ladder and soon sunshine began to filter through the tall windows once more. When they had been cleaned properly, inside and out, the light coming through would be even better.

'Yet another job,' Phyllis remarked. 'This place is like painting the Forth Bridge, no sooner have you finished one bit, then you have to start all over again.'

'We are going to need some help running this place I think Mum, it's going to be too much for us.'

The following day the telephone was re-connected, and Hugh passed on the good news that Angus was quite happy for them all to contact whomever they wished. He would get the solicitors to ring India and ask her to come back up again. He did not want to discuss any details with her over the phone; he wanted to talk to her face to face.

'I do hope she comes back, it will be such a lovely surprise for her,' Susan said.

'Do you think when she finds out about all her relatives and why she was invited here it will improve her manners? I don't think I could stand her living here if she doesn't change her ways.' Phyllis was not looking forward to the prospect of that spoilt girl coming back. What with Linda after the men and Shelley acting strange, what was it with all these women? Was she the only normal one?

Marilyn was the first to phone home and Ken sounded delighted to hear from her; she did not think he would be so pleased when she told him about the baby. He was surprised that the four weeks were not up and wanted to know what had changed with the situation.

'I am not going to tell you anything over the telephone,' Marilyn said, 'but I would love you to come up here, see where we have been staying and tell you some simply amazing news.'

'Can't you tell me now? What has happened that is so exciting? Come on Marilyn, tell me, I won't be able to come up there until the day after tomorrow at the earliest, I have meetings that I cannot possibly change at such short notice.'

'No, you will have to wait; will you be driving up? If so here's the address so you can satnav it, just give me a call on this number and give me your arrival time.'

In some ways, Marilyn was quite pleased that he would not arrive until Saturday; it gave her a bit more time to decide what to say about the baby. It wasn't immediately obvious that she was pregnant, although there was already a small bump and her breasts were larger and her face a bit more rounded, so with a bit of luck he might just think that she had been over-eating whilst here. If he doesn't want the baby, he can jolly well do without me as well she thought, hoping that once he knew he would change his mind. She really did not want to bring up this baby on her own.

Well, only one more day before I find out, I could just do with a nice glass of wine to calm my nerves. Can you believe it, that cellar full of wine and I cannot have any, you had better be worth it little one and with her hand, as was her habit these days, covering her stomach protectively, she went to find the others.

When Marilyn had finished, Linda telephoned her son. She hoped to catch him at his digs, before he went to the bar where he worked part-time to supplement his student grant. As luck would have it, he had changed his shift so was at home.

Tim panicked when he heard her voice. 'What is it Mum, are you all right? Are you ill? Is it awful there? Do you want to come home?'

'Tim, calm down, it's none of those things; but something simply wonderful has happened, I need you to come up here as soon as you can. Get the first train tomorrow, get a taxi from Strathdown, I will pay for it when you get here, you really must come, I have such great news.'

'I thought the whole thing was a bit mysterious to start with, now it's just got more intriguing; do I really have to wait until I get there to find out what's going on?' Tim laughed at the enthusiasm he could hear in his mother's voice, he had not heard her talk like that in a long time; it must be something special. 'I will do my best to get there Mum, see you tomorrow. Is it alright to ring back on this number, and let you know what I've arranged?'

'Yes, of course you can. See you tomorrow, Tim, I love you.' Linda put the 'phone down with a big grin on her face. She could not wait to see him.

It was Shelley's turn to phone home. She delayed as long as possible before picking up the receiver and dialling, her fingers crossed hoping for the answer phone. She knew she would go home. There was no point in staying up here. The news about Dunnbray and all these women being related to her, well what a load of rubbish; she was just not interested, especially with Susan becoming the next Laird; and how easily she could decide to stay without a thought for anyone else. She wished it were that easy for her. All this was out of her league, she was an ordinary woman for God's sake, and she worked in a supermarket. All this talk of running a family business, she wanted no part of it. She regretted telling the others now that she might look for work up here at the end of their stay.

Brian answered on the third ring.

'Hello Brian, it's me, how are you?'

'Oh, it's you; I thought you couldn't get in touch for four weeks, have you got fed up with your holiday already?' She heard the unkind tone in his voice.

'I have some news, but I don't want to tell you over the telephone, I'll be coming home in the next day or two.'

Shelley replaced the receiver to cut short any more conversation.

Hugh had joined the others out in the garden again and was listening contentedly to their chatter. The talk was all about the news their families were going to get in the following couple of days.

'When's Brian com...' Susan was about to ask when she saw the look on Shelley's face.

'He isn't coming,' she replied shortly, 'I'll see about getting a train back in the morning. Could you take me to the station Hugh, please?'

'But, Shelley, I thought you didn't want to go...'

Susan was cut off in mid-sentence, 'I am going home, that's all there is to it. I'll go and start packing.'

'Well I never, it's one rude girl after another here, I can't understand her,' Phyllis was surprised at Shelley.

'I know, I can't believe she moaned about her husband and kids so much and now she's going back. Perhaps it was all talk, Mum.'

'Did she really say she wasn't happy with her husband?' Hugh interrupted.

'She told us she'd had enough, he wasn't interested in her. In fact, it was her main topic of conversation. They did not love each other; all that stuff. I thought she might have stayed, especially if Douglas does come and work here. I think she is quite taken with him. He'll be sorry to see her go.'

Chapter 42

Angus took great delight in the girls' visits every morning, and would sit and listen contentedly as they chattered away about their plans. This morning they could not make it because Shelley was catching the early train and they all wanted to go to the station with her. She had already been to say her goodbye to her uncle, and was very negative in her responses to his questions about her leaving. In the hall, as she stood with her case waiting for Hugh to load them into the vehicle, she said to the others, 'You don't need to come to the station.'

'Don't be silly Shelley, we want to come and anyway we all want to go into Strathdown again, and Marilyn has to register at the doctor's, so we are coming whether you like it or not.' Susan was upset about Shelley's attitude, she felt they could have become good friends; they were quite close in age. Why was she acting like this?

It was a quiet trip into Strathdown. Shelley obviously did not want to talk and the rest of them did not know what to say. When they arrived at the station, Hugh jumped out of the people carrier and lifted Shelley's case out of the back and they were all just about to get out when Shelley stopped them.

'Don't bother seeing me off, I'll say goodbye here; might see you again sometime.' She took the suitcase from Hugh and without a backward glance headed for her train.

'Well, that's the end of her then, is it?' Phyllis watched her walk away. 'Come on everyone,' she said trying to jolly them along, 'let's go and get Marilyn registered at the doctor's then we'll have a cup of tea at that nice little café.'

Their timing at the doctor's was perfect. When Marilyn explained what had happened, she was whisked in to see a Dr. McFarlane who just happened to have a free appointment. The wheels were set in motion for regular visits and eventually meeting the local midwife if she did not return to London. Marilyn was assured that all was well.

'I shall have to go shopping for some larger clothes now; I don't want maternity tents though.'

'Marilyn, elasticated trousers and loose tops will be fine; you are not going to get that big.' Linda told her.

Marilyn had a fleeting thought of ending up looking like Susan, but pushed it firmly to the back of her mind.

'I don't think I can do this too often Angus, they've worn me out this afternoon, and we'll have to get them put on the insurance so someone else can drive.' Hugh groaned and held his head in mock weariness, when they all returned.

'Good point; we'll sort that out in the morning.' Angus said, 'and by the way Marilyn, you have a visitor.'

It had to be Ken, he had come early and Marilyn rushed off excitedly to find him in the sitting room. 'Ken, darling, it's wonderful to see you, sorry I wasn't here, but we wanted to see Shelley off. Oh, of course you don't know who Shelley is do you? Come on up to my room and I will tell you all about it, and then afterwards I will introduce you to everyone.'

Ken gave Marilyn a huge bear hug and a long lingering kiss on the lips.

'I'm so sorry for being such a jerk before you left, what must you have thought of me?'

'Honestly? I thought you were a pig. I wasn't expecting you until tomorrow; did you cancel your meetings?'

'Yes, I know I said I couldn't, but then I thought, what was more important, my wife or my work and you won, so here I am, what's the big secret?'

Marilyn suddenly panicked and realised the biggest secret was the baby, but decided to leave that to the end, she would tell him all about her new family first.

'Would you believe it Ken, all the women I came on holiday with are my relatives; I have cousins, aunties and a great uncle, the man who owns this place is my Uncle Angus. My mother and India's mother were sisters.'

'Whoa, slow down, I can't take this all in, can you repeat it all, slowly this time.'

Marilyn explained it all again, and why they had been invited in the way they had been, why it had been kept a secret and how they had come to discover the secret before they were supposed to.

A discreet tap on the door disturbed them. On opening it, Marilyn saw Phyllis standing there.

'I just popped up to see if you two would like a cup of tea or something. Linda and I are cooking dinner tonight, so you can spend time with your husband.'

'Oh, God, I am sorry Phyllis, this is Ken, Ken this is my Auntie Phyllis and I have not introduced him to anyone else either, how rude am I hiding him up here, we will be down in a minute.'

'Don't worry, we all understand you have a lot to talk about,' she said winking at Marilyn, 'I'll bring you up a tray.'

'What did she mean by that? Why was she winking? Is there something else you have not told me? By the way, I hate to say it but you look like you have put a bit of weight on since you have been up here. Your face looks quite chubby. It's back to the gym for you when we go home, I can't have a fat wife.'

He looked her up and down and instinctively she clasped her hands over her expanding stomach and said, 'There is something else I have to tell you, but I'm scared, you will be so angry,' and with that she burst into tears.

'What is it Marilyn? What has happened? You sounded so happy just now telling me about your new found family, I think it's wonderful news, what can possibly have happened to spoil all that?'

'I'm pregnant Ken; I'm pregnant with our baby.'

'What! You can't be.'

'I am about three months now, isn't it wonderful news, aren't you pleased?' A feeling of dread began to spread through her as she saw the expression change on his face.

'I thought we agreed no children, isn't that what we said? How could you let this happen?'

'It does take two you know, I did not do it all on my own and anyway, we didn't actually agree to no children, that was your decision, it was you who said you didn't want any.'

Ken had stood up to be introduced to Phyllis but sat back on the bed with a jolt.

'OK, so it was me who said no children, ever, but you never disagreed. You're not that many weeks, it's not too late to…' his voice tailed off.

'To get rid of it, is that what you're saying? You cannot make me get rid of it. I know you don't want children, but I do, so if you want to divorce me you had better go ahead and do it, because I am keeping this baby.'

Marilyn walked over to the window and gazed out over the gardens. She held her breath as she waited for the outburst of anger that was sure to come. But all was quiet, he must be so angry, she thought. Not able to wait any longer she turned and looked at him. He was still sitting on the bed, head in his hands.

'Well, say something Ken.'

They heard another tap on the door. It was Phyllis with their tea.

She opened the door, took the tray from Phyllis and shook her head, tears welling in her eyes.

Phyllis touched her hand, and then left the two of them together.

'I can't believe you let this happen, after all I have said about children. You know I don't want them, but you deliberately get pregnant and expect me to go along with it.'

'But Ken,' she interjected, 'I didn't deliberately do it, I didn't know myself until after I came up here.'

'Yes, but you are the one on the pill, you are the one to take responsibility for not getting pregnant.'

Silence fell like a curtain between them, she standing, he still sitting.

After a few minutes, Ken spoke. 'Marilyn, I repeat, I don't want children, not now, not in the future, never, so it's up to you, what do you intend doing?'

Marilyn looked at the man she loved, had loved, for in that moment she hated him with a passion. He was asking her to choose between him and her unborn child. She knew, with great certainty which one she would choose and it was not him. Turning back to look out of the window, with hands held protectively around her, she said, 'if that's how you feel, then there is no point in you stopping a moment longer. I will not be coming home, you can send all my things up, I am going to live here and bring up my baby with my family. Goodbye Ken.'

He came up behind her and went to put his arms round her, but she shrugged him off and he turned and walked out of the room.

Marilyn stayed gazing out of the window for what seemed hours. She heard the front door slam and watched him and his car disappear out of her life. A little later, she heard her bedroom door opening and someone came up and put their arm round her shoulders. It was Susan.

'I am so sorry Marilyn, Ken introduced himself and said he was not stopping, I guess he would not accept the baby. You never know, he might come round when he has had time to think about it. It must have been a bit of a shock for him.'

'But you didn't see the look on his face,' Marilyn started to cry, 'he blamed me, it was all my fault he said, he won't change his mind, Susan, my marriage is over, you will let me stay here with you won't you. I can work; I will do anything as long as I can stay here with my baby. Oh God, you won't mind a baby in the house will you?'

'Oh, Marilyn, of course we won't mind a baby in the house, just think how many babysitters you will have and how many 'aunties' will be fussing over your little baby. It'll be alright, we'll all support you, please don't worry about anything, promise?'

Marilyn wiped her eyes. 'You are all so kind, I would be lost without my family now.'

They gave each other a hug and Susan left her gazing out of the window again.

Dinner that night was a quiet affair, due to Marilyn's disastrous meeting with her husband. She refused to come down and Phyllis had taken her something up on a tray. None of them could understand how Ken could have been so cold and hurtful to her. Douglas and Hugh and as a special guest, Angus himself had joined them. They ate in the dining room and would have waited for Linda's son to arrive, but decided that it would be far too late for Angus to be eating, and agreed that they would do it all again the following night, so that Tim could join them.

Coffee was just being served, when the doorbell jangled.

'That'll be Tim, I'll go,' said Linda rushing to the door. She opened it and gave her son a big hug, then dragged him into the dining room and introduced him to everyone, her uncle, her cousins, her nieces, laughing at the expression on his face.

'Sorry Tim,' she said, 'I just couldn't resist that. Come into the kitchen, I'll rustle you up something to eat and explain what is going on.'

In the dining room, the conversation turned to plans for the future for some or all of them, before Angus decided to call it a day and turn in. It had been another long day for him.

'Anyone else left to arrive now?' Angus asked as he was leaving.

'No that's it now,' said Susan as she linked arms with her grandfather and escorted him back to his rooms.

'I get the impression Douglas will miss Shelley,' he said, 'I have noticed he talks about her rather a lot and likes coming to visit. And what about you and Hugh, he seems quite taken with you, you know.'

'Grandfather! Stop trying to marry us off. I would like to know though, is he married? We can't find out, he never talks about himself.'

'He was, but his wife died several years ago and he has never shown any interest in anyone else until now, so it could be interesting, Dunnbray's first wedding maybe?' He chuckled at his own joke.

Susan's thoughts drifted to Hugh, as they so often did these days, and then she remembered she had not mentioned to Angus about offering Douglas a job. It had just slipped out in conversation.

When she told him, Angus laughed. 'Not wasting any time, that's what I like to see; I would love Douglas to come and work here, he is a good man, reliable, trustworthy, just the sort you need around you.'

'He hasn't agreed to come here yet though, so we'll wait and see.'

Susan gave Angus a kiss on the cheek as she left him.

Meanwhile Linda and Tim were still in the kitchen. Tim absolutely amazed at Linda's story. He now had second cousins and aunties and a great uncle too, he could not take it all in. Just seeing how excited his mother was made him happy, and when she said that she would like to sell the house and move up to Dunnbray, but she wasn't sure how he would feel about that, he said exactly what she had thought herself. He didn't come home that often and he could just as easily get up to here as down to Exeter. In fact, he was already planning on inviting some of his university mates up for a holiday if she didn't mind.

'I can't see that will be a problem, they could have a working holiday, and there must be loads of work to do on the farm. I believe they are going to continue farming in some way.'

'That's it then Mum,' he said, 'that's settled, the bank holiday is coming up, would you like me to go home and get the house valued, so that you can stay up here and do whatever you need to do to help Susan get this business up and running?'

'That would be brilliant Tim, if you wouldn't mind, and make sure you keep it tidy. Get at least three different agents to value the house, as they all charge differently, then let me know and we can ask them to show prospective clients around, we don't need to be there for that. I will have to write to Jack and explain that I am not coming back, but I am sure he will understand when he knows the reason, and Tim, thank you for taking this all in your stride, I am going to be so happy here, I can feel it.'

'Mum, that's all I want for you.' He gave her a hug and they went to join the others. Little did Tim know that Linda's plans for him did not involve working holidays on the farm. Oh no, her son would be the only surviving male member of the McPhail clan, that must count for something. She did not discuss any of this with Tim of course, that could come later.

Chapter 43

Taking a taxi from the station, Shelley arrived home before the rest of her family got in from work. None of them knew she was coming home today, it would be a surprise; she would see by their reaction just how much they had missed her, and more importantly how she felt about seeing them again, especially Brian.

She let herself into the quiet house and walked into the kitchen; something tickled her leg, and looking down she saw Molly. She picked up the purring cat and hugged her tightly; ashamed to admit she had missed her more than she had missed any of the others. Noticing Molly's water and food dish both stood empty and unwashed she said to the cat, 'Oh, poor Molly, I am so sorry for leaving you, haven't they been looking after you?' Molly meowed in response. Shelley quickly put food and water down and was shocked to see how greedily Molly ate and drank.

The kettle had just boiled when she heard the key turning in the lock, and Brian entered. He stared first at her case then at her.

'You're back then? Why didn't you let me know you were coming today?'

'Why, would you have met me?' She challenged.

'I might have been able to, still you are here now, what's for tea then?'

'Aren't you the slightest bit interested in the news I told you about?'

'If it's that good why don't you wait until the girls come in, then you'll only have to say it once.'

The girls walked in at that moment and seeing their mother rushed over and gave her a hug, saying they were glad to have her back, not having had a decent meal for weeks. They had been living off fish and chips and take away Chinese and all that fast food had played havoc with their skins. Was she going to cook them something nice for tea? And had she brought them a present?

Shelley stared at them, blinking back tears of frustration and told them about the family she had discovered in Scotland; how her cousin was to be the future Lady of Dunnbray and how they were going to run a family business and asked her to join them, but she thought they needed her more at home.

'You're right there,' said Brian as he switched the TV on. 'you are definitely needed at home, none of us can use the washing machine properly, the beds haven't been changed and the fridge is empty. Are you going back to work tomorrow?'

'I can't believe I thought you might have missed *me* as a person, not what I do for *you,* and what about Molly, who was supposed to be feeding her? She was starving when I got back.'

She saw the sheepish looks, which passed between the girls; Lily said it was Jane's turn and Jane said no it was not it was Lily's. Shelley wondered how many times they had forgotten to feed Molly. Looking in the freezer for something to cook that was quick, she found some chicken pies, frozen roast potatoes and peas, which would have to do; she switched the oven on, with a big sigh, put the pies and potatoes in, and then carried her case upstairs to the bedroom.

She wrinkled her nose with distaste at the crumpled sheets of the unmade bed; fetched clean ones from the airing cupboard and remade it. There that looked better already. Dirty linen was overflowing out of the basket in the bathroom. She looked round in despair. Discarded toilet roll tubes lay on the floor, open tubes of toothpaste lay near the washbasin, and the towels obviously had not been changed since she left. What an idle family they were.

Back in the bedroom, she sat at the dressing table and stared at her sad expression in the mirror. Reaching out, she touched her reflection. She did exist; tears rose in her eyes then slowly trickled down her cheeks; she brushed them away angrily, her thoughts straying to Douglas; she pictured his dark wavy hair, which she wanted to run her fingers through, his handsome smiling face. What was she to do? Did he think about her, the way she thought about him? If she went back to Dunnbray, would they want her there after the way she behaved? Would they think as badly of her as they did of India?

Knowing with sudden certainty, she could not stay here. The family's reaction to her coming home had been enough to prove it to her. Why was she so jealous of Susan? thinking she had no ties; of course she had ties; Phyllis was a big one for a start. It could not have been an easy decision for Susan to make. So many questions, but what were the answers. Perhaps she would ring Dunnbray in a few days, apologise for her behaviour and have a chat about the future, hopefully a future there. It was a beautiful place and like the rest of them, she had fallen under its spell. She wondered what India was like, the relative she had not met yet, would she go back?

She forced herself to go back downstairs, drying the tears as she did. Brian heard her enter the kitchen again and shouted through, 'What about money then? Is there any inheritance coming your way? It would come in useful.'

'I have no idea, Uncle Angus isn't even dead yet and all you think about is the money? What's the matter with you Brian?'

'How old is he then, this Uncle Angus?' The girls asked, 'do you think we would be left some money too?'

'Is that all you can think about? Not the long lost family I have discovered. Are you not interested that I have a sister, you have aunties and an uncle?'

Without waiting for an answer, she dished the dinner up. What a fool she had been. She had her opportunity, her one chance to make a break for it and what had she done. Screwed it up that is what, by feeling jealous and being rude to everyone. She had let her niece down badly by her reaction. Susan and she got on so well and she could understand Susan's reticence about Linda. Shelley was thrilled she had a sister, but at the same time thought that Linda was not someone she could easily trust.

Chapter 44

It was Saturday and no one had yet seen around the estate properly, so Hugh suggested a ride out. Phyllis didn't feel like being bumped around in a Land Rover, so was quite happy to stay behind. She wanted to spend some quality time with Angus; to find out more about his life and her husband Bill's family when the opportunity arose. Marilyn didn't fancy going either, she was still feeling the shock of Ken's hurtfulness.

The first stop on the route was a cottage, about half a mile away, looking very neat and well kept, with roses growing round the porch and a tiny front garden. A picture postcard home.

'Whose place is this Hugh?' Susan asked as they all stared at it.

'Mine,' he replied, 'this is where I have lived for the last few years. I won't show you around today, but some other time, as it will be getting dark soon.'

What a lovely cottage. Was he happy here with his wife? Susan thought; did he miss her?

He showed them the small flock of sheep wandering across the moorlands and a bit higher up, in the distance, some deer.

'You won't be able to get too close to them,' Hugh explained, 'the deer are far too timid.'

'Some of them must be shot for venison Hugh, do you do that?' asked Tim.

'No, would you believe it, I am the estate manager, but I couldn't shoot one of those, I am too soft. We get a professional marksman in to cull them and take them away. We have some of the venison and the rest is sold to the local butcher. The same with the sheep, someone takes the lambs away every year and we have some of the meat, the rest go to market.' Seeing their faces he said, 'Don't laugh at me.'

'We're not laughing,' said Linda, 'we think it's rather sweet.'

He is such a lovely man thought Susan as their eyes met in the rear view mirror.

Turning the vehicle round Hugh headed back to lower ground, where crops should be growing, but the fields stood barren and bare.

'We haven't done much with the land,' Hugh told them. 'We might be better re-cultivating the vegetable garden with organic stuff and selling that locally. That's what Angus's mother did to make money for her and the three boys.' They were approaching woodland now and in between the trees, they could see the sun glinting off water.

'That's the lake, fed by the River Bray, hopefully with trout still in it. I would like to start offering trout fishing again. It has been left over the last couple of years. In fact, the last few years have been extremely difficult; Angus has been getting more and more tired and losing interest. I have kept things ticking over, but not a great deal I can do, without any control over the purse strings. Several times, I have felt like moving on, but I love it here and I did not want to leave Angus. You girls have done him so much good in such a short time; he is like his old self again, raring to go.'

'Right, that's another idea. You will have to tell us when the fishing season is and we can then target the right clientele.' Susan was thinking that's another job to be done.

They approached Dunnbray from the other side this time and were able to see the part of the house that had been closed off to them. More outhouses came into view and a small barn.

'So much space,' said Tim, 'there are so many things you could do with this place. You could turn those buildings into self catering chalets for instance, then me and my mates could stay in them while we come and work on the estate.'

They all turned and looked at him. 'What? Have I said something wrong?'

'No, indeed you haven't young man,' Hugh told him, 'I think you have just come up with another project for the McPhail team.'

'I can't keep up with all this,' said Susan holding her head in her hands, 'so many ideas, so much to do, we must start making plans, right? Am I right folks?'

'Yes boss,' they all shouted in unison.

'Well that's alright then,' she laughed.

'Well, ladies, have you a campaign plan yet?' Angus asked at dinner that night, as they tucked into a Raspberry Pavlova smothered in cream, which Marilyn had whisked up in no time at all. 'And by the way, this is delicious.'

'I'm still recovering from the shock of seeing the ballroom. The possibilities for this place have grown even bigger since seeing that space. Tomorrow, we are going to have a quiet day, sit down and draw up a proper plan,' replied Susan. 'We were thinking that perhaps a party of some sort would be good to remind people of Dunnbray once again, let them know that we are still here.'

'Good idea, I like it,' said Angus, 'but what sort of party did you have in mind.'

'We haven't got any further with the idea yet,' replied Susan thoughtfully.

'What about a garden party?' Tim suggested, 'the grounds would be great for that, and if it's wet then hold it in the ballroom.'

'How long have you got left at Uni?' Angus asked him. 'We could do with someone like you up here, that's a really good suggestion.'

Tim could feel his face glowing; he glanced at his Mum who was beaming with pride. He would not have felt so happy if he could have read her mind.

The meal carried on late into the evening, until Angus announced that he was tired and could not keep up with this partying every night; he needed his beauty sleep.

The rest agreed that they too would call it a night and headed off in their various directions.

Chapter 45

Saturday came and Tim told Linda he could only stay for a couple more days. His workload at Uni was quite heavy, and he could not afford to take much time off.

'I can't wait to come up again Mum, but I'll go back to the house at Easter and get the house valued and put on the market. It's the best time to sell, the spring, we shouldn't have any problems.'

Susan visited her grandfather.

'Why don't you join us in the garden this afternoon,' she said, 'we are going to make plans for the garden party; that's if you are still happy with the plan.'

'Of course I am, my dear, can't wait.'

Marilyn had been very quiet since Ken left and was causing them a bit of concern.

'Are you feeling alright Marilyn?'

'I've been thinking about money, we have a joint account, I don't have any money of my own. You don't think Ken will cancel my cards do you?'

'Didn't you keep your own bank account?' Linda could not believe that she hadn't some independent means.

'There didn't seem much point when I gave up work, anything I wanted I just got on the joint account; it has never been a problem until now.'

'Don't worry about it,' Susan told her, 'he can't cut you off without any money, he has a child to support whether he likes it or not. Next time we go into Strathdown you can check at the bank.'

'Men!' came from Phyllis.

'Come on, you need something to take your mind off things, go and find a notebook and pen and you can make notes for the party.'

The date was chosen. The garden party would be in four weeks time, Saturday 21st May 2008. It would give Susan and Phyllis time to go home, get the apartment and house sorted and in the hands of the estate agents. Flyers would be printed and pinned up around surrounding villages and an advert placed in the local paper. Angus suggested a visit to the local vicar to see if they could borrow chairs and tables from the church hall, also cutlery and china.

The list of items grew as they discussed food.

'Linda, I think you are the most experienced of us on the computer, so can you find out if we can order online and get one of the supermarkets to deliver, that would make life easier.' Susan said, 'but our biggest problem is we will not know how many to cater for, we cannot ask everyone to let us know whether they are coming or not, how many shall we allow for, any ideas anyone?'

'I think a hundred should be enough.' Phyllis said.

'A hundred! Are we going to get that many?' Marilyn put a hand to her face.

'We could do, especially if we put it in the paper, you know what people are like, when they realise there is free food and drink; they'll definitely want to come and have a nose round.' Linda replied.

'We need to think about this very carefully then. If we provide alcoholic drinks, we will need a licence, so soft drinks only, because people will be driving any way and perhaps we should consider charging for them too. One hundred people is far too many to provide free drinks for; they will only take advantage.' Susan was thinking of the cost.

'And what about the house, do we allow people in there or not?' Marilyn asked.

'Well,' said Susan, 'if it is wet they will have to come inside won't they? We will have to keep some of the rooms out of bounds. We can put a rope or something across the stairs, so there is no access above the ground floor, but I think they will need to see the rooms that we could be using for weddings, such as the dining room, sitting room and ballroom, don't you think?'

'At this rate I think we'll need to employ a couple of people for the afternoon just to stand guard in the house,' Phyllis said, 'I don't like the idea of people wandering round inside, if we are out in the garden.'

'I think you're right Mum, something else to think about. So, tomorrow morning, shall we go into Strathdown and place the advert? Can you design and print the flyers Linda? Is that something else you can do?'

'Yes, why not, I enjoy that sort of thing.' A big grin spread across her face.

The rest of Saturday passed uneventfully.

Chapter 46

Breakfast over and done with, Susan went to the study to phone India. The solicitors had not been able to speak to her in person, but had left messages, which India had not responded to. Susan thought she might get more of a response from her.

'Wish me luck,' she said. Picking up the receiver, she dialled India's home number. It rang for several seconds and Susan was expecting an answer machine to cut in and was just wondering whether to leave a message or hang up, when she heard a click and India's voice.

'India, it's me, Susan, yes Susan from Dunnbray, did you get the solicitors' messages? Oh you did, but you haven't replied?' India's tone suggested a sudden put down, and Susan panicked and blurted out, 'you'll never guess, but Marilyn, one of the women who arrived after you left, well she is your cousin, you must come back to find out the rest of the story, it's absolutely amazing.' That got India's attention, the desired effect, but Susan felt guilty, as she had promised her grandfather not to tell India anything. After a few more minutes chat with India pressing her to tell her more, she hung up. India hadn't said she would come back, but surely, she must now.

Susan was worried over letting slip that Marilyn was her cousin, but Marilyn said that if that was what was needed to get her to come back, then she had done the right thing. India would not be able to resist wanting to find out more.

Hugh had sorted out the vehicle insurance and Susan, Marilyn and Linda could now drive the people carrier; the insurance documents were in the post.

'Let's go then, and get that advert in the paper.' Susan grabbed the keys from Hugh as they headed out to the vehicle. 'Who's coming with me? And am I driving, or do you want to, Linda?'

'I am quite happy to let you drive; it looks a bit big for me.'

'I'll stay here if you don't mind. My brain and my baby could do with a rest, have a good time.' Marilyn was still in shock.

The three women climbed into the black people carrier, but not before they finally checked out what make it was; A ford Galaxy

Diesel Automatic. Susan took a few minutes to find her way round the controls, and then they were off.

'Hold on ladies, you could be in for a bumpy ride,' she laughed.

'I suggest you take it easy to start with, at least there is quite a way until we reach the main road, so you can get some practice along the lane.' Phyllis commented as she hung on to her seatbelt.

Strathdown was reached without any mishap, and Susan was complimented on her driving. The advert was placed to go in the local paper in two day's time and the Editor promised to send a reporter along, so they could have some free editorial in the paper. They were thrilled to be offered this. The three women then headed to their favourite coffee shop and sat round a small table in the window.

'We've done it girls,' exclaimed Susan, 'there's no going back now, no changing our minds, we are committed to Dunnbray, the McPhail Musketeers, one for all and all for one, how do you feel?'

'I feel as if I have been waiting for this my whole life,' said Phyllis, 'does that make sense to you? I now have a purpose.'

'Of course it does, we both feel the same way.'

The conversation shifted to India and Shelley. 'I can't believe I am going to say this, but I would like India to come back.' Phyllis held up her hands. 'Now I know she's family, I feel differently towards her, silly I know. I hope you won't mind me saying this Susan, but India is a bit like a granddaughter to me. You know the saying: *A leopard doesn't change its spots,* well just for once I think they've got it wrong, I think she could change.'

'You and your sayings Mum; will you ever run out of them? At least you use them in a kinder way now, so perhaps you have changed your spots too!'

They all laughed, but underneath Susan felt a sudden stab to the heart at her mother's comments. It obviously hurt Phyllis having no grandchildren, but she had never said anything, leaving Susan to think all these years that it was not a problem, but apparently, it was.

'I don't know what to make of Shelley; do you think all the information was too much for her, and she couldn't handle it? I can't believe we are sisters and she would just walk away from us. Do you think she will change her mind too?' Linda was disappointed in her newly found sister's reaction.

On their return, Linda rushed off to start designing the flyers and a little later appeared with a mock-up.

'That's great, has Grandfather seen it?' asked Susan.

'Yes he's really impressed, and he says we must sort out another computer and a better printer, so that's another trip into Strathdown I think. And he mentioned TVs. Do we want any? I said I would speak to the rest of you, see what you think,' Linda said.

'Talking of TV's, do you think the guest bedrooms will need them?' Susan asked. 'Or do you think that could be part of Dunnbray's charm, no television?'

'Why don't we put one in the small sitting room, with a DVD player, which could become the TV room for guests and then perhaps get one for each of our bedrooms if we want? Would funds run to that expense? I must admit I have missed the soaps. And could we have a DVD too?' Phyllis was wistfully thinking of all her favourite programmes she had missed. It would be nice to have an hour or so's peace and quiet in her room if she needed a break from everyone. It was going to take some getting used to, a house full of people after all these years on her own.

'That sounds a good idea, five small television sets with DVDs built in and a larger one for the sitting room. We need to decide which bedrooms we are going to use too, we won't be able to stay where we are if we are to have paying guests; we have the best rooms in the place.'

'Another project for us then,' laughed Susan, 'it's never ending.'

'Yes, but so much fun.' Marilyn smiled. She was trying hard to get involved and feel part of the family.

Chapter 47

'Bedrooms today, ladies, can we sort out our bedrooms please? My thoughts are that we should move along the corridor to grandfather's side of the house and keep all this side for guests. We can open up the big bedroom with the balcony, which can be the bridal suite, then there are our six bedrooms and the two over the kitchen and utility, so nine bedrooms in all, I think that is plenty, don't you?'

Susan sat at the kitchen table with notebook and pen in hand.

It was quite an easy decision for them all in the end choosing which rooms. Susan and Phyllis were to have the two bigger bedrooms on the front, similar to the ones they were in now. Marilyn was to have the bedroom with a small box room next to it, which would become the nursery. Linda would have the room next to Marilyn at the side. There were also rooms for Shelley and India if they came back.

'I hope India doesn't mind us making the decision for her, but we do need to get things sorted,' Susan said to the others. To which they all agreed, so it was settled.

Phyllis looked at Linda and said, 'More bedrooms to clean, shall we get started then?'

'*Strike while the iron's hot* Mum? To quote one of your sayings.' Susan gave her Mum a hug. 'We aren't going to argue with you.'

The weather had gradually deteriorated through the day, so afternoon tea was served in Angus's sitting room; cups were passed round accompanied by another of Marilyn's superb cakes, this time a chocolate sponge with gooey cream running through the middle.

'I am going to get so fat,' groaned Hugh, who had been asked to join them. 'Marilyn, you are going to be the death of me.'

'Perhaps it's just as well Shelley isn't here then, it would be double the trouble as her cakes are even better,' replied Marilyn, 'talking of Shelley, I do miss her.'

'I think Douglas does as well, he's always popping in on some pretext or other, but I'm sure it's Shelley he wants to see. I have asked him if he would like a job here and I'm waiting for his answer, and talking of jobs,' Susan said, 'what are your plans Hugh. You are going to stay on at Dunnbray aren't you?'

'That depends.'

'On what?'

'On whether the future Lady of Dunnbray wants me to stay, or not.' He gave her a quizzical look, which implied that he was not only thinking of work.

'Don't be silly, of course I want you to stay.' Susan blushed in confusion. 'We all want you to stay, don't we girls?' She looked at the others for confirmation.

'See, they all agree and anyway I don't know one end of a sheep from the other and the deer are scary, someone needs to look after them and then there's the fishing to set up.' Susan smiled at him.

'That's settled then, because I really want to help get this place back on its feet.' Hugh smiled back.

A voice calling out from the hall interrupted their chat.

'That's India,' Susan said jumping up so quickly her drink spilled on the floor. Rushing out she saw India and a man she did not recognise and grabbing hold of the young woman, she gave her a big hug.

'Oh, it's so good to see you again, I'm so glad you have come back, but that was quick.'

'Ugh, get off, that's enough of that.' India gasped for breath.

'Come on in, we are all here.' Susan caught hold of India's hand and dragged her into the sitting room. Everyone by then had stood up. Introductions were made. The man with India was her father, Sir Harry, who had decided that if India was going back to Dunnbray, then he should go too, to find out for himself what was going on. He had had such a garbled story from his daughter, that he could not make head or tail of it all.

'Sorry to just burst in on you all with no warning, India was so determined to come as soon as she could, I hope you don't mind me turning up too, but I am intrigued by India having a cousin; you, Marilyn is that right?'

'It is indeed,' she laughed, 'but I think we will let Susan and Angus tell you the full story while the rest of us leave you in peace and go and get rooms ready for you. You are staying for a couple of days I hope.'

Two long hours passed. What was going on in Angus's sitting room? They were dying to know. Linda was getting impatient; she stood at the front door gazing over the grounds, then taking the steps slowly walked over to the lawn. The damp grass tickled her ankles and her shoes left footprints, because it was so long. We must get this cut, she thought as she bent down and ran her hand over the soft tufts. Her hand came away wet and she wiped the dew on her cheeks, how lovely and fresh it smelt. All this would definitely be Tim's one day, she was sure of it.

She was roused by a call from Marilyn. 'They are back, are you coming in?'

Linda entered the hall to find everyone congregated there. India came over and gave her a big hug.

'Hello cousin,' she said, 'I bet you heard all the horror stories about me when you arrived, but even I must have appeared nice compared with that awful Edna.'

'*Do unto others as you would have them do to you,*' Phyllis answered for Linda. 'There's to be no more cheek from you my girl if you are going to stay, is that clear?'

'Mum, don't talk to her like that in front of her father; now you're the one who is being rude.'

But Sir Harry just laughed and said he knew exactly what his daughter was like and not to put up with any of her nonsense.

Susan explained to India that a bedroom had been chosen for her in Angus's wing, so she would show her, hoping she would accept a smaller bedroom this time. She eyed all India's luggage with dismay; it would never fit in the small fitted wardrobe, but was pleasantly surprised at India's reaction to the smaller room.

'These rooms are ideal for us aren't they?' India said, going to the window and looking out, 'the other bedrooms will be much better used as guest rooms; are you really going to have weddings here?'

'Hopefully, if all goes well, we will start with wedding receptions and the bride and groom can stay, and guests too if they want. We are so far off the road I expect people will want a drink and they will not want to drive home afterwards. I am looking at information on the internet to see how, eventually, we can apply for a licence for the service to be held here. What do you think of the idea and are you really interested in staying; now you've had the whole story?'

'I would love to stay if you will have me, I am so sorry about how I acted when I arrived. There was no need for that behaviour. My father was so annoyed with me when he heard. He seems to be quite taken with the place; I could almost hear his mind ticking over when he was talking to Angus. He has a plan up his sleeve I bet. And Susan,' this said tentatively, 'could I be the wedding organiser if no-one else wants to do it, I am sure it would be something I would enjoy and I must do something with my life, how do you…'

Susan held up her hand to stop India. 'We would like nothing better than for you to be our wedding organiser, we have already talked about it. I think you will be far better at it than the rest of us and you must have so many contacts; just think if you could get one of your London friends to get married here what a great advert that would be. Madonna got married in a Scottish Castle after all.'

'Susan, you are such a lovely person, I can't believe I could have been so unkind to you. I will try to be nicer to all of you, even your mum. Oh and would you mind if I put some of my clothes up on the top floor for now, they are not all going to fit in that wardrobe.'

'Of course, there's plenty of room up there, we could have a dressing room couldn't we. Whatever has been said is all in the past, forget it, let us make plans for the future. My mum is already thinking of you as a granddaughter she never had, what do you think about that?'

'Did she really say that?'

'You can ask the others, they heard her say it.'

Going back downstairs, Susan thought how well India coming back had gone, and that they would probably have the best-dressed wedding organiser in the whole of Scotland.

Later that night, over dinner, Angus and Sir Harry told them that they had been discussing Dunnbray, and Sir Harry wished to invest in the family business, if nobody minded. He could see a good business venture when he saw one and the fact that his daughter would be involved made it even more interesting. He especially liked the idea of the trout fishing; with so many colleagues in the business world who enjoyed fishing as a relaxation, he knew they would jump at the chance of a weekend in Scotland.

Susan went to bed that night an extremely happy lady. Dunnbray was coming to life again. Thank God, she and all the others had replied to the letter. She wondered what would have happened if they had not. Her last thoughts as her eyelids grew heavy were of poor Shelley, what was she up to? Would she ever come back?

Chapter 48

The phone ringing in the hall brought Phyllis running to answer it.

'Hello, yes it is; how are you? Did you get back all right? And were they pleased to see you?' There was a pause as Phyllis listened to the replies.

Susan was hovering. 'Is that Shelley?' she mouthed. Her mother nodded.

'I am sorry to hear that and yes, Susan is right here, I'll pass you over.'

Susan took the phone, said hello then was silent as she listened to Shelley. After a few minutes' conversation, she put the receiver down.

'Well?' Four voices said all at once.

Laughing, Susan repeated what had been said. Shelley was coming back if they would have her. Her family had been so unkind, she couldn't wait to leave, and she was sorry about her behaviour before she left, she had felt jealous because it had seemed so easy for Susan and Phyllis to decide to stay, and of course, there was Douglas, she was confused about her feelings for him.

'Why don't I ask Douglas to go and pick her up from the station, she is travelling up tomorrow, so she will be here by the evening, isn't that good news? He will be so pleased; and by the way she is bringing her cat; the family were starving it apparently.'

The local paper came out on Tuesdays, so Linda suggested another trip into Strathdown to pick up a copy to make sure their advert was in. She had printed off some flyers so thought they could hand some of them out too.

'We had better call at the local church, to make sure we can borrow some tables and chairs. Let's not bother with crockery and cutlery; it's too much hassle, what if it gets broken? Or worse still, pinched; we will just use paper plates, plastic cups and cutlery.' Susan had given it a lot of thought and decided this was best.

Douglas was thrilled at the news. Shelley was coming back. He had missed her.

The advert was in, flyers were stuck in strategic places, the tables and chairs would be available to collect on the Friday before the garden party. The local minister in Strathdown was very accommodating, and very much looking forward to attending.

Just after ten o'clock the following night a tired, but happy Shelley opened the door to be greeted by hugs and kisses of welcome. Douglas followed her in with her cases, a silly grin on his face.

'Welcome home Shelley,' Susan said, 'we are so happy you are back. India's come back as well, so now we are all here at last, and India's father is here too. Shelley this is Sir Harry.'

'Please, call me Harry. I keep telling them to drop the Sir. Pleased to meet you, Shelley.'

'And this must be Molly.' Susan pointed to the cat carrier. 'She is certainly going to love it here, with all this space. We bought a basket, litter and tray for her until she gets her bearings and some food too.'

'Thank you all so much. You don't know how pleased I am to be back with you all. This is my real home; this is where I feel I belong. I really am sorry about my stupid behaviour. I suppose I couldn't believe that something like this could happen to someone like me.'

'Shelley, you needn't say anymore, we all understand. It cannot have been an easy decision to make, but we all think you have made the right one. All of your family will be welcome to come and stay whenever they like. You can go back for holidays; perhaps spending time apart will make Brian appreciate what he has lost. Who knows what the future holds for any of us.'

'That's enough speeches for one night, let's just get the wine out and drink a toast to the future.' Phyllis said. She had been watching Douglas's face while Susan had been talking and knew that he did not want Brian back in Shelley's life.

Chapter 49

Sir Harry was expected in London for an important meeting, so he offered Tim a lift back to University. He would drop Tim off, he said, stay overnight in Leeds and be home by the following day. Tim leapt at the opportunity of a lift back in Sir Harry's Rolls-Royce. Wait 'til he told his mates. Sir Harry was impressed by Tim's level-headedness and maturity for his age; the oil business could do with young people of Tim's calibre and he welcomed the opportunity to have a chat with him.

Linda moped about after they left; she had enjoyed having her son with her for a few days and showing him off to the rest of the women. She was the only one of them with a son, and a good one at that. She was quite disparaging of Shelley's daughters, what a waste of space they sounded, but then they were adopted, who knew what sort of family they had come from and Shelley was far too soft, not like her of course.

Discussions on the garden party took up most of the day, now they were all there, plus Hugh who volunteered to collect the tables and chairs and do anything else he was asked. The various jobs were being divided up. Phyllis thought they could still do with a couple of people to help with security in the house; she was still worried about anyone getting upstairs.

'Don't worry Phyllis; I know a couple of girls from nearby who would be glad of a few hours work. They are still in school, but I know they have been looking for a Saturday job. If they are okay, perhaps you would be able to use them for chambermaids once you start letting out the rooms.'

'Great idea, we will definitely need help then, thanks Hugh.' Susan was so glad to have him around; it was reassuring to have a man about the place.

The telephone rang in the hall. 'I'll go,' said India rushing to answer it. They could hear her animated voice saying, 'Yes...Yes, of course, no, that should be fine, let me find a pen, I'll take your telephone number and get Susan to call you back when she has looked at the figures. Yes, that's right. She's Angus's granddaughter. Bye.'

India came rushing out the door to where they were seated, pen and pad in hand, hair streaming out behind her. Flinging herself into a garden chair, she sat and grinned at them.

'Well, don't keep us in suspense girl.' Phyllis still got niggled at India's attitude sometimes.

'We have a wedding reception to organise, first week in August, fifty for sit down meal and one hundred and twenty for evening buffet and disco. I said you would ring her back this evening Susan. Isn't this exciting our first wedding, I can't wait, can you?'

'Honestly? How come?' Susan looked at the others with a stunned expression. 'We have only just advertised. Who is it?'

'Someone called Hilary Scott, her grandmother can remember Isobel McPhail apparently and when she saw our advert for the garden party, she recalled what a beautiful place this was and suggested Hilary give us a call. We can do it, can't we; you are not going to turn it down are you? Susan, say something.'

'But that's only just over three months away; do you think we can do it?' She looked around at all the smiling faces seeking reassurance. Their dream was about to become a reality, could they cope? Had they done the right thing?

'Of course we can cope, August is ages away. We will have a trial run with the garden party and iron out all the creases. The property already has planning permission as a hotel, so there is nothing to worry about there. Positive thinking Susan, we will do it.' As always, Linda took everything in her stride.

Susan was grateful for Linda's support, she was gradually warming to her, Linda was strong, capable, and everything Susan thought she wasn't.

Notepads produced, pens at the ready, the wedding plans were under way. A menu quickly put together for the sit down meal, as India did not have any details on what the bride would like. They could always change it but at least they would have some idea of cost. Suggestions were put forward for the buffet food.

'A bar, we will have to have a bar and I've no idea about costs of alcohol, and we'll have to get that licence.' Susan was starting to panic again. 'And what if they want to stay or guests want to stay, how many rooms are we going to say are available? What on earth have we taken on, none of us have any experience have we?'

'We can do it, Susan, stop panicking.' Phyllis banged the table. Her daughter needed to show more leadership, she would own this place one day; she had to show them she was more than capable. Phyllis secretly worried about Linda, nice enough woman, but if Susan were not careful, she would take over.

'You are right Mum, we need to visit a few wedding venues, and pick their brains if they will let us, but I don't think we should do it around here, they might not be forthcoming if they think we are competition. We should have got some prices worked out before we advertised.'

'I'll check out places on the internet, that's the best way. I can make a few phone calls too if you like and I'm sure India has contacts, she could get some information.'

'Linda, what would I do without you?' Susan hugged her as Phyllis looked on with the familiar tight lips.

What is the matter with her? The fleeting thought went through Susan's mind as she glanced at her mother.

Hugh was going to pop in on Angus, and tell him the great news. He would be thrilled at things moving so fast.

India and Marilyn could not stop talking about the wedding.

Susan telephoned Hilary Scott, and discussed the bride's needs and came off the phone with an A4 sheet of paper covered in numbers and indecipherable scribbles that she needed to write out again legibly before she forgot everything. She took it off to the library to sit in peace. She would get back to Hilary as soon as Linda and India had put some costings together.

Phyllis was getting concerned about her house and suggested to Susan that they should go back and get both properties sorted out. Susan's flat was easy, it was rented and she had already phoned up and given notice on it. But what was she to do with hers. Susan had suggested renting it as well, which would be the easier option for now and it could always be sold later. There were many happy memories in that house, she would be sorry to leave, but she had a future to look forward to at Dunnbray.

Chapter 50

Phyllis and Susan sat on the platform at Glasgow, waiting for their connection back to Dorchester. Hugh had dropped them off at Strathdown in plenty of time and given Susan a quick hug and kiss before they boarded their train.

'He's quite taken with you; do you feel the same about him?'

'I think so Mum, he's so kind and caring, but I get the feeling he's holding back now that I will inherit Dunnbray. Do you think he thinks I would think he was just after me for my money?'

'I think you think too much!'

The garden party was now only three weeks away. Luckily, Susan's flat was rented through the Estate Agents where she worked, so she only needed to give a month's notice, which was up in two weeks; giving her a few days to pack up her belongings. They had decided to rent Phyllis's house out. Houses were not selling too quickly in the area and they did not want to lose money on it just for a quick sale, and demand for rental houses was high.

There was a lot to sort out in Phyllis's house, she had lived there so long, but they had given themselves ten days at the most to get it all done and get back up to Dunnbray.

Susan had not wanted to leave yet, there was so much to organise, but she knew that if she stayed until after the garden party, they would be into planning for their first wedding and she would not want to go then, and her mother was fussing about her own house.

Another reason for not wanting to leave was Linda, if she was honest. She would have to keep a tight check on her; otherwise, she would take over. Phyllis had voiced her opinions on several occasions, telling Susan to watch her. She did not like the way she kept on flirting with the two men either. Shelley was getting annoyed at her interference between herself and Douglas, who paid regular visits to Dunnbray but still had not committed himself to giving up his other job and Susan was afraid that Linda would put him off working for her.

She sometimes thought about her life before Dunnbray, how she had liked the routine, how she enjoyed selling houses, was she really doing the right thing, giving it all up?

Surprised at how quickly she cleared out her flat, Susan realised how little she had in the way of possessions. The flat was rented fully furnished, so there were only clothes and personal items to be moved. Many of her ornaments and an assortment of clothes went to the local charity shops and she had already decided to treat herself to some new clothes once she got back to Dunnbray. The rest of her stuff, she boxed up, gave the flat a good clean, then locked the door behind her for the last time, which she found surprisingly easy in the end. She said goodbye to her neighbours and moved in with her Mum for a few days to finish off there.

The Estate Agents were sorry to lose her, but wished her well in her new venture. Secretly they were amazed at the change they could see in her; she was more confident, more sure of herself. They would have no problem in renting out the flat again and were looking for a tenant for Phyllis's house, which they assured Susan wouldn't take long, and then an income for her mother would come from that.

'Hi Mum, I'm here,' Susan called as she opened her Mum's front door. There was silence. 'Mum, where are you?' She thought she heard a sound from above and quickly ran up the stairs. Pushing open her mother's bedroom door, she found Phyllis sitting on the bed with a photo of her father in her hand. She was crying.

'What's wrong Mum? What ever is it?' She put her arm round her Mum's shoulders and gave her a hug.

'It's such a big step, you know, at my age, leaving this place after all these years. Are we doing the right thing Susan?'

'Yes, we are, I have no doubts at all.' Susan did but she was not going to tell her mother that. 'Come on Mum, what needs packing up here? I have finished the flat and handed the keys in so I can help you now. We only have a few days left.'

There was another pile of stuff in the small front room for the charity shop, so Susan packed it all in her car and took it away. Phyllis was going to rent the house out fully furnished so that made things easier. She would leave all her crockery, cutlery and everything in the kitchen. All she would take with her were clothes and things of sentimental value, like photos and little things that Bill had bought her over the years. They all went in boxes. . Later that day Susan's work colleague, who had bought her car, came to pick it up. She didn't feel like driving all the way back to Scotland, and there were already a couple of vehicles at Dunnbray.

The two women were ready to leave after a couple of days. The Agents thought they had found someone for the end of the month, so that was good news. They were put in touch with a man with a van, who did small deliveries and had relatives in Glasgow who agreed to take their boxes up to Dunnbray for a good price, and they felt it was a safer way of carrying their valuables and clothes.

The boxes were loaded onto the van, which set off on its long journey; Phyllis locked her front door and they both popped in to Amy's to say goodbye, before checking into a local bed and breakfast for the night. Amy said how much she would miss Phyllis living next door; who was going to clean her windows and sweep her doorstep now?

They were sure the new tenants would do it for her once they got to know that she was on her own, and told Amy to make herself known as soon as they moved in. The new tenants would like to see a friendly face next door. Coming back out of Amy's while they waited for the taxi, Phyllis stood and looked up at her home, her eyes glistening with unshed tears.

'Honestly, are we really doing the right thing?' She said holding on to Susan's arm.

'Definitely, but if it does not work out the way you would like at Dunnbray, you always have this house to come back to you know. It's not final, it's not as if you have sold it, it's only going to be rented for six months at a time.'

'You're right, here's the taxi, let's be on our way, before I change my mind.' Phyllis jumped in the taxi without a backward look.

The next morning saw them on the train again, for their long journey back to Dunnbray. Susan felt a little shiver of excitement run up her spine as she thought of Hugh waiting for them when they arrived. She was looking forward to going back, now that all the arrangements for her mother's house were completed.

'How do you feel now Mum?' She asked as they settled themselves into their seats for the first part of their journey, 'are you happy to be going back?'

'I am now; I wasn't sure at first. Do you know the W.I. ladies were really nice to me when I called in to say goodbye, they were so interested to hear about you inheriting a castle and they all said if they went to Scotland, could they come and visit? What do you think about that?'

'I think you were right all along about them Mum, you have suddenly become more important, more wealthy in their eyes, so they see you as an equal now. I'm always amazed at how important wealth and status are to some people and that others are judged by their lack of them.'

'Susan, I can't believe I heard you say that, there I am saying nice things about them for once and you are contradicting me?'

'I might be coming more confident, but at the same time perhaps I am becoming more cynical, it must be catching.'

They both laughed and sat back in their seats looking forward to their arrival. What a difference a few weeks made; even her relationship with her mother was much improved. They did not get on each other's nerves any more; it was lovely. Susan's thoughts drifted to their first journey up to Scotland, and how nervous she was. She hoped it had not all been a dream and she would wake up to reality.

Chapter 51

The train pulled into the station. Susan gazed eagerly about her. She thought she had caught sight of Hugh, but of course, she could be wrong, no, she wasn't, there he was, standing with Douglas, his eyes scanning the passengers. Suddenly their eyes met and forgetting all about her mother, Susan rushed up to them, flinging her arms round Hugh, who lifted her up and spun her round, a big grin on his face.

'Welcome home my Lady,' he said.

'Oh Hugh, don't say that.' But she was secretly pleased, what a welcome.

She turned to Douglas, and said hello to him and held out her hand, suddenly embarrassed at the show of affection between her and Hugh. He grasped it and gave her a quick kiss on the cheek. 'Welcome back Susan, we have missed you.'

'I have missed you all too and oh my goodness, Mum, I have forgotten all about her.'

'Yes, never mind me then, good job we haven't got any luggage, leaving me to struggle off the train on my own.'

'Phyllis, my favourite person in the whole world,' Hugh said, picking her up and spinning her round like he had with Susan, 'it's so good to see your miserable face again. I'm only joking,' he laughed, as she hit him with her handbag.

'You'd better be my lad or I shall have to deal with you.' She tried to keep her face in its usual tight-lipped way, but could not keep it up; she was delighted to be back. She enjoyed the easy banter that had developed between her and Hugh.

'How's everything at home? Hey listen to me Dunnbray is already our home.' Susan chattered away as they climbed into the people carrier.

Hugh's face lost its smile as he said, 'I will be totally honest with you before we get back, things aren't brilliant. The three witches and Shelley are not getting on. They need you to sort them out, get them back on track. If they are all to stay and work together then they need a tough boss, which unfortunately is going to be you. I wish you luck with that lot.'

'I think calling them the three witches is a bit strong, but Hugh's right, things are a bit strained, your grandfather is getting worried. He will be so pleased to see you back,' Douglas said.

Susan's mood changed in an instant, she looked at her mother uncertainly.

'What do I do, Mum? I was so happy to come back and now this.'

'Start as you mean to go on. Be firm, be fair, but put them straight. You will not stand any messing, and there is a garden party next weekend that has to run smoothly. I will support you all the way.'

Susan smiled gratefully at her mother. 'Thanks Mum. Oh dear what have I let myself in for? Why do things keep going wrong?'

The rest of the journey passed in silence, Susan filled with trepidation now, the nearer they got. Her spirits picked up as they turned in through the gates and she saw Dunnbray again in the dusk, with the lights shining a welcoming light, drawing her back.

As they entered the hall, everyone rushed out to greet them.

'Welcome back Susan.' Her grandfather hugged her, and then hugged Phyllis. The others all crowded round, giving them hugs and kisses.

'It's lovely to be back, I have missed you all,' Susan said as she looked around, 'what have you all been up to while we've been gone?'

'Come on through and we'll make you a cup of tea. Linda has made a cake to welcome you back,' Shelley said as she escorted them through to the kitchen.

The two women sat down, feeling slightly puzzled at the news that Linda had been baking. Tea was poured and slices of fruitcake handed round.

'What do you think Susan; it's a good cake isn't it?' Linda said smiling broadly at everyone.

'Mmmm, very nice, but I thought Shelley and Marilyn were the cooks and cake makers.'

'Yes, well, they are not the only ones who can cook are they? We should all take it in turns don't you think?'

Susan looked discreetly at Shelley and Marilyn who both sat tight-lipped.

Phyllis sensing the atmosphere decided that as it was late and it had been a long day, perhaps an early night was called for and they could catch up with all the news the following day.

Susan nodded. 'I think she's right, we have been packing for days, and then a long train journey, I think we will have an early night if you don't mind. Sorry Grandfather, hope you will excuse us tonight, we will both pop in and see you tomorrow. Your new housekeeper needs to know what her duties are.'

Angus laughed. 'That's right, she needs to start work straight away, I have loads of washing and ironing waiting to be done. '

They all agreed on an early night and one by one drifted off to various parts of the house.

As they went upstairs Susan and Phyllis realised that they needed to get their rooms changed, they had not had chance before they left. That was the first job for tomorrow.

Susan had just entered her bedroom, when she heard a discreet tap at the door and called out, 'Come in.'

It was Shelley. 'I must speak to you, I hope you don't mind, but I can't leave it until tomorrow. Can you spare me a few minutes? I know you're tired.'

'Not as tired as I am pretending to be. Hugh told me there have been problems and I could feel the tension in the air downstairs, and did not want to get involved tonight. Whatever is going on?'

They sat side by side on the bed and Shelley told her all that had happened in the week or so that Susan had been away. It appeared to be Linda, who was causing the problems, and she kept interfering with everything. She had muscled her way into the cooking, even though she was not very good at it.

'I noticed,' said Susan with a grimace, 'that cake was awful.'

Shelley said that was just one example. Linda insisted on Angus and Hugh eating with them all the time and Douglas too when he was around. She was making the meals at least every other night. She was drinking too much and was bossing Angus around and treating him like some geriatric patient, drawing up a rota of who did what for him.

'What about the others?'

'Well, India isn't speaking to Linda at all. India has been working hard on the wedding venue idea, she has been trying to get information on how to get a licence, but Linda tries to stop her using the computer, she says that is her job. She has upset Marilyn, talking about her husband and what an awful man he must be, and telling her to get a solicitor to sort out her money.'

'And what about you, has she upset you too?'

'It's Douglas, she keeps chasing after him and telling me that he is going to take her out for a meal, he isn't interested in me at all and that I should go back to my husband. I should be grateful I have one.'

'Thanks for telling me all this, I shall be ready for it all in the morning. Now go to bed, it will all get sorted, don't worry.' She gave Shelley a hug.

Shelley left, Susan got ready for bed, but she could not settle. Perhaps it would have been better if none of them had stayed. It seemed such a good idea at the time that they all work together as they were family and it was what her grandfather wanted, but was it ever going to work? Why couldn't women work and live together without all this friction? If this was what it was like to have a predominantly female family then she was not too enamoured if she was honest.

She got her journal out with a heavy heart and started to write. She realised that she had not written anything whilst she was away.

Chapter 52

The next morning, Susan took her time getting showered and dressed, putting off the inevitable show-down that would take place today. Realising she couldn't put it off any longer, she made her way quietly down the other staircase to Angus's side first. She managed it without anyone seeing her, and hearing low voices she knocked on his sitting room door and entered to find Angus and Phyllis sitting together, chatting.

'Susan, come in,' Angus greeted her with a big smile, 'come and sit down, there is fresh coffee here, have you eaten my dear?'

'Thanks I will have some coffee and no, I haven't eaten yet.'

'Phyllis, would you mind making Susan some toast, while I have a chat with her?'

The two of them were left together. Angus's expression changed as he told her about the other women, how they were not getting on, how he and Hugh had spent several evenings discussing it, and he was worried for the future. Susan told him that Shelley came to her room the previous night to tell her about the problems.

'Shelley is a good girl, she has tried to keep the peace, but it hasn't been helped by Linda making eyes at Douglas all the time. I don't think she is even interested in him; she just does it to wind Shelley up. Douglas is not the slightest bit interested; but did not want to make a scene with you not around. Thank goodness I have a granddaughter to take over the reins, I really do not know what I would have done if you had all been nieces of mine. It would have been a far larger problem.'

His words weighed heavily on Susan's shoulders. She could not let this kindly old man down, but so much depended on her. She had to make a success of this estate.

'What shall I do Grandfather, I am not used to all this, what can you suggest? I need help.'

'You are stronger than you know, my dear, and you must show them that you are more than capable of running this place. Don't stand any nonsense. You will have to make it clear that they all work together or they leave, it's as simple as that. I would like everyone to stay, but not if it means upsetting you.

One thing I have done is get Charles to draw up some draft contracts for everyone, I will get you to have a look at them, to make sure you agree, and then you can interview them all. Everyone's role, as I see it, in the business, will be defined; obviously, there will be some overlapping, but their main duties will be written down and they must agree to them. That will solve a lot of the problems. I get the impression Linda is trying to be top dog around here. You will put her straight, I have no doubt.'

'What a great idea, a brilliant way of dealing with it if I might say so, you are clever Grandfather.' Susan smiled at him; already she was feeling better about the situation. 'Could I look at those contracts this morning do you think? I suppose if we are to run a business then we must all have some sort of contract and salaries and things like that. I must admit I had not thought about that side of it at all. I could use them as a way of seeing everyone on their own, then they will not think I am favouring one more than the others. There's so much to running a business, am I up to it?'

'Of course you are, have faith in your ability, you may not have experience of running a business, but you have been the driving force behind everyone for the last couple of weeks and you have the right temperament and the will to succeed. You will find the contracts in that file over there.' Angus pointed to a coffee table. 'I suggest you have your breakfast and look the contracts over and if you are happy with them, tell everyone that you will meet with them individually, to discuss their role in the business and until they have their meetings, there will be no discussion about Dunnbray.'

'Thank you, what would I do without you?' Susan brushed a small tear away.

He smiled at her; she would manage to knock them all into line, this granddaughter of his. He was certain of it.

The rest of the morning was spent reading the contracts. She was very impressed with what Charles had come up with, and pleased to see one for Hugh as well, in his role as estate manager and also very surprised to see one for Douglas – the horse riding enterprise, and the overseeing of the conversion of the outbuildings into holiday lets. Hopefully, he was going to stay after all. She would leave his until last.

Lunchtime came and she put in an appearance in the girls' part of the house. Where had she been, they all wanted to know, they all wanted to talk to her.

'I have been with grandfather and he and Charles have had draft contracts drawn up for you all,' she announced as she sat down to home-made soup, made by Marilyn together with a big chunk of granary bread. It was worth being here just for the food, she thought. She continued, 'I am going to see you all this afternoon, one at a time, I think in the library would be best, where we won't be disturbed. We can go through them together and discuss anything you are not happy with. If everything is satisfactory, Charles will draw up final contracts, which we will all sign and obviously they will be binding, and we will all keep a copy.'

'Sounds okay,' Linda said, 'who do you want to see first?'

'I think Shelley first, and then Marilyn; India, then you Linda, Mum, Hugh and finally Douglas, that's if he is around today, if not I will see him next time. I'll start at two o'clock if that's alright with everyone, so I'll see you at two in the library Shelley.'

Susan glanced at her mother who gave her a discreet thumbs up signal. Phyllis could see that the chat with Angus had done her daughter no end of good.

Chapter 53

Scanning through the contracts in front of her, Susan sat in the library waiting for Shelley. Her fingers tapped nervously on the desk, for this was her first time in the position of offering employment to people, and it did not sit easy with her. Contracts for the Dunnbray employees; it sounded very formal, but exciting too. Angus had not mentioned a contract for her, but she felt sure there would be one. She wiped her perspiring hands down her trousers, and called out to Shelley as she knocked on the door and entered.

'Come and sit down Shelley; this feels really strange to me talking about your position here, which is why I wanted to start with you. I feel that you and I can work together and hope it is the same for you.'

'It is weird isn't it? But my feelings are the same as yours. We will be fine.'

'Right then, let's have a look. Grandfather and I would like you to carry on with cooking main meals for the family to begin with, then hopefully for the paying guests and of course the wedding receptions. I hope Marilyn will join you, at least until she takes maternity leave. We will take someone else on to cover that of course and we will get extra casual help for the weddings, and we can all muck in, there is enough of us. If we keep the menus simple, I'm sure we can manage. Also the shopping needs to be taken on by you and Marilyn. How do you feel about that?'

'I would be happy to do it, especially if Marilyn joins me, we get on well together and I know we will get help from everyone if we need it. It will take some getting used to cooking for large groups, but it can't be that difficult can it? Just one thing, I know it's not my place to ask, but can you tell me what Linda will be doing? Only I don't want her in the kitchen and I know Marilyn definitely won't.'

'I can't discuss Linda's role until I have spoken to her. I will just say for now that if we all sort our own breakfasts and lunches out, that will be the only time we will need to use the kitchen. Not forgetting of course, that we do have two kitchens, so make sure you and Marilyn choose which one you want to use, then the other one could be for casual use for the rest of us, how does that sound?'

'That's great; I think you have answered my question. I am so excited, when can I sign?'

'If you are happy, then I'll get Charles to draw up the final one. Thanks, Shelley, now you are sure that you will stay? You won't be changing your mind again and disappearing back home.

'This is home now; I won't be going anywhere soon.'

With a big smile on her face, Susan asked Shelley to send Marilyn in and asked her not to discuss anything with the others apart from Marilyn until all the interviews had been carried out.

Marilyn came in next and sat down. She looked scared to death. Susan smiled at her. 'You look as nervous as I do Marilyn, this is not something either of us are used to doing is it?'

'I haven't had an interview for over five years, it's really scary. Are you sure you want me to stay? Being pregnant, it rather messes up the plans doesn't it? Most employers would want to get rid of me, not take me on.'

'Don't be silly Marilyn, how many times do I have to say that you being pregnant is not a problem and anyway you are family, it's different.' Susan then went on to offer Marilyn the same position as Shelley. She hoped they would work together, and asked her to decide with Shelley which kitchen they would rather use, and then the other one would be the communal one. She explained about maternity leave, which would be covered.

Marilyn was more than happy to accept the terms of the contract, but had one small question if Susan didn't mind her asking. Susan could guess what was coming.

'What will Linda be doing?'

Susan laughed at that. 'You sound just like Shelley, I do get the message, but obviously I need to talk to Linda first. Don't worry; it will all be sorted. I will ask you not to talk about this with anyone other than Shelley at the moment, until I have seen the others. Can you send India in now please?'

This was all going well, she thought as she waited for India. She didn't think she would have any problems with India's job, but she wasn't looking forward to seeing Linda, that would test her patience and interviewing skills.

India was thrilled with her job description – Wedding Organiser. She was to be given her own computer and printer and be in charge of placing adverts in suitable magazines. She was to attend wedding fayres with information and literature to hand out. Deal with any enquiries for wedding receptions. Start the ball rolling for wedding services to be held at Dunnbray and to liaise with Susan over menus, prices, and of course, how many they were to cater for. She would need to work within budgets given and not make any decisions before discussing them with Susan.

When Susan had finished, India rushed round the desk and hugged her. 'Thank you so much for having such trust in me, I won't let you down, now, where do I sign? Can I sign my contract now? I am so excited.'

'I'll have to get the official one drawn up, which you will sign. Can I just ask as well, that if there is anything else we need doing, if there is a problem, can I count on you to muck in and help? This is quite important.'

'Of course I will, I'm sure my hands can deal with a bit of washing up or cleaning if you need it. I was such a diva wasn't I? It's no wonder Phyllis was so annoyed with me.' They both laughed, remembering India's first visit to Dunnbray.

After a few more minutes chat, India left the library with a beaming smile and Susan knew that this opportunity would be the making of this young woman. Finally she had found something worthwhile to get her teeth into.

Next, was Linda, the most difficult one? Susan was dreading this, but knew she had to be firm and stick to her guns.

'Come in Linda, sit down please. Now, everyone seems to be happy with the positions they have been allotted so far, so I hope you will be too. As you seem to have more experience of running an office than the rest of us, you will be invaluable in setting up the accounts system. There is a small accounts package on Grandfather's old computer, but I suggest we get a decent new one with a better accounts package.'

Susan continued, 'I would also like you to get the Bed & Breakfast side up and running, with adverts, brochures, information, that sort of thing. Look at other accommodation in the area; find out what they are charging. Sort out the tariffs for the different rooms, special offers for two night stays etc, in fact any information that you can put together. Also what other places are charging for evening meals. We are a bit off the beaten track, so guests might want to eat here at night too. When you have everything together, then we can sit down and organise our first paying guests. The sooner the better I think. That will keep you busy, I am sure. How do you feel about the position?'

'Yes, that's all very well and sounds good, but what about the catering side, who's doing that, because I quite enjoy cooking and I have some great menus I could come up with for the weddings and things. And what about Angus, he needs looking after.'

'Those areas are all covered. Shelley and Marilyn are becoming the cooks for Dunnbray, it is what they both do best and they work well together.'

'What if Shelley goes back to her husband? What happens when Marilyn has the baby? Have you thought about all that, and the weddings? You will need some help with those, I can do all that.'

'I am sure you would offer to help out if and when we need it; but the position you are being offered is what I have already told you Linda. I am trying to use everyone's skills in the right areas. Now will you accept it or not, I need to know, because the only other position at the moment is that of cleaner, would you rather do that?'

'Cleaner? I don't think so. All right, I will accept what you have offered, but don't blame me if it doesn't work out and you haven't offered the right jobs to the right people. You are not used to employing people, are you? I can tell. Of course, I have had lots of experience in that field.'

'Linda, please, either you want to work here with your family, or you don't, it's up to you. Are you agreeing to your role in the business?' Susan wished with all her heart that Linda would say she had decided not to stay, but it wasn't to be.

'Yes; but there is no need to take that tone with me. Before I go can I ask about Tim, would there be something here for him to do?'

'I have thought about that and I like the sound of working holidays that he suggested, that sort of thing could be really useful. He and his friends could have free bed and board in return for helping on the farm or anything else that may be going on. I am sure Hugh could find him plenty to do.'

'I wasn't exactly thinking of holiday times, but something more permanent, when he finishes University.'

'We need to get up and running before we start employing any more staff, Linda, and perhaps Tim has plans of his own, he's studying Maths and Science isn't he? He does not need a degree to round up sheep. We'll discuss it later, if and when he is interested, is that okay?'

'Yes, I suppose so. Thanks.'

A huge sigh of relief slipped from Susan's lips as Linda shut the door behind her. What a difficult person she was. Well, with the amount of work she now had, that should keep her quiet. Susan just hoped that she was not making a mistake letting Linda do the accounts. She must get a bit more au fait with that side of the business, and in fact that was something she could ask Hugh to help her with, as he would continue with the accounts for the farming side of the business. It was also a way of spending some time alone with him. She smiled to herself at that pleasant thought.

She was very pleased to see her mother come through the door with two cups of tea.

'You don't know how welcome the sight of that tea is.' She smiled at Phyllis. 'That was horrible, I'm glad it's over.'

'Linda didn't look too pleased when she came out. Is she not happy with her position?'

'Hard to say, but time will tell, the others are happy, that is the main thing. Now, are you happy with becoming housekeeper, not only for Angus, but for the whole place Mum, it is not going to be too much for you is it?'

'I'm not sure I can physically do everything Susan, it's a huge place to keep clean; will I have help?'

'Of course you will Mum, you'll have me for a start. I have given all the good jobs away and I need something to do other than swan around telling everybody else what to do. I thought that every one should keep their own rooms clean for a start, so there will only be Angus's for you to do. The main rooms I will help you with, and once we start getting paying guests, we will employ someone as a chambermaid. We should be able to cope with the washing between us all and we can each do our own ironing. You will need to make sure Grandfather has his breakfast and lunch, but Shelley and Marilyn are doing the evening meals. Washing up can go in the dishwasher. Is that better, do you feel happier now?'

'Much better, now you have explained it, but are you sure you want to be doing the cleaning?'

'Yes, until I know how long it takes, and what needs to be done every day, I need to get a feel for it before I take on someone else. I'm no good at cooking, which you well know, and I am not experienced on the computer and I am only good at selling houses, so I think I have everybody else in the positions that they know best. I know how I want this place run, I just need to make sure it all happens.'

Tea finished, Phyllis went away happy. Now Hugh next, that would be easy, he was already in his role as Estate Manager, he would just continue along the same lines. Hugh came in and sat down, with a big smile on his face.

'There are some happy faces out there, you're doing a great job Susan, it can't have been easy this afternoon.'

'No, it hasn't, especially with a certain person, but I think we're sorted. I don't need to change anything with your contract. Are you happy with things as they are?'

'Quite happy, we can get the farm up and running again if that's agreeable. I'll have much more time now that I haven't got to keep running around after a bunch of nagging women who have been living here recently.' He laughed and ducked as Susan aimed a book at him. 'Even Angus is showing more interest in the farming side again now. He wants to increase the flock of sheep and get the fishing going.'

'Can I leave you to deal with all that then, I know nothing about farming; you will have to teach me when we get some spare time. And I would be very grateful if you would show me how you do the accounts for the farm. I have given that position to Linda on this side of the business, but I think I need to keep my finger on the pulse, not that I don't trust her or anything, but…'

'You need say no more, Susan, and by the way *is* there going to be any spare time, with all that's going on?'

They both laughed, comfortable in each other's company.

'Before you go Hugh, can I just ask you about Douglas? His draft contract mentions the stables and horse riding and converting the outbuildings into holiday chalets, is that something he has suggested or is it your idea?'

'Both really. We have had a few chats about it while you have been away. He is a nice fellow, very genuine. Angus likes him too. The riding stables were his idea, he told me you had offered him a job, but did not know what and he would love to work here. He comes from a horse owning family, so has been riding for years. He has contacts that could help with the purchase of horses and he would be quite happy to take on all of that. Young Tim gave us the idea of converting the outhouses, so he said if there was no one else he would get involved with that too. Of course I can help out there, I know local builders.'

Susan leaned forward. 'That's absolutely wonderful, is he here today?'

'No, unfortunately, he has a small job in Edinburgh, but will be back the day after tomorrow. The other thing we discussed is where he is going to live, so I have agreed that he moves in with me as soon as he starts work here, as a temporary measure, but perhaps one of the outhouses could be converted into a cottage for him, what do you think?'

'Good idea, there's also the loft in the stable too, perhaps that could be converted instead, it might be more private for him.'

'I hadn't thought of that, that's a brilliant idea. I will get him to come and see you as soon as he arrives, then perhaps we could talk to him together. We need to organise a surveyor quick to see what we can and cannot do, as it is such an old building. I will look into that if you like.'

'Yes please Hugh, I know from my old job how difficult it can be sometimes to get alterations passed by the local council.'

Susan sat back in her chair when Hugh left, the effort of the afternoon had left her exhausted, but knowing Grandfather would be waiting she stood up, stretched her aching back, then headed towards his sitting room.

That night round the dinner table, the excited chatter revolved around their new jobs; when they would start; and how they could not wait.

Angus told them that the new contracts would be available in two days time. They had all been told what their salaries would be. Not a huge amount as they would be living rent-free and all their meals paid for, for which they all expressed their gratitude. They were also told that each one of them would receive a cash payment of five thousand pounds including Tim, payable immediately to cover any personal expenditure incurred by the upheaval in their lives. There were gasps of astonishment around the table at that news and one by one they gave Angus a big thank you kiss on the cheek.

He told them to enjoy a couple of days of freedom and relaxation as work would start in earnest all too soon. The garden party was looming up on them.

Chapter 54

Escaping from the crowd for a few minutes, Susan opened the French windows and stepped out onto the balcony to look over the garden. She could not believe the sight that met her gaze; there must be about two hundred people, all sitting at the tables or milling about on the lawn. Thank goodness, they had catered for more people. Both kitchens had been put to full use with quiches and sausage rolls, cakes and pastries and this morning the worktops were covered with loaves of bread being turned into dainty sandwiches. Shelley, Marilyn and her Mum had done most of the hard work. She would never be able to thank them enough.

Hugh had roped in the two schoolgirls mentioned, and they were happily guarding the stairs and the ground floor rooms, which weren't open to visitors; and taking coats, not that there were many, it was a glorious spring day. Thank goodness, the weather was being kind to them. The last week had been quite wet and windy, but on Thursday the sun made its welcome appearance and the lawn, freshly mown, was just dry enough to stand the onslaught of all those feet.

From her vantage point, she could see Hugh circulating through the crowd, what a joy it was to have two such nice men as Hugh and Douglas around. Douglas and Shelley were becoming close; Shelley had not heard any more from her husband, he just accepted that she had left, just like that, how strange that he could just let his wife go without a fight. Showed what sort of man he was. Shelley was probably better off without him.

She watched Hugh stop and chat to her mother; Phyllis was laughing and patting her hair as she listened to him with rapt attention. Susan felt a twinge of jealousy; she wished it could be her. She often caught him looking at her, but whenever she caught his eye, he would look away. She got the feeling he wanted to say something, but never quite got around to it. Since his impetuous act at the railway station when she had come back, he had been careful not to have any physical contact with her.

It was no good, she would have to make the first move if she wanted their friendship to blossom, but she was not that sort. Why couldn't she be like India or Linda, both full of self-confidence? They wouldn't be having these thoughts; they would have been straight in. Still, he had accepted his contract and wanted to stay at Dunnbray.

She caught sight of her grandfather; he was sitting at one of the tables with some other elderly gentlemen and pointing over towards the lake. Perhaps he was telling them about the plans for the fishing.

'Susan, Susan, come on down.' She heard her name being called and looking down, saw Shelley holding up a couple of glasses. She smiled and waved, then turned to go back downstairs, her few minutes of peace and quiet over. She joined Shelley in the garden, and then spent the next two hours introducing herself to local people, all wanting to know about her plans and all offering assistance if she needed help. She took the names of three young women who were looking for work in the area, and a young man called Colin who was looking for work as a gardener.

Later, she mentioned Colin to Hugh, who had been cutting all the lawns himself because the old gardener decided not to return to work, due to his bad back. Hugh knew of Colin and could vouch for him, so Susan went in search of him again and offered him the job, starting the following Monday. Colin was thrilled to have found a permanent position.

'Thank you my Lady, I won't let you down, I'm a hard worker.'

'First of all Colin, please call me Susan and secondly I must tell you that I will be out here interfering with what you are doing, I love to come out and potter, you will have to tell me if I get in your way.'

'I won't do that ma'am, you can come out here any time you like, thank you ma'am.'

'See you on Monday then, and please call me Susan.' She walked away with a big smile on her face; she quite liked being called ma'am. What a nice polite young man.

Seeing her grandfather sitting alone, his companions having left, she sat down beside him. 'Are you alright Grandfather?'

'I am fine my dear,' his eyes twinkled as he gazed on this special girl of his. 'I have just been telling Barry and George over there about starting up the fishing. They are interested and want all the details as soon as we have them. It is all go isn't it? It has been a grand turn out today. Well done to all of you, you have worked hard. I'm a bit tired now; I think I will go back inside, if you will excuse me, and have a little nap before dinner.'

'Do you want Mum to fetch you anything; shall I give her a shout?'

'No, no don't bother her; I don't need anything, just a bit of a rest.'

With sunglasses on to hide her eyes, Linda watched as Susan sat talking to Angus. She must be careful, not let her true feelings show. Who did Susan think she was? Why only a few weeks ago she was a sales negotiator in an estate agent's office in Dorchester, now look at her, acting as if she was already the Lady of Dunnbray. Angus, silly old fool, absolutely doted on her. And why couldn't he have just paid off Shelley and India, why did he and Susan have them back? It would have been two less to deal with.

How to make her Tim the Laird? That was her goal in life now. She must come up with a better plan than poor old Edna. Linda secretly admired Edna for trying to get rid of them all and she was only doing it for her son. Now she, herself, had to rise to the challenge and put Tim in his rightful place. But for the time being, she would work hard at ingratiating herself with everybody, hard as that was. She would do everything she was asked, make herself indispensable while giving herself time to come up with a plan.

That night at dinner, quickly rustled up from leftovers from the party, with some fresh salad, the talk was all of the afternoon. How well it had gone, the contacts they had all made, the enquiries, the request for leaflets. They had amassed a large mailing list already. India and Linda would have to sort out which people were interested in weddings, and which for bed and breakfast.

Angus declined to join them and Phyllis had popped along to see him. Coming back into the kitchen she said, 'He did look tired, he's having his dinner on a tray in front of the fire, and then is going to have an early night.'

'So much has happened in such a short time, it's no wonder he is tired. He has enjoyed it though hasn't he?' Susan had grown extremely fond of her grandfather; was it only a few weeks since she had met him?

When Angus finished eating, he pushed the tray away, not able to manage it all. Those girls were wonderful cooks, but tonight he had no appetite. He reached over and picked up his little notebook, in which he jotted down all the every day happenings, and in doing so noticed the envelope containing the riddle that he kept forgetting to give to Susan, he must let her have it tomorrow.

Chapter 55

Phyllis was the first up as usual, and peeping into Angus's sitting room on her way to the kitchen to make his breakfast, she noticed his head leant against the wing of the chair, his eyes closed. Such a silly man she muttered looking at the unlit fire. He got up far too early; she would get his tray ready before she disturbed him.

She made a pot of tea, put two cups on the tray, buttered some toast, fetched the marmalade, plates and cutlery and carried them through.

Phyllis shivered; the room was chilly. He was still asleep. She noticed the tray, left from the night before, with his half-eaten dinner still on it, placed on the coffee table beside him. Hadn't he gone to bed? Had he slept all night in his chair? She tutted and spoke gently to him.

'Angus, I've brought your breakfast, wakey, wakey.'

She stared at him, he had not moved; she reached out and tentatively touched his cheek, it was so cold.

Phyllis's scream woke everyone with a jolt. What was that? Who was screaming?

Susan rushed down to where the scream emanated from; it was Angus's sitting room, what on earth? 'Mum what is it, what's wrong?'

Phyllis just pointed at Angus. 'Dead,' she sobbed, 'he's dead.'

Susan was rooted to the spot, no, he couldn't be. Too shocked to do anything, she just stood, icy cold fingers creeping round her heart.

Everyone had been roused by the screams, and poured into the room.

'What is it? What is going on? Oh, my God, Angus is he…?'

Linda just caught Susan in time as she was about to collapse to the floor, trembling, in shock.

'Come on Susan, let's go to our sitting room, you need to sit down, someone fetch her a cup of sweet tea, it will help. One of you ring Hugh, he'll know what to do.'

Linda helped Susan down the passage and into their sitting room where she guided her into a chair and crouched in front of her, brushing the strands of hair out of her eyes. Susan began to cry, great racking sobs, tears streamed down her cheeks.

Hugh rushed in, already having telephoned the doctor who was on his way. His face registered the same shock as the rest of them. While they waited for the doctor to arrive, tea was made just to give them something to do, and everyone moved as if in a dream.

Linda went back in to Angus to cover him with a rug and noticed the envelope on the coffee table addressed to Susan and a small notebook that had fallen down on the floor at the side of the chair. Picking them up, she realised the notebook was in fact his diary, and about to close it and leave it on the table, she spotted that the writing had changed into a squiggly pen line drifting off the page. Too curious now to put it down, she read the last entry.

'Did anyone know Angus had a bad heart?' she asked entering the sitting room again.

All eyes were drawn to the book in Linda's hand.

'What have you got there?' Hugh asked crossing over to Linda and taking the envelope and book from her, and slowly read aloud the last entry.

My dear, dear family, and Hugh and Douglas.

I was diagnosed with a bad heart eighteen months ago and was told I didn't have long to live. The only people who knew were Charles MacDonald and Dr. McLeod who were both sworn to secrecy. I feel the end is very close now and I am grateful for the time I have been given to spend a few wonderful weeks with my girls. And to you Susan, I know you will make a terrific Lady of Dunnbray. I was so pleased with the success of the garden party, and I know the wedding venue idea will be every bit as successful. I know Hugh will support...

'It looks like he would have written more but obviously ....' Hugh could not finish. He was too choked up. He handed Susan the envelope without speaking. Shelley approached him with her arms open wide, tears in her eyes and he gave her a great bear hug, burying his face in her neck.

Susan opened the envelope as the others watched curiously, wondering what it contained. She removed a single sheet of paper. 'Why it's a riddle,' she said, reading it.

'Read it out then.' Phyllis told her.

Susan read

'The secret of Dunnbray is never far away.
Is it under ground? Where the secret can be found?
Find four legs and a tail and the secret will unveil
Security for Dunnbray always, forever and a day!
Solve this riddle and your money worries will be well and truly over.'

Underneath, a note was written in her grandfather's hand. It said that his father had been left this riddle by his own father. No one had ever managed to solve it and now he was passing it on to Susan and the others to see if they could unravel the mystery and he wished them good luck.

Doctor McLeod, a small man with the look of a worried bank manager arrived, examined Angus and wrote the death certificate. There was no need for a post mortem, he said, Angus had been in his care for more years than he could remember and he was amazed at how Angus had kept going the last few months. It must have been the arrival of his long lost family, and when they all arrived, he knew Dunnbray was in safe hands and he could go in peace. The doctor arranged for the body to be removed and told them to register the death in Strathdown and let him know the funeral arrangements.

Charles MacDonald was the next to arrive, shaking all their hands, offering his condolences and apologising for having been sworn to secrecy.

'He really didn't want any of you to know how ill he was, he didn't want you to come here or even stay here through pity. It was to be your own choice. I think he held on until he was satisfied that you would all do your best to stay. Susan, he was so proud of you, his only granddaughter, he was ready to let go the reins and pass them to you. I would be so happy if our company can continue our association with the McPhails and anything I can do to help please do not hesitate to ask.'

Susan thanked him and said, 'We would be happy for you to remain our solicitor and we will let you know when the funeral's to be.'

A little later Angus was moved to the funeral directors' and they sat about, not quite knowing what to do next. It had been a long exhausting day.

Susan let herself out of the front door and breathed in the fresh air of late afternoon. She walked down the drive towards the gates; it was good to see them standing open. Hearing the crunch of gravel, she turned. Hugh had followed her out.

'I don't know whether this is the right time to suggest this, but here goes. We have to organise some sort of wake for Angus, it would be nice to hold it here. I know we have only just had the party, but there would be many people wanting to pay their respects. We will have to put something in the paper.'

'Hugh, can I leave that to you? Would you mind? As soon as we know when the funeral is, get it in the paper.'

'Of course, don't worry; you have enough on your plate.' He put his arm round her and walked her back to the house.

India phoned her father to tell him and Linda phoned Tim, who said how sorry he was for their loss, Angus had been a very kind old man, but he could not wait to tell Linda about his trip back with Sir Harry, he was full of it. There could be a position for him in Sir Harry's company; he was very impressed with Tim's mature approach to life.

'Don't go making any rush decisions Tim, you have another year to go yet and you don't know what your results will be, I thought you might like to come and work here.'

'Yes, I would, but that's more of a holiday job isn't it? I've plenty of time anyway.'

Linda said goodbye and put the phone down with a thoughtful expression on her face. Tim had to become Laird now, he was the only male in the family, surely, it would be better if there were a man at the helm, and he could take over when he left University. She had the use of the computer; she would look at the possibility, discreetly though, of course.

A sad group ate in the kitchen that night. Conversation was muted. News had spread quickly and they had received many phone calls from people in the surrounding areas all offering their condolences and asking when the funeral was. Charles left them with another note from Angus to say that he would like his ashes to be spread beside the lake on Dunnbray land.

'I'm tired of telling people it's too soon to make the final arrangements. When we know we are going to have to put it in the paper quick, so people can find out.' Susan sighed, what an absolutely awful day, she was shattered. 'I think I am going to turn in, I can't cope with any more, goodnight everyone.'

'Good night Susan,' they all called after her. 'Try and get some sleep,' Phyllis told her. 'Poor Susan, she doesn't know what's hit her,' she said when her daughter was out of earshot. 'So much responsibility now.'

'Can she handle it, do you think?' Linda would have to be careful what she said. 'Do you all think she is up to the job? I only ask because she doesn't give the impression of someone able to take on this place.'

'I don't know about that, look how quick she was to jump on Edna when she got the chance,' Marilyn leaped to her defence, 'I think she's more than capable, and look how quickly she sorted all our contracts out.'

'I agree with you.' Hugh stepped in quickly. 'She has the support of all of us; she'll be fine, let's just get the funeral out of the way.'

'Well, I still think it should be a man who runs Dunnbray, people would have more respect for a Laird. Well, goodnight all, I will see you in the morning.'

'I don't know about the rest of you, but I think we should keep a watchful eye on that one,' Phyllis whispered, 'she obviously thinks Tim should become Laird.'

'Phyllis! You don't believe that do you?' Hugh was shocked.

'Look at it logically, Angus had an older sister and if the estates come down through the eldest in each generation, then it should be Jamie by rights who should be Laird, but it's only due to circumstances that Angus ended up Laird here, and his direct descendant is Susan, so Linda might decide to challenge it at some stage. I'm worried for Susan that's all.'

'You have been doing some thinking Phyllis, but I wouldn't worry about it. We are all behind Susan one hundred percent, and she would have to make a right mess of things for any title to be challenged. And of course Jamie's grandmother was illegitimate. Let's not give it a second thought.' Hugh tried to dismiss Phyllis's word of warning over Linda, but it kept creeping into his mind, was Phyllis right? She was a canny old bird.

Susan pulled the riddle from the pocket of her jeans and read it repeatedly. Whatever did it mean? Was it genuine, or a cruel joke left by Angus's grandfather to his own spendthrift son Archie? Her head ached; she put the piece of paper on the bedside table, then unable to hold back the tears, lay in bed sobbing into her pillow and finally fell into a disturbed, dream-filled sleep, her damp hair stuck to her cheeks as she tossed and turned.

Chapter 56

The date for the funeral was set for the following Thursday. They managed to get the details in the local paper in time. The service was to be held at the church in Strathdown.

Hugh suggested that he and Susan went out and selected a place near the lake where Angus had requested his ashes to be spread, near to where the ashes of his beloved mother, Isobel had been scattered. They walked out of the door on the far side of the house, nearest the lake and crossed the drive to the heath land and beyond until they reached the pine forest. A little way in they found a clearing with the lake in the background.

'What about here? Hugh suggested. 'This looks a good place.'

'It's so peaceful Hugh isn't it? I think he would like it here. We are just out of sight of the house too, so it won't be visible every time we look out of the window, I wouldn't like that.'

'I'll get things organised then, how are you coping, are you okay?'

'Yes, I'll just be glad when next Thursday's out of the way. Thanks for your help Hugh; I would be lost without you.'

'Do you fancy a longer walk? We could go back via my cottage if you like. Would you like a look around? It will give you something to occupy your mind.'

Susan looked at him in surprise; she had not been expecting that. 'I would love that,' she said, 'it looks such a lovely place.'

'Come on then.' He took her hand and together they walked through the trees until they emerged into the open and Hugh's cottage could be seen in the distance.

It looked even prettier than Susan remembered. The white picket fence surrounding a small garden filled with shrubs and flowers, the short path up to the brightly painted blue front door. The windows, with their small panes gleaming in the sunshine. She could just imagine what the inside would be like, cosy, chintzy and very welcoming, which it was. She found out a few seconds later when Hugh unlocked the door and ushered her in.

The front door opened straight into the small sitting room with an inglenook fireplace with its shiny brass ornaments and a fire laid ready and waiting. A cottage style suite of furniture, comprising sofa and two easy chairs were grouped round the fireplace. This room led directly onto the kitchen, which held a small table and two chairs, placed to look out of the rear window onto a small garden. A staircase at the side led up to what Susan could only guess was one bedroom and a bathroom, which Hugh confirmed as he saw her glance up the stairs.

'How about I make us some coffee,' he said as he stepped into the kitchen area.

Susan could not help herself. 'What happened to your wife?'

'Angus must have told you that I was married did he? What else did he say?'

'Nothing, all he said was that you were married, and your wife died, that's all.'

'She died in a car crash on the road to Glasgow.'

'Oh, Hugh, I am so sorry.'

'She had met someone else, she couldn't take to living here, in the middle of nowhere, she was from Glasgow, she missed the bright lights, and we should never have married. The night she died, she was leaving me for this other man.'

'That's terrible. What an awful thing to happen.'

'We weren't happy, but she never deserved to die like that, but at least it was instant. There hasn't been anyone else since, until...' Hugh paused and looked at her, 'that is until I met you. There I have said it, I have been wanting to say something but didn't know how to, out of practice, I suppose.'

'There hasn't been anyone else in my life since my divorce either. I have become very fond of you Hugh, but I didn't think you were interested in me, and especially now I am taking over the estate.'

'I know, it crossed my mind, you might think that I am just after your money, which is why I haven't said anything before, and it is only a few weeks.'

'Let's get the funeral out of the way, I can't think of anything else at the moment, and then we'll take it from there shall we?' Susan stepped towards him, put her arms round his neck and kissed him gently. He held her in his strong arms and she felt an overwhelming sense of warmth and security, she had truly come home.

'Our secret for the time being?' Hugh asked as they drank their coffee, smiling at each other.

'I think so, if you don't mind.'

'Hey look who's arrived, that's Douglas's car,' Hugh said later as he and Susan headed back to the house. 'When I rang and told him about Angus he said could he come up and stay for a few days, I told him it was alright; if you don't want him staying in the house, he can stay at my place and if you want me to move out too, just say so.'

'No, I want you to stay please Hugh, I feel we need a man about the place, at least until after the funeral, if you don't mind and of course Douglas is welcome to stay too. The more the merrier especially at mealtimes.'

They entered the hall and greeted Douglas, who hugged Susan and told her how very sorry he was for their loss. Angus was a good man, he had liked him very much, and he would be sorely missed. He thanked her for allowing him to stay in the house. Susan pointed upwards and reminded him how many bedrooms there were; one more person would not make that much difference.

Hugh glanced at Susan as she turned and told Phyllis there was an extra person staying; she was so very attractive, perhaps a bit old-fashioned in her ways, but he loved the way the unruly wisps of hair were escaping from the wide band she wore round her head and curling in ringlets around her face. He wanted to push them away for her. He knew he wanted to take care of her for the rest of her life. He was so glad of his impulsive move to show her his cottage.

The days leading up to the funeral passed in a blur. Susan couldn't remember anything about it. The early service in the old church was well attended; many came to pay their respects, but even more came to catch a glimpse of Angus's granddaughter. She was the talk of the town. And all those other women too, all related they had heard; gossip was rife. Would they all be able to carry out Angus's wishes now he was not around? Time would tell, they told themselves. Only the family travelled to the crematorium for the final farewell, it was too far for many people and Susan wanted to say a private goodbye.

The wake was held later in the afternoon for whoever would like to come, and a great many people came back to Dunnbray, many of whom had attended the garden party just over a week ago and here they were again. This time it was a more sombre occasion and one held indoors, the weather was not so kind to them, it was cold and wet, with a blustery north wind. A buffet had been laid out in the dining room; India had seen to it all, while the rest were at the funeral, she said there was no way she could cope and did they mind if she didn't come.

Susan said it was fine, not to worry and she would be very grateful for India laying out all the food, otherwise they would have had to employ someone to do it.

Subdued voices filled the hall and dining room. Susan wished they would all go home, but she circulated, thanking everyone for coming and yes, she would let them know if there was anything they could do. There was a request for no flowers, but kind visitors still brought bouquets of flowers for the girls and the rooms were filled with the scent of lilies.

Finally, everyone left; the family plus Hugh and Douglas congregated in the sitting room having a much-needed alcoholic drink and a sit down. Susan said she was going upstairs for a lie down for half an hour if nobody minded.

Instead of going to her room, Susan walked along the corridor to the bedroom over the front door. She opened the French doors and stepped out onto the balcony. The wind had dropped and watery evening sunshine breaking through the clouds was just making itself felt over the distant hills. She loved this room. Soon it would have its first bride and bridegroom sleeping in it.

Leaning on the wrought iron railings, her gaze drifted to where only recently her grandfather had sat with his friends on the lawn the day of the garden party. He had been so happy that day. The tears that she had been holding back all afternoon coursed down her cheeks unchecked.

'Oh, Grandfather,' she whispered to the air, 'I wish you were still here. I feel so alone, help me, and give me the strength to care for Dunnbray.'

A small white feather floated down on the evening breeze and landed at her feet.

She looked up to see what bird it might have come from, but there were no birds around. Something stirred in her memory, about feathers. That was it; a friend told her once, that sometimes people in times of despair would be sent a sign, an unspoken message of love and support from a departed soul. She gazed at the feather again, and then picked it up; it nestled in the palm of her hand. The tears dried on her cheeks and a small smile flitted across her face; it was a sign from Angus, it had to be. He had heard her cry for help.

Susan lifted the feather to her lips and kissed it, whispering, 'thank you Grandfather.'

Be Mindful

If you have enjoyed **Every Why** then look out for the exciting sequel **Be Mindful** which keeps readers guessing as to whether Susan can decipher the riddle, and what Linda's plans are to instate Tim as the Laird of Dunnbray.

    A story of plotting and intrigue, which tests Susan's abilities as Lady of Dunnbray to the utmost. 'You can choose your friends, but you cannot choose your family.' – A saying, which Phyllis would have been proud to quote.

You can find me on www.shirleyford.co.uk

http://fordsthoughts.wordpress.com

https://www.twitter.com/@ShirleyFord11

or Shirley.ford@mail.com

I would love to hear from you.

Acknowledgements

I would like to thank my husband, Alan for all his support during the writing of this book. I would also like to thank my good friend Eve Cox, for producing the original artwork for the cover of Every Why. It has created something unique.

Shirley Ford now lives in the South West of England with her husband and little rescue dog called Bailey. Writing is how she now spends her retirement.

Made in the USA
Charleston, SC
31 July 2013